LEFT FUR DEAD

"Is there anything else you wanted to know other than information on the sheriff's investigation?" I asked Andrew.

Bun sidled up against my ankle. I couldn't tell why, though he might have thought Andrew could become aggressive. Again, I had no idea why he'd think that, but there are times when Bun often gets weird vibes from people and his imagination takes over.

"Are you sure that's all he wants?"

I glanced down at him, raised a brow, and then turned back to Andrew, who said, "It occurred to me that you have quite a stake in Arty's death. How far are you willing to go to find his killer?"

His words gave me pause. Was he aware of my intrusion into Arty's home? Did he know more than what he'd heard from me and Jessica? If so, how did he come by that knowledge?

Bun thumped the floor with one foot, and I looked down.

"Take care, Jules. The man is riddled with discontent. I have no clue why. . . ."

Left Fur Dead

J.M. GRIFFIN

KENSINGTON BOOKS
www.kensingtonbooks.com

KENSINGTON BOOKS are published by

Kensington Publishing Corp.
119 West 40th Street
New York, NY 10018

All Kensington titles, imprints, and distributed lines are available at special quantity discounts for bulk purchases for sales promotion, premiums, fund-raising, educational, or institutional use.

Special book excerpts or customized printings can also be created to fit specific needs. For details, write or phone the office of the Kensington Sales Manager: Attn.: Sales Department. Kensington Publishing Corp., 119 West 40th Street, New York, NY 10018. Phone: 1-800-221-2647.

Kensington and the K logo Reg. U.S. Pat. & TM Off.

First Printing: July 2019
ISBN-13: 978-1-4967-2057-3
ISBN-10: 1-4967-2057-1

ISBN-13: 978-1-4967-2060-3 (ebook)
ISBN-10: 1-4967-2060-1 (ebook)

10 9 8 7 6 5 4 3 2 1

Printed in the United States of America

CHAPTER ONE

"It's quite blustery today," I murmured as a fine sheen of ice-crusted snow crunched under my feet while a steady wind buffeted us. The edge of the water, glazed with shards of ice, reminded me of broken glass. Tall grasses, stiffly encrusted with snow, barely swayed in the wind coming off Lake Plantain. Frosty boulders dotted the landscape. New Hampshire in March was frigid. I stopped abruptly when Bun's voice entered my head.

Bunny, my black-and-white rabbit, snuggled against my chest in the baby sling he rode in. Bun's head protruded from the sling opening, and his ears twitched as he glanced around.

"That looks odd, like a frosty hand rising from the tall grass over there." Bun dipped his head to my left. I followed his lead, slanting a look in that direction.

Holy crap, it did look like a frozen hand reaching upward. My heart began to pound, my breath came short and fast, and I veered toward the area.

"You don't think it's real, do you?"

"I'm sure it's just the way the frost has clumped the grass together. We'll have a look."

My name is Juliette Bridge, better known as Jules. I'm the owner of Fur Bridge Farm, where I raise rabbits, find good homes for them, and care for others that have been rescued from difficult and often abominable situations. Bun, my best buddy, lives in my farmhouse as my resident housemate. He has a personality that warms my heart, that is, when he's not poking his sweet little nose where it doesn't belong.

Not your average rabbit, Bun's smart, sociable, talkative, and very talented. His specialty is pure nosiness. He communicates with me by way of mental telepathy, which adds another dimension to an ongoing list of my problems. I know, it sounds ludicrous, but when Bun talks, I've learned to listen. I never thought I'd have a talking pet, but there you have it. He's never mentioned how this ability came about, and I've never asked. Uncertain if everyone can hear him, I can only assume they aren't willing to acknowledge his ability.

We've shared the farmhouse for the past couple of years, after I rescued him from a despicable family with no respect for animals. They were glad to see him go, saying he was in league with the devil. I figure they could hear him talk.

The first time I heard his voice, a soft, lilting, somewhat musical sound, I wondered if I'd imagined it. As time went on, he kept talking to me, and I continued to ignore him. One morning, about a year ago, we were taking our usual walk, when I ran into Margery Shaw. Margery had been Bun's previous keeper and there was no love lost between us. Having seen Margery coming before I did, Bun had huddled down inside the sling, burrowing as far as he could, trying to disappear. I heard a warning to take care before there was only silence.

The woman marched up and asked if I'd heard the rabbit talk. That was the dawning realization that Bun could, and often did, communicate with me. Unwilling to admit it to Margery, I shook my head and asked if she was imagining things. Her anger evident over my remark, I left her standing on the path as I jogged off, holding Bun close to my chest.

From that day forward, Bun and I have conversed on a regular basis. I doubt I can answer him telepathically and haven't tried. I'm careful where and when I speak aloud to him. It doesn't look good to prospective rabbit owners if I'm blathering on about something to Bun when they've come to the farm in search of rabbits of their own.

My face numb from the wind, I slipped and slid our way through the snow, focused on what looked like a hand, all the while mentally denying it was one. As we drew near, Bun started to quiver, a clear sign of his excitement. Bun always likes to be right, especially under these circumstances.

I came to a stop and leaned forward. The hand, a real hand, was connected to the arm of a man lying amid grasses that arched tunnel-like over his lower extremities. He seemed to reach out, maybe in hope that someone would take hold of his hand and lift him off the ground. I trembled, and then shook, before pacing back and forth while I muttered that this must have been an accident. I pulled my cell phone from the pocket of my jacket and dialed 9-1-1.

A female dispatcher answered the call and listened as I babbled on about my find and where it was located. Finally, she asked, "Are you still at that location, ma'am?"

"Y-yes."

"Stay there, emergency services will be with you shortly. Please remain on the line until they arrive." Her voice, calm and soothing, left me less frantic, and I stopped pacing. I detest murder, or violence of any kind, though I admit I'm a curious sort, though Bun is much more inquisitive than I am. My intuitive, long-eared pal is right quite often. That's why I listen when he speaks to me.

Moments later, sirens blared, and a police cruiser slid to a halt not fifteen feet away from us. A rescue vehicle parked, and four men scrambled over the snow, closing the distance between us.

Sheriff Jack Carver gave me the once-over as he came abreast of me, Bun, and the deceased.

"When did you find the body?"

I slanted him a look, shut off my phone, and tucked it into my jacket pocket. "Just now. I walk every morning, but not usually here."

"Why come this way today?"

"I wanted to see if there was an ice buildup around the lake. It's quite beautiful, without a dead man, that is."

Carver gave our surroundings a sweeping look and shrugged. "I guess beauty is in the eye of the beholder. All I see is frozen ground and a slippery road."

Bun popped his head out of the sling. He sniffed the air, twitched his ears, and settled against my chest. *"He might have a point."*

"I suppose you're right," I said, not speaking just to Carver, but also to Bun. We watched as paramedics pulled a sleigh-type basket over the snow-covered ground. They stood back until given the go-ahead to take pictures and do their job before collecting the dead guy for his ride to the morgue. Ice chips dropped off his face and clothing as the crew wrestled him into the sleigh. Once he was strapped in and tightly secured, the team took him away. All that was left on the ground where he'd lain was a dark patch of something I thought might be blood.

The sheriff noted the spot at the same time I did, leaned forward, ripped one of the mashed stalks of grass from the ground, and held it to his nose. He bagged the grass and tucked it into his coat pocket.

Who was this dead person, and what was he doing by the lake? Inwardly, I shivered at the thought of him dying in the cold, and then turned my attention to what the sheriff was saying.

He waited for an answer to the question I hadn't heard and then repeated it as he tipped his head in the dead man's direction.

"Are you familiar with him?"

"No, I don't recognize him. Do you?"

I pointed to the dark spot. "Is that blood on the ground?"

"It doesn't concern you."

Bun moved around, then wiggled his head out

of the sling again. He watched the sheriff with keen eyes.

Jack gave Bun a glance, then offered me a cool attitude that surely meant he'd be asking the questions. "You're certain you've never met him before? Maybe he stopped by the farm, or you ran into him in town?"

"Not that I know of. If I did come across him somewhere, he didn't make an impression. Sorry, Jack."

We walked from the beach onto the upper part of the road where his patrol car sat running.

"Do you always walk with the rabbit?"

I smiled a bit. "Every morning. It's good for us both."

With a smirk, he nodded. "If I think of anything else, I'll be in touch." Jack tipped his hat-covered head and got into the cruiser. He drove off without a backward glance as I walked on while Bun chatted up a storm.

"Why was he so insistent on you knowing that man? Do you know him? Has he been by the farm? Why didn't I see him if he did?"

"Stop talking long enough for me to answer you. I have no idea why Jack thinks I've seen the guy. He hasn't been at the farm when I've been there, and that's why you aren't familiar with him." I heaved a sigh. "And, by the way, we aren't going to get involved in the investigation, so get that idea out of your head right now."

According to my Fitbit Surge watch, we'd reached the three-mile mark. It was time to return home. My face was so cold, I wondered if it might crack and fall off. The icy dead guy came to mind as Bun asked why we couldn't check into the death.

"Because it's none of our concern. Now stop asking questions and brace yourself while I jog back to the farm."

"If I had known you were going to jostle me around like a sack of potatoes, I wouldn't have come along. Though, if I hadn't come, I wouldn't have found the corpse, nor would you have."

Ignoring his jibber-jabbering, I picked up the pace and we made it to the farm in half the usual time it took. Unbuckling the sling at my shoulder, I leaned down, and Bun jumped free. He scampered into the house and ran into his bedroom before he hopped onto his cushioned bed and settled in. I poured food into his feeder, added fruit bits and lettuce to a bowl, then added water to the one next to it before leaving for the barn.

A short breezeway connects the barn to the house to keep me and my farmhands from becoming soaked by inclement weather. I'd had it erected about a year ago, after the wettest winter I'd ever encountered. At first my workers thought it was ridiculous, but they soon changed their minds when heavy rainstorms blew in.

Halfway through the breezeway, I met Jess Plain, my right-hand helper. A breath of fresh air, Jessica was a student at a veterinary college about fifteen miles from Windermere. Willing to do just about anything I asked of her, Jess adored the rabbits, had named them all, and they became excited when she entered the barn.

Tossing my jacket onto a peg near the door, I caught sight of my windswept, burnished-copper hair and tried to bring it under control using my fingers as a comb. My facial skin had returned to its normal peach tone, rather than the redness the wind had brought to my cheeks and nose. Tears seeped from the corners of my eyes and trickled down my cheeks from the sudden change in temperature. I gave up on my hair, dried the moisture around my blue eyes, and turned to listen when Jess started talking.

"Have you heard the news? Arthur Freeman is dead. It was on the news radio station."

"Is that the man I found dead on the lakefront? Bun and I saw him when we were there. It sure didn't take Sheriff Carver long to make an identification."

A look of surprise filtered across her face. "Good grief, don't tell me you're going to investigate Freeman's murder?"

"Since I'm not familiar with Arthur Freeman, why would I bother?"

"You didn't recognize him?"

"Hardly, he was frozen like a Popsicle. His name isn't familiar to me, either."

We'd walked into the barn and moved bags of rabbit feed from the trolley. We stacked them on shelves. I handed Jess the last bag when she said, "I can't believe you don't remember him. He was known as Arty the Mime."

It only took a second for me to make the connection from Arty to the dead guy. "You're kidding, right? I never saw him without mime makeup on. That's why I didn't know who he was. Son of a gun, who'd want to kill a man whose goal in life was to do magic tricks at children's parties?"

"Did Jack ask if you knew him?"

I nodded. "He must have had an idea who the corpse was because he asked me a couple of times." I rolled my eyes and drew a deep breath. "He probably thinks I lied."

With a shrug, Jess remarked, "True, but then, it won't be the first time he's thought someone lied to him." When I glanced at her, she hastily added, "I didn't mean you, of course. You and Arty had a run-in at the fall festival last October, didn't you?"

"We had a disagreement, nothing more. It was simply a matter of different opinions. While we weren't friends, we had respect for each other."

"What was his problem?"

I thought back to that day. "We differed on whether animals should be free or kept. He wouldn't listen when I tried to explain what we do and how we rescue rabbits who have been mistreated or maimed." I considered how much more to say. "The situation became heated until I invited him to come out and visit us. He stomped away, and never mentioned it again."

Jess prepared to feed the fifteen rabbits we housed and medicate those who needed it. Finished charting the dosage information, I set the clipboard on its peg and walked back to the house.

Later in the afternoon, a car rolled into the driveway. I looked out the window and thought Jack Carver must have had more questions. I scooted across to Bun's room and murmured, "Stay in here, the sheriff has arrived. The dead guy is Arty the Mime."

One ear flipped forward, which I took as a sign of agreement. Bun remained on his bed as I closed the door to his room. With his superb hearing he'd know what Jack had to say. I didn't want Bun underfoot and blabbing while I spoke with the sheriff. I flipped the coffeepot on and opened the front door as Carver reached for the doorbell.

"Come on in, it's cold out there. Can I get you a cup of coffee?"

His nod was answer enough, and I filled two cups with steaming brew. Setting them on a tray along with a sugar bowl and creamer, I carried it to the end table next to an overstuffed armchair in the living room, where Jack was seated. I handed him a mug of coffee and added cream to my cup.

Seated across from him, I rested my elbows on my knees cupping the mug with my hands. Not giving Jack the opportunity to accuse me of misleading him, I said, "Jess mentioned the dead man was Arthur Freeman. It was announced on the news."

"You knew Mr. Freeman, didn't you?"

I nodded. "Only in a professional manner, and only as Arty the Mime. We attended many functions as the entertainment du jour. He'd do magic tricks and I had the educational rabbit petting pen. I never saw him without his mime makeup on. Honest to God." I crossed my heart.

"I'm glad you admitted that, Jules. After all, everyone is aware that you two were frequent entertainers at kids' events and public affairs the town hosts. Especially the festival last fall. Didn't you have a falling-out of sorts?"

"I didn't make the connection, sorry. Arty was

great at kids' functions, and we shared a few jokes now and then. He took miming seriously and was in tune with his audiences, no matter their ages. As to the falling-out, it was actually a difference of opinion."

"Different in what way?"

Quick to explain what had caused us to disagree, I mentioned Arty had been disgruntled. I left out the fury he had shown and how he'd walked away ranting about unfairness to animals.

Jack sipped his coffee. "Are you aware of anyone who might have had a grudge against him?"

"Not that I can think of offhand. If something comes to mind, I'll gladly let you know. Have you contacted his family?"

"He doesn't have any family that I can find."

"That's a shame. He was a nice sort, we enjoyed our stints together, and parents appeared to like him."

He placed the half-empty cup on the table and rose. "If you remember anything, anything at all, call me. I don't want time to get away from us. The longer the investigation goes on, the colder the trail becomes." At the door he reached for the knob and then said over his shoulder, "I know you might want to help out because you knew this fellow, but please don't interfere."

"I have no plans to," I blustered.

"I'm glad we're clear on that. Don't poke your nose where you shouldn't, I won't stand for it."

"What was the cause of death, by the way?"

"The pathologist is doing an autopsy on Arty's body now. He said it appears Arty was stabbed with a sharp instrument that pierced his skull. He won't have a full report until he's finished, but he thinks the man might have suffered hypothermia while cranial bleeding slowly killed him. Miserable death, for sure."

The thought of such a slow, horrible death sent shivers over my body. "What kind of weapon was used?"

Heaving a sigh, Jack rolled the brim of his hat with his fingertips and then put it on. "Nothing definite on that. And, before you ask any other questions, I have nothing else to say. Good day, Jules."

The door closed with a snap as I grimaced over his attitude. Scratching sounded at Bun's door. I swung the door wide and, hands on hips, I stared down at the furry creature.

"There's no gratitude for our brilliance."

"We haven't been brilliant, not yet anyway. Besides, the sheriff doesn't want our assistance."

"I think we should investigate, if not to satisfy our curiosity, then to get justice for Arty. After all, you might still become a suspect if Sheriff Carver finds out how bad your disagreement with Arty was."

"I had thought of that. If Jack presses me, I'll have to admit the situation got out of hand. Until then, I intend to keep that information to myself." I walked away before Bun could insist we become involved.

CHAPTER TWO

Never let it be said I don't listen. The problem is that I don't follow orders. Just because Jack Carver wanted me to stay out of Arty's murder investigation didn't mean that I wouldn't check into a few things on my own. I owed Arty that much. I had questions that needed answers, too. Answers I wouldn't get from Jack, that's for sure. Besides, if he asked around, he might find my disagreement with Arty had ended in a screaming argument.

A couple of weeks after our tiff, the barn had been broken into and the rabbit cage doors were left open. While I hadn't thought Arty was to blame, it gave me pause to think he'd been involved somehow. The furry little darlings had remained in their homes for the most part, since they were wary when those unfamiliar to them entered their domain. Unusual, I know. Several of the rescue rabbits had been traumatized by the event. It took weeks to coax many of them out of their homes, so they could get some exercise. Jess and I had constructed a huge playground where the rabbits could scamper about and jump around, as well as run through a clear plexiglass tunnel.

I'd been angered by the action that caused the rabbits mental harm. The barn doors had also been left wide open for escape. Thankfully, only one rabbit took advantage of his freedom. He'd eventually come back, looking for a meal and his own pen. Initially, Jess had named him Willy, but after his escape, she'd renamed him Walkabout Willy. We've kept a close eye on him, lest he take another trip around the farm.

"What's for supper?" Jess asked, tossing her work gloves in the laundry basket.

"Shepherd's pie is on the menu. Hungry?"

"You bet. Is it ready now? I have clinical work tonight and have to be there soon." She washed her hands at the kitchen sink and dried them with a nearby hand towel.

"It is. Get the rolls and butter so we can eat."

She brought them to the table and took a seat. "What did Carver want?"

The casserole steamed as my serving spoon sliced through the whipped mashed potatoes, digging into the corn before I scooped ground beef from the bottom of the pan in one big generous helping. Jess lifted her plate and I plopped the shepherd's pie onto it, then filled my own dish.

"He asked about the argument at the festival. I made light of it, which seemed to satisfy him. I never mentioned the barn break-in we had a few weeks later, because I didn't believe Arty was behind it. I hadn't notified the police department because only Walkabout Willy went exploring."

"You should have called them," Jess remarked, and then thought for a moment. "Maybe it's better that you didn't. You'd be a suspect."

Slathering butter on a warm roll, I said she was right. "I still might be on his list if he asks others who were present at the festival. Arty was some ticked off, and I don't know why. He ranted on about the cruelty of keeping animals penned up, and how they should roam freely."

After swallowing a mouthful of food, Jess said, "While that freedom is fine in theory, domesticated animals are less likely to survive when left on their own. We know they fall prey to larger animals, like foxes, wolves, bears, and wildcats. We do live in the countryside. I suppose you pointed that out?"

I nodded, ate my dinner, and asked after her classes. When she graduated later this spring, I was sure Jess would go off on her own, and I'd have to find a replacement. Not a chore I relished, since we'd become friends.

Her jacket flung over her shoulders, Jessica raced from the house, started her Volkswagen Jetta, and took off for her clinical shift. I packed away the leftovers, started the dishwasher, and then sat by the fireplace with Bun, who'd been quiet for some time. This was not a good sign.

"Do you think Arty argued with someone else who wasn't as forgiving as you are?"

"I wouldn't know, it's possible, I guess. He never spoke of friends. Ours was a professional relationship. Did you see anyone, at any parties or functions we were at, who might have had an issue with Arty?"

"At the party we attended for that little dark-haired girl, Racinda or something like that, I saw Arty in a heated discussion with her father, or maybe he was an uncle. I don't know who the man was, but I'd recognize him if I saw him again."

"Her name is Racine Corando and her father's name is Richard. She has an uncle who was there, whose name is, um, let me think, it's Jose. What was said? You do have excellent hearing."

"The children bustled about and made a lot of noise, so I didn't hear the men. I merely saw them argue. What does Richard look like? This man had a deep scar on his hand that was very ugly." Bun twitched a bit.

It was such a human action, I instantly wondered if he'd been reincarnated from a human into a rabbit. I shook off the thought and snickered.

"What's so funny?"

"Bun, it isn't like you to twitch over a scar. Why now?"

"I can't say. It's just how it struck me. Kinda like the one Fredo has on his back. Very ugly."

Fredo, a lop-eared rabbit who'd been abused by his owner, had received sixteen stitches to close his wound. He'd come to us by way of Windermere's animal rescue personnel, who'd asked Jess to deal with his injury. Fredo was a loving creature with a tan-and-white coat. His ears were edged in gray, as was his nose. His fear-filled eyes had been watchful on our first encounter with him. When the woman in charge of the unit requested we take him into our care, the immediate answer was "yes." Jess and I had worked with him for a long time to gain his trust.

"It isn't the scar that's ugly, Bun, it's the people who inflict them on animals. Try to remember that, okay?" A loud banging interrupted our conversation. I rose and peered out the window toward the barn. The double doors swung back and forth in the wind, striking the building.

I shrugged on my jacket. "Stay here. I'll check the barn and secure the doors. Be right back."

I rushed through the breezeway, catching sight of a shadowy figure running the length of the corridor that separated the rescued rabbits from the ones I raised. "Stop, you there, stop!" I yelled, and ran in his direction. His stride was longer than mine and he left the barn by the rear door.

I reached the doorway, stepped a few feet into the darkness, and listened. Other than the wind, I didn't hear anything. No feet pounding the frozen ground, nothing. I went back inside, bolted the door, and turned toward the cages. A cold blast of wind funneled its way through the barn. I hurried to shut and bolt the front double doors. Heat blasted from the furnace, and though the air was still chilly, I knew the barn would soon warm up.

Grumbling, I wondered why they'd been left unlocked in the first place. It wasn't like Jess to forget. Angered by the episode, I made the rounds, checked on each rabbit, and spoke softly as I went. I reassured them of their safety, and that I would take good care of them. Rabbits are intelligent animals, aware of what's going on around them, and are very sociable.

I'd reached the last pen when I heard a noise. It took but a second to figure out I wasn't alone. "Come out, right now."

My heart thumped, as if trying to escape my chest. My pulse raced, and I grew angrier by the second. "I don't know who you are, or what you think you're doing, but get out of my barn and off my farm before I call the police."

"You didn't call the last time and you won't this time. Besides, if you do, I'll tell them your secret."

Confused, I froze mid-stride. "Wh-what secret?"

"Why, that you killed Arthur, of course."

"B-but, I didn't kill Arthur. It's likely that you did and want to cast the blame on me." I scanned the dimly lit area and wished I'd flipped on every switch in the barn to brighten it. Shadows loomed as I cautiously moved toward the breezeway. One step, then another, before I tripped and fell.

"Oomph."

"You are so clumsy, Jules. Didn't you hear me calling you?"

"No," I whispered, and felt Bun climb into my lap where I sat on the floor.

"Who were you talking to? Jess left, didn't she?"

I answered with a light whisper. "She did. Go back to the house, we have an intruder."

Bun bristled as I told him of our visitor. *"I'll do no such thing. I'm staying put, who else will protect you?"*

I smiled and ran a hand over his thick fur while listening for footsteps or sounds indicating he'd gained ground on us.

"Are you still there?" I called out to him. How had he gotten back inside? Unless he'd left by the rear door to sneak around the exterior of the barn, then reenter by the front and hide when I closed those doors.

"Yes, I haven't finished what I came to do."

"What's that?"

"Free the rabbits, of course. Arthur tried and failed to get you to do it, but I won't." His words sent chills up my spine as I heard one hutch door after another open.

Unwilling to have the animals placed in danger, I set Bun aside and reached for the pitchfork. Holding it upright, I walked toward the electric switches. As I flicked each one, light filled the barn and the sound of footsteps began to recede. It was clear the man didn't intend to be seen, nor did he want to face me down.

When the rear door slammed against the barn, I hurried in that direction. At the doorway, I knew he'd gone. Lights cast a glow over the partially snow-covered ground, and I could see fresh footprints. It had been dark when he'd left the first time, and I wouldn't be stupid enough to ignore the light switches again.

I closed and bolted the door, wondering once again if the intruder had run from the rear door to the front of the barn to reenter before I could secure the entry. Making my way to the main area, I spoke to the rabbits, soothed their fear, and promised them a quiet night.

I picked up the phone and dialed the police department.

"Officer Langley."

"Could you connect me to Jack Carver?"

"He's gone home for the evening, ma'am. Can I take a message?"

"This is Jules Bridge, there's been an intrusion at my farm."

"I'll send someone out immediately. Are you all right?"

"Yes, thank you."

"Stay on the line until an officer arrives."

"That's not necessary, he's gone." I hung up and dialed Jack's home phone. Jack's wife, Meredith, answered the call.

It took some doing, but I remained calm. If not for my sake, then for that of the rabbits. Bun hovered at my feet in what I believe he considered protective rabbit mode.

"Hi, Meredith, it's Jules Bridge, is Jack home?"

"He sure is. Hold on a second."

I heard muffled words before Jack came on the line.

"What's going on?"

"I've had break-in. I called your office but was told you had left for the day. A policeman is on his way, but the situation is more complicated than it sounds. Could you come out to the farm?"

I heard him make a *tsk* noise before he answered me. "I'll be right there. Where are you presently?"

"In the barn. It's locked up tight. I don't think he'll be back, but you never know. The house is secured as well."

"Stay there."

I hung up and strolled the length of the barn, talking to the rabbits as I went. They didn't appear traumatized or fearful, which was a miracle. I rubbed a few bunny noses as they came close to their doors, then ended up back where I started. Bun announced a car had arrived.

Knuckles rapped against the wooden entry

door as a deep voice announced, "Deputy Adams, open up."

It took a moment to unfasten the locks to let him in. He entered and scanned the room. "You had a break-in, ma'am?"

"Earlier, I came to check the rabbits for the night and found an intruder. He was trying to let the rabbits loose."

He gave me a long look before he turned to the door as it opened. Jack walked in and the officer immediately stood at attention.

Carver nodded at him and then looked at me. "An intruder, huh?"

"I was telling Deputy Adams the man was trying to free the rabbits. He said Arty wanted them freed. I tried to coax him out from the shadows, but he refused and threatened me. I had my trusty pitchfork handy and turned the lights on as I followed the sound of his voice."

"That was foolish. You should have called us right away," Adams remarked.

"He threatened to say I killed Arty. I didn't, but he said he'd claim otherwise. I finally decided to protect myself and my rabbits from the likes of him."

Jack's bushy eyebrows hiked a bit. "What would you have done if you'd come face-to-face with the man? Attack him with the pitchfork? It's a deadly weapon that most likely would have been used on you instead."

"I know, I know, I wasn't thinking clearly, but it angered me that this jerk might harm us all. The bunnies had already been scared senseless in the past." I stopped talking so abruptly both men trained their attention on me.

"When was this?" Adams asked as Carver opened his mouth.

"Um, uh, well . . ."

CHAPTER THREE

"Don't hem and haw, just tell us," Carver demanded.

"Okay, fine. In November, someone entered the barn after the rabbits were settled for the night. I have no idea how he got in, there was no damage to the doors or windows, but he tried to set the rabbits loose. They're quite comfortable here, usually never afraid, and are well cared for, so they didn't budge, except for Walkabout Willy."

The rabbit's name brought snickers that turned into chuckles. Indignant that I wasn't being taken seriously, I snapped, "He likes to go out and explore. He's the only rabbit that does."

As always, Bun hovered near my feet, once again in protection mode. *"Can't they see that you were protecting us?"*

I looked down and gave him a wink before I faced the two policemen. "You asked," I remarked grudgingly.

"You're right, of course." Carver glanced at Adams and then said, "Continue on, then."

"The rabbits were stressed over the incident. Jess and I worked for weeks to regain their trust."

Adams held back a smirk. "Why didn't you report this?"

"I figured it was a kid making mischief."

"You didn't think it was Arty?" Jack asked.

I shook my head. Never would I admit that Arty might have been the culprit or the incident might have been connected to him. It would lead to suspicion of me as a murderer, and who needed that?

His pen and notebook in hand, Adams quickly scribbled what I'd said and mentioned he'd have a report on Carver's desk first thing in the morning. Carver instructed the deputy to check the footprints left outside the rear door and then dismissed him, while he alone stayed behind. Oh boy.

Noting the barn and its layout, Carver said, "Take me on a tour, if it won't stress the rabbits too much."

I gave him a keen look. "Do I sense a smartypants attitude?"

His nod was my answer. We walked the length of the single-floor, low-roofed, squat barn. I explained the rabbits, their needs, and where they came from, before taking a quick detour to check on Walkabout Willy. He lounged in the three level, wood and wire frame hutch near his food and water dispensers. Willy didn't seem any worse for wear after our visitor had tried to free him.

"Many of those rabbits, to your left, have been treated abominably. They've been tortured, and even attacked. One needed sutures from a knife wound." I sighed and continued, "These are endearing creatures, and more than that, they're loving. There's nothing mean about them, which is more than I can say for humans."

"I see you're dedicated. Tell me about the argument with Arthur. I know there's more than what you said earlier."

He matched my stride as I slowed my pace. "We were at the festival, where the petting pen was located, with kids enjoying the rabbits. No one was harming any of them. Arty, dressed in his mime costume, strode over after the last child had wandered away. I was about to wrap up our part of the event and return to the farm with the rabbits. He started to ramble on and on about animals needing to run free. His rant grew louder by the minute. I tried to explain how we provide for, and consider, our furry friends, but he refused to listen."

"Then what happened?"

"Things got a bit out of control. We struggled over him opening the pen gate. By that time, he'd grown downright angry. He was shouting, people stopped to gawk, and he pushed me to the ground to gain access to the pen. That's when the festival manager intervened."

"Why didn't you tell me this earlier today?"

"I didn't want to become a suspect. I liked Arty, we were professional, not personal, friends. In the end, he was asked to leave and did so raving like a maniac. I packed up the bunnies and came home. A couple weeks later, the barn was broken into."

"You never saw Arty after that?"

"Not that I recollect. We had done some birthday parties together before his outburst, but nothing afterward. It was as if he went on vacation or something. We had never moved in the same circles, other than those types of events."

Carver's attention, seemingly centered on the various rabbits in their cages, left me to wonder if he'd even heard that last part.

"You've created a great haven for these critters. I can tell you feel strongly about them and they receive good care."

I leaned down, picked up Bun, who had followed along behind us, and held him close. "They're intelligent and wonderful, that's all there is to it. People who harm animals should be put in jail."

"If you have this problem ever again, call the station immediately. No pitchfork, no weapons of any kind, understand?"

"Yes, sir, I do. But understand this: I won't tolerate having animals in my care harmed, frightened, or anything else. This place is my responsibility."

"I realize that." Carver moved toward the door. He turned at the last moment. "Other than you and Jessica, who else works here?"

"Two high school kids, Ray Blackstone and Molly Perkins, come in a couple times a week after their classes are over. They need to do a certain amount of community service hours before they graduate. Nice kids, and they're great with the rabbits. I also have a college student, Peter Lambert, who gives me a hand a few days a week. He needs the money to help pay for his studies. These people are young, but good workers."

A twinkle in his blue eyes brought on my smile. "What?"

"You can't be more than twenty-five years old and you call your workers kids?"

"Sometimes I feel older. After my parents moved to Georgia and gifted me this sweet little farm, I thought life would be idyllic. Instead, I've found a lot of hard work goes into owning any type of business. The effort is worthwhile, and I wouldn't give it up, but one must stay focused."

With a nod, Carver opened the door. "Lock up and don't worry, you'll be safe. I'll have a car drive by every so often to check on you."

"Thank you. I'll keep you posted should any further problems arise. I appreciate you coming by. Give Meredith my regards."

I watched as the fiftyish, stout man walked to his vehicle, started it, and drove away. It would be foolhardy to think I'd get a wink of sleep. Bun and I went into the house after I'd checked the doors again and taken a last stroll around the barn to make sure all was secure.

If ever there was a time to fess up, it had been last night. A tad relieved that I'd told Jack what had happened between Arty and me, I contemplated what conclusion he'd drawn. I'd mainly confessed due to the fact an intruder had offered to place Arty's death on my doorstep. Life was difficult enough without dealing with that.

I'm hungry, are you feeding me today?

Bunny never let mealtime pass, and rightly so. I disliked missing a meal, too. Maybe that's why I wasn't model thin or even slim. I enjoyed food, not junk food, just good cooking. My mother always called me stocky; I figure I'm more along the lines of fluffy.

His dish filled with his favorite blend of oats, wheat, and barley, I replaced the remnants of the timothy hay with a new bunch of stems and left Bun to his meal.

Bacon sizzled, eggs boiled, bread toasted, and coffee perked when Jess entered the kitchen with a wide smile on her face. "Is there enough for me? I'm late because my car wouldn't start. I think it needs a new battery." She poured coffee that had just finished perking and set the table for two.

Toast popped from the toaster. Jess slid them onto a plate and brought the butter tray to the table with her.

"We had an incident last night. A scary one. Before I explain what took place, did you leave the barn unlocked?"

"No, I checked both sets of doors before I left. I even checked the one in the shop."

Chewing a bite of toast, Jess listened to what had taken place. Her brown eyes widened, and shock lay on her features as I followed up with the sheriff's visit.

"What did you plan to do with that pitchfork?"

"No idea. Just use it to appear fearsome, I guess. Carver wasn't happy about it, but what was I supposed to do, huddle like the rabbits?" There'd been a time in my life when that's exactly what I'd have done, but those days were long gone. I now stood up for myself and for my furry charges. There'd be no crippling fear in my life ever again, if I could help it. After my car accident, I'd been jumpy over the least little thing. Being forced off the road and left to die can crush all the confidence a person might have. My healing process, both mental and physical, had taken some time, but fear no longer controlled me. At times, I wondered if Rusty Cardiff would once again appear out of nowhere and try to get even for my sending him to prison for his actions.

"You're pensive. Are you thinking back to when you were run off the road and left for dead?"

I shoved the memory away and forced a smile. "That was a long time ago. I refuse to allow fear to be my master, no matter the circumstances."

Slouched against the back of her chair, Jess nodded. "I'm glad you have the ability and fortitude to handle these situations. I can't be here all the time to be of use should another episode take place. Any idea who broke in?"

I shrugged. "I didn't get a look at his face. He ran out the rear door. He wore a long jacket with the hood up. I couldn't make out if he was thin or heavy. I'm a good runner, but he was fast, so maybe he wasn't heavy, and it was the coat that made him seem so."

"Write down what you saw, what you heard, and the tone of his voice, whether it was high or low, soft or lilting, you know what I mean."

"Good idea, I'll do that later. Right now, we should take care of the hutches and fill feeders with fresh food and water. I think Peter is due in anytime now to give us a hand. I'm fortunate to have a great staff. Even the high school kids work hard. They've offered to run the shop on Saturdays, so I can take a break from doing both jobs. It's tough to run back and forth when customers come in and the rabbits need attention."

"I know of someone who would be delighted to work here on Saturdays. She might fit in. Her name is Lizzy Fraser. I'll give her a call if you'd like to set up an interview."

"Just for Saturdays?"

"Yeah, her full-time job has been reduced to part-time and she's looking for extra cash. I think she'd be perfect."

"Sure, go ahead and call her. I would rather not have the teenagers operating the shop. It involves a lot of responsibility and then there's the money end of things." The students were great with the rabbits and working in the barn, but allowing them to sell merchandise was another matter altogether. I wasn't ready for that, and I didn't think they were, either.

The appointment with Lizzy was set. Jess and I watered, fed, and cleaned up after the rabbits while Bun happily hopped around. Peter arrived and gave us a hand finishing up before we took a break and went into the house.

"Got any of my favorite apples left, Jules?" Peter asked with anticipation.

I handed a plate of sliced fruit and cheeses to him and watched his face light up. I always bought natural peanut butter by the one-pound tub and brought that to the table as well. Jess poured hot water for tea, and we settled in. Like I said, I'd rather not miss a chance to eat.

"Are you breeding rabbits this year?" Peter asked.

"We might, but I'm not sure who will get to do the

honor of bringing babies into the world. Peaches had difficulty delivering her litter of kits last time around. We should select another rabbit. Any ideas?"

Warming to the subject, Jess offered her opinion. "Jazz would be perfect, and I think her kits would be lovely. Her long fur can be sheared and used for yarn in the shop, too. People in town have asked if we planned to have more of that type of merchandise for sale. A couple of parents want bunnies for their kids, as well. We could give another class on the care of rabbits should you sell the kits or find homes for the other rabbits we have. It was successful the last time around."

Interested, I noted the suggestions that flowed from the two of them. The cheese and fruit gone, our teacups empty, my two helpers went back to work while I headed into the yarn and gift shop attached to the barn.

The large room featured vaulted ceilings and a stretch of windows that ran around its two exterior sides. An enormous gas fireplace filled half of one wall and could heat the entire space. It blazed when I reset the thermostat, warming the room quickly. I listed merchandise to be added to the yarn stock that was left before taking inventory of rabbit toys, gifts for rabbit lovers, and rabbit paraphernalia that Bridge Farm Shop had on hand. The additional income from sales defrayed costs at the farm. Locals purchased the yarn and supplies I carried that wasn't available anywhere else in town. Always surprised by those who could, but didn't, order from online companies, I was happy to serve my customers and have a chance to chat with them. A personal touch is worth more than dealing with strangers on the computer. At least, that's what I'm told.

Sheriff Carver, accompanied by Officer Bonnie Jones, arrived as I lifted the last basket of yarn onto the counter. *What now?* I turned back to the yarn and kept counting, noting what was what and how much of it I had until they entered the shop.

"Jess said we'd find you here. I take it there wasn't any further trouble?" Carver asked, setting a loaf of bread, wrapped in a clear plastic bag, on the counter. "This is from Meredith, she knows how much you enjoy her sweet bread."

I worried when the law came bearing gifts. Why? I had no idea, it simply seemed that it might be used as a segue into more questions that I didn't have answers for, or didn't want to answer at all.

"Very nice of her, tell her I send my thanks, Jack." I held the bag opening to my nose and sniffed the fragrant bread. My mouth watered in anticipation of hot chocolate and toast for tonight's snack. I imagined the addition to my waistline and set the bread on the counter.

Bonnie withdrew an envelope from her jacket and held it out to me. "We have a suspect who might be connected to your intrusion. Would you mind giving this photo a look?"

"Sure, but I didn't see his face." I studied the photograph, my hand shook slightly, and I set the picture on the countertop. Rusty Cardiff, the idiot who'd run me off the road three years before and left me for dead, stared up at me. I took a breath, let it out slowly, and then faced Bonnie and Carver.

"He's in jail, how could he have broken into the barn?"

"He was released in October. You haven't seen him then?" Carver asked as Bonnie pocketed the photo.

With a shake of my head, I said, "He hasn't been around, at least I haven't seen him, and no one has mentioned him to me, either. Where does he live?"

Bonnie opened her mouth to answer, but Carver interrupted her. "He has a place on Rockland Way, a few miles east of here. He said he'd get even with you for testifying against him. We thought he might be the one who broke in here twice."

"If he wanted to make me pay, why would he mess with the rabbits?"

"They're your concern, and you feel deeply about them. That would be enough to hurt you, Juliette," Carver said in a gentle tone.

"I didn't see the man's face, and didn't recognize him from the way he moved as anyone I'm familiar with. As far as Rusty Cardiff goes, he hasn't been around that I'm aware of."

With a warning to keep my eye out for him or strangers lurking about, Carver and Bonnie took their leave. I heaved a weary sigh as they drove off. The memory of what happened three years ago came back in vivid color.

A party at the Coral Bar, in Windermere, had begun around nine on a Saturday night. Dancing, drinks, and lots of partygoers had filled the room. High spirits had abounded until a bar fight broke out between two guys who had decided they wanted to dance with the same woman. Namely, me.

Try as I might, I couldn't get between them to break up the fight and received a few punches for my effort. I'd backed off and let them go at it until sirens wailed and cops arrived to arrest those who were involved in the fray. Not wanting to be one of those people, and sporting a bloody nose, I'd known I looked like I belonged in the arrest group. I sidled out the back door of the bar with the intention of driving home.

Out of nowhere, a man had stepped into the dim light and grabbed my arm. He dragged me toward his vehicle and tried to force me inside. I fought like a wildcat, scratching and clawing at his face while kicking out and shoving against his chest. When he tripped and fell, I ran to my car and raced off into the night, happy to have escaped.

It wasn't long before headlights drew closer and closer. The horn of the vehicle behind me had sounded. I'd increased my speed and the car shot forward, momentarily leaving him behind. He pulled up close and slammed into the rear bumper, sending my car careening over an embankment. The car flipped over and that was the last thing I remembered.

Sheriff Carver had filled me in on the accident that should have killed me, but didn't. The driver had left me for dead. His footprints had been embedded in the hillside when he'd come to see if I was among the living. Jack had said I was so bloody they couldn't tell where it stemmed from. In my haste to get away, I hadn't secured my seat belt tightly, the airbags hadn't deployed, and I was injured badly because of it.

Eventually allowed home from the hospital, I had started my recuperation. Rusty Cardiff was arrested for assault and a slew of other things, and I testified against him. The skin under my fingernails had proven to hold his DNA. It took months before I went out on my own. My parents worried every time I'd done so, and I think my father had followed me once or twice just to be sure I was all right.

I leaned against the counter. I was no longer that person. Instead, when I'd gotten well enough, I took a women's safety class held at the Windermere YMCA. I'd proven to be the best student and maintained my skills.

The door opened, and Jess marched in with Bun right behind. I gave a start at the angry look on her face.

"What's the matter?"

"Bonnie said Rusty's living in Windermere. How could he have gotten out of jail so soon? He was sentenced to six years, for God's sake."

"It may have been due to good behavior or overcrowding at the prison."

"Yeah, well, I'm moving in."

I snorted. "You're not serious?"

"I am. I'll move in this afternoon. I'm not on the clinical schedule tonight or tomorrow, so I'll have time to pack my stuff and bring it here. You don't mind, right?"

I shook my head. First Bun went into protection mode and now Jess had joined him. A caring duo was forming, and it warmed my heart.

Left to inventory the rest of the merchandise, Jessica went about her chores. Finished for the day, she headed off to pack some clothes, while I organized a bedroom for her. Later in the afternoon, we hauled boxes and bins of her belongings into the house and up the stairs. It took some time to get her settled into the room facing the front of the property.

"This is great. The view is wonderful, and I can nearly see the entire barn from here. Whose room was this, anyway?"

"It has been a guest room for as long as I can remember. My aunt Ginny used it when she visited my parents. She lives in Maryland now and hasn't visited since my parents moved to Georgia."

"Nice digs, thanks for letting me stay, even if it's temporary."

I nodded, wondered how good an idea it had been, and then realized it would all work out, especially since my intruder had become brazen enough to threaten me. It seemed he had an agenda of his own, and I didn't believe it was simply because he was following through on Arty's plan. No, this guy had a reason for his actions, and I intended to find out what it was.

CHAPTER FOUR

The interview with Lizzy Fraser went well. Her positive attitude and sweet disposition were exactly what I was in search of. I had no doubt she'd be great with customers, and her knowledge of knitting and supplies needed for any yarn work fit my needs to a T.

"Finish filling out the paperwork, and I'll be right back," I said, and left her to it. I roamed the barn in search of Jess and found her giving Walkabout Willy his usual injection. Poor Willy hadn't been his chipper self lately. When Jess and I had checked the inoculation charts and found he needed his yearly shots to help him stay healthy, I'd also changed his food to a higher vitamin level to see if he'd perk up.

"Is Willy any better?"

She looked up, a sparkle in her brown eyes. "He's coming along nicely. I think he needs to go into the exercise pen, though. He hasn't been out of his hutch for a long period of time lately. What do you think?"

"You're right, he's probably anxious for a walka-bout," I snickered, as did she.

Moments later, Walkabout Willy joined a few of the other bunnies in the exercise pen. Jess said she'd watch them, lest Willy become frisky with the females. I nodded and returned to the shop.

Her paperwork in order, Lizzy asked a slew of questions, made stock and yarn suggestions, and agreed to generate advertising for the farm and shop. Happy with her willingness to get started, I agreed. Bunny popped into the room, took one look at Lizzy, and said, *"She has purple hair."*

I gazed in his direction, bent down and picked him up, and introduced him to Lizzy.

Noticing my gaze and that of Bun, she remarked, "I have purple hair. Do you like it?"

Dumbstruck, I wondered if she had heard Bun.

Lizzy said as she scratched Bun's head, "He's adorable."

I went on to give her Bun's history with his past family. "For some odd reason, they think he's in league with the devil."

She lifted Bun from my arms and hugged him to her. "Nonsense, he's simply intuitive. No other animal would stare at my hair the way he did."

"Another woman who appreciates my attributes."

Lizzy walked about the room with him in her arms, speaking quietly. Bun gave her his complete attention, and I left to make dinner.

In the kitchen, I mixed spices, ground beef, and a few secret ingredients together for meat loaf, then set it to cook in the pan alongside carrots, sliced onions, and potatoes. I enjoy making one-pan meals. They're easier for cleanup and tasty once the ingredients blend together.

An hour later, Jess strolled in with Bun on her heels. "Lizzy has left for the day. Two of her friends stopped by to purchase yarn. Imagine? Two new customers on her first day."

I chuckled. "Did she call them to say she'd gotten the job?"

Jess nodded and peered into the oven. "Is that meat loaf and veggies?"

"It is. I left the biscuits for you to make." I gave her a grin and walked into the living room. In the week she'd been living here, Jess had taken on her fair share of the household duties, for which I was extremely grateful. I was nobody's maid, and thankful she didn't think I was.

After dinner, we checked in on the rabbits, did the last of the chores, and returned for the night. The living room was toasty warm, inviting conversation.

"You'll be graduating soon, won't you?"

Nodding, Jess glanced in my direction, then turned back to the blaze. "I've had offers to consider from large practices in the state. I'm reluctant to leave you without enough help to manage the farm and all it takes to keep it running smoothly. You do realize I have to consider these offers, though, don't you?"

"Absolutely, that's as it should be. I'd expect nothing less. You've put in a lot of time completing your education."

She breathed deeply, then explained which veterinarian clinics had offered her a position.

"Do I hear a *but* in there?"

"I'd like to open my own clinic after I pass my state board exam."

It wasn't surprising to me that she'd want to do so. She'd mentioned it a few times, just not lately. "Do you know where?"

Setting her glass on the end table, Jess leaned on the chair arm and said, "Here, at the farm. You've got enough room for it, and I'd carry my weight with finances, rent, and all that. What do you think?"

"We both should give it serious thought. Owning your own business comes with a lot of expense and responsibility. I know from personal experience. Insurance costs alone are enough to choke on. If you're serious, then come up with a plan for the space you require, and let me know. Then, we'll decide if it'll work."

Her excitement was palpable, her smile enthusiastic, and I laughed out loud. That's when the phone rang.

I reached for the call, said hello, and listened intently for a minute or two. Bun lay at my feet staring up at me. I said, "I'll be right down."

Her face a mask of concern, Jess asked, "What was that about?"

"I'll be at the police department. Jack wants to have a conversation. Gosh, I think I'm in trouble." I petted Bun and readied to leave.

"What kind of trouble?"

"What did Jack say?" Jess asked.

"He didn't, he just asked politely if I'd come down for a chat."

"Uh-oh."

"You should have said it was inconvenient."

With a nod in his direction, I said I'd return soon.

The Windermere Police Department was of medium size in comparison to larger cities. With a population of fifteen thousand residents, Windermere was a hub of activity fueled by industry, both large factories and smaller home businesses. I considered my farm in the latter category.

I parked in the first available spot and sauntered across the lot toward the station. I wanted Jack's questions to be over with as soon as possible. I'd reached the door when I heard a voice behind me.

"I can't believe you'd think I would harm your stupid rabbits."

I whirled to face Rusty Cardiff. The overhead light showed craggy features. He seemed much older than I remembered. I guess prison ages people. It isn't a country club, and New Hampshire prisons could never be called such, nor would their county jails. Those places weren't for the faint of heart.

My chin went up a bit as I stood my ground, while my stomach flip-flopped like a bowl of Jell-O. "What are you doing here?"

With a cold glare, he said, "Probably the same thing you are." He reached past me and opened the door, then strode into the building.

The duty officer asked our business. Before Rusty could utter a word, I asked to see Sheriff

Carver. He picked up the phone, murmured into it, then pointed to a nearby bench and told us to wait.

There was only one bench. Neither of us wanted to sit near the other, so we sat at each end. Within a few minutes, Carver showed up, summoned us with a crook of his fingers, and turned toward a hallway. Uncomfortable as I was in the presence of a man I'd helped send to prison, I refused to scurry away from him. It would only let him know I was nervous, though I was sure he'd mistake it for fear.

I slid a glance in his direction. His brown hair was cropped short, his clothing clean and pressed. He didn't look like a former convict, but then, I'd never seen one, so my viewpoint might be skewed. His face held a closed appearance, as if he hid behind a mask of indifference.

Carver ushered us into his office and took a seat behind his desk. We took the two seats in front of it. Wary of what was about to take place, I thought of Bun and my life at the farm, and my nerves stopped whining like a strident violin out of control.

His stern features gave nothing away. Carver's steady gaze was on us in turn as he said, "You're both here to clarify a few things."

I raised a brow. "What things, exactly?"

"You said you didn't see the face of the man who broke into your barn, is that correct?"

He was all business, no friendly smile, no bread from Meredith, nothing. Carver was direct, in search of chinks in my answer that might let Rusty off the hook or put him behind bars. Again.

I nodded. "The man was running away from

me. Due to the way he was dressed, I couldn't tell if he was fat, thin, bald, or had a full head of hair. I stated this before."

With a dip of his head, he turned to Rusty and asked, "You haven't been to the farm or near Juliette since you were released?"

"That's right. On the date this happened I was in Manchester, visiting my sister, Amy. She was in the hospital at the time. I know you checked my alibi, she told me. What's this about, Sheriff?"

"I wanted the two of you here to clarify we aren't looking at you as a suspect. Juliette didn't think you were the culprit and had no idea you had been released from prison early. It was a matter of police follow-through on the investigation of who might have an ax to grind where Juliette is concerned. I know there's no love lost between the two of you, though she was certain you had nothing to do with the intrusion. Are we clear on that?"

"As a bell," Rusty remarked. "Are you finished?"

I watched Carver, saying nothing in response to his words. It occurred to me he might be playing a game of sorts. I couldn't figure out what it might be, or why he'd do so. In my opinion, cops can be sneaky. For what reason? I have no clue.

"I am. There will be no backlash toward Juliette over our investigation of your whereabouts, Cardiff, understand?"

"I do. Good night." He rose and left the room without a backward glance. I watched as he let the door close behind him.

"Was this necessary?"

"I thought so. He wasn't very happy when we started poking around in his life. His sister was in the hospital, she'd broken her leg skiing. The shift nurses verified his visits as well. He stayed in Manchester for a couple of days until Amy was released. Are you worried that he'll harass you?"

"Not at all. I can handle myself if I must, and you're only a phone call away. Besides, Jess moved into the house last week, so I'm no longer there alone."

"Glad to hear it. Meredith has been nervous over you living out there by yourself."

"She's such a dear." I readied to leave. "Give her my best, and tell her we have a new shipment of yarn arriving on Monday."

He heaved a sigh as we walked along the corridor and out the front door. I was about to be escorted to my car. So much for him believing I was safe from the likes of Rusty Cardiff.

"That woman has more yarn than she needs now. I suppose this next bunch is alpaca or some fancy must-have yarn she'll drag home and put away?"

I chuckled, opened the car door, and said he'd better give her the message, or I'd call her myself. He gave me a pained expression and then glanced around the parking lot. "Fine, fine. You win."

The evening hadn't turned out so bad. I wondered why Carver had thought he needed to make everything clear with Rusty and me present at the same time. Did he want to see how we reacted to each other? Was there another motive behind his actions?

Neither Rusty nor I wanted anything to do with each other. The fact that he'd stayed clear of me after he'd left prison said a lot. Rusty hadn't appeared to be angry or holding ill will, not like he'd been in court when he was sentenced. He'd ranted like a nutcase, leaving me rattled.

With a sigh of relief for having gotten the meeting over with, I drove home. Two miles from the farm, I noticed a truck behind me. It was gaining on me. I accelerated, and my car shot forward, leaving the truck behind. At the driveway, I took a sharp right, slowed when the car fishtailed, and then drove into the yard. The truck went by, not braking or slowing in the least. Anxiety over another left-for-dead episode had reared its head, but not enough to leave me fearful, just cautious.

The front door opened as I went up the stairs and onto the porch. Jess waited until I took my coat off before tossing a slew of questions at me.

I folded my arms, waited until she stopped blathering on, and then said, "All is well. It was an interesting and somewhat curious meeting." I poured a glass of wine for each of us, took it into the living room, and explained what had happened.

When I stopped talking, Jess jumped in. "That must have made you uncomfortable. You haven't seen him in years, right?"

"Not since he was taken away. He wasn't angry, that I could tell, and he doesn't seem to have a grudge against me, either. At least I didn't feel any animosity coming off him. I'd like to think he's making a decent life for himself, and that trying his hand at kidnapping again isn't on his agenda. As it was, I hadn't been his intended victim back then. He'd been waiting for someone else. His attorney said so in court."

"At least Sheriff Carver cleared up any misconceptions for both of you. You haven't been worried about Rusty showing up, have you?"

"It had crossed my mind once or twice. I think if he'd been going to come by, he'd have done it sooner rather than wait until now. I refuse to live in fear. I've moved on and sense that he has, too."

"Let's hope so." Jess finished her wine and went to bed.

I heard her footsteps on the stairs and her bedroom door close. I lingered, soaking up heat from the fireplace. Bun came out of his room, snuggled against my feet, and stared up at me.

"Were you scared?"

"No, only a tad uncomfortable. I think Carver wanted to see our reaction to each other."

"That could be a good thing. He now knows what to expect. Officers are sneaky like that, don't you think?"

I agreed. Hadn't I thought that very same thing?

"How do you like Lizzy?"

"She's interesting. Something is off, but I can't tell what. She was very friendly, though. You know how intuitive I am."

Full of himself, too. "You can read people, no doubt there."

"I was thinking that since we have Lizzy on our crew, it would allow you and me to investigate Arty's death. You haven't forgotten we are going to do that, have you?"

I shook my head.

"Great, we should get started as soon as possible. Carver was right when he said a cold trail makes investigating more difficult. When do you want to begin?"

"Let's consider where to start. Even with Lizzy onboard, there's work to be done every day. We can't run off on a whim, Bun."

"I know, I'm just excited to be hunting a killer."

"I'd hardly call it that. But we will look into Arty's background and ask around about his lifestyle very soon."

Satisfied with my answer, Bun twitched his ears in what I assumed was agreement.

"Jess is gonna be our in-house vet, huh? I heard what she said earlier tonight."

"She'd like to set up a veterinarian clinic here at the farm after she passes her state exam. It'll work out well for all of us, don't you think?"

"Where you gonna put her clinic?"

"There's enough space in the barn right behind the gift shop. I'd never considered opening it up as part of the shop or to increase the amount of rabbits we have here, so that could be where she probably wants to open her clinic. We both need to think things over and then discuss the matter. There's time, she doesn't graduate and become licensed for a while yet."

"She's the best gonna-be vet I've ever come across. We'll be most fortunate to have her so close by. It'll be great, I feel it in my lucky foot." Bun hopped toward his room, snuggled into his pillow, and sighed happily.

I lowered the fireplace thermostat, slipped a wool sweater on, and went through the breezeway, into the barn. Everything was quiet. No intruder, no nervous rabbits, nothing. On soft-soled shoes, I took stock of the animals. That done, I included the shop in my rounds and flipped the light switch as I went in.

A scrap of paper lay at the base of the front entrance. Not giving it much thought, I plucked it up, gave it a cursory glance, then tucked it into my sweater pocket. Lizzy had rearranged baskets and racks of knitting tools and yarn to draw customers' eyes to the colors and texture. The beauty of it made me wish I had enough time to knit more than a simple scarf. She'd arranged my grandmother's small spinning wheel off to the side of two armchairs grouped in front of the hearth. A small, rectangular table sat tucked between them, creating coziness. I smiled at Lizzy's creativity and considered her a bonus to my business.

A door lay off to the right, leading into a section of the barn I used to store what wasn't immediately needed, some of it being furniture and boxes filled with belongings my parents left behind when they'd relocated. I surveyed the long, wide space that spread from the shop to the back of the barn. I imagined walls erected to section off treatment rooms for animals that would work for Jess's needs.

Closing the door, I glanced once more around the shop. A slight movement at one of the windows caught my eye. The interior lights cast a glow across the empty, silent yard as I cupped a hand at the corner of my eyes to peer through the glass into the night. Nothing moved, other than stray leaves that had refused to drop until winter set in. They tumbled across the yard in the wind and rain. I shrugged and knew I was merely jumpy due to previous events that had taken place. Was my imagination running out of control? Had I become paranoid, and was I seeing danger lurking in every corner? Disgusted to think any of these questions were viable, I left the shop.

There was only one thing to do to stop this feeling of angst that constantly haunted me. I'd have to find out who was behind Arty's death and the break-ins and put an end to it. Bun would be excited to think we'd begin the search for those who had done us wrong. Hopefully, the sheriff wouldn't get in my way while I solved Arty the Mime's murder.

Being uneasy all the time was annoying to say the least.

"Has something happened? You appear upset."

I shook my head. Bun had been awaiting me when I'd entered the house. "Just my nerves worrying me." I rubbed my hands over my face. "I'm tired of feeling this way. I've decided you and I should get started immediately on our investigation into what happened to Arty, what caused him to behave the way he did, and why someone is using his viewpoint to ruin my business and possibly harm the rabbits. By the way, I thought you went to bed."

Gleeful, Bun ran circles around the kitchen table. *"At last, I thought you'd never see things my way. No more dragging your feet, hooray!"* He stopped hopping and sat some distance from me, his head turned to the side a bit. Rabbits have a small blind spot directly in front of their nose and can't see very well up close. Being far-sighted, they have a vision field of nearly three hundred and sixty degrees. All of Bun's senses were exceptional.

His expression made me smile until he added, *"You know I'm always right about these things. I did go to bed, but couldn't sleep. Glad I waited up for you. We're gonna get justice for Arty."*

With a groan, I picked him up, smoothed his soft, plush fur, and snuggled him tight against my chest.

"Okay, okay, don't get mushy. Just admit I'm right, and we'll get started first thing tomorrow."

Amused, I put him on the floor. "We'll visit Arty's house to see if we come across something that will help us out."

I watched him happily scamper into his room and jump up on his pillow.

CHAPTER FIVE

The delightful aroma of perked coffee wafted into my nostrils. My mouth watered. I blinked at Jess, who held the cup out to me with a question in her eyes and a smile on her face.

"Oh, thanks." I took the cup from her, inhaled the coffee, and then took a sip. Still dressed in yesterday's clothes, I stood up and took stock of myself. I'd fallen asleep in a comfy chair next to the fireplace after my discussion with Bun. Surveying the room, I noticed he wasn't with Jess.

"It's been raining all night. Thankfully, the snow is nearly gone. I put Bun in the barn with a few of his pals in the playpen. You must have been exhausted to have fallen asleep down here."

It wasn't as much of a statement as it was a question. I nodded and slurped more coffee. In the kitchen, bacon sizzled, toast was piled high on a plate, and orange juice sat in a clear pitcher, waiting to be poured.

"I made oatmeal for breakfast. Yours is a bit

soupy, sorry about that. Hurry and eat it before it grows cold."

Truthfully, I detested oatmeal, and soupy or not, I rarely ate it, unless it was in cookie form. As a kid, my mother made thick, lumpy oatmeal, saying it was a good way to start the day. I'd gag it down and then give the rest to the dog when Mom left the room.

At the table, I chewed a slice of toast, downed a glass of orange juice, and stirred the oatmeal in hope that Jess would go out to the barn, so I could dump it in the trash. I only kept oatmeal in the cupboard because I liked to bake cookies.

"Well, are you going to eat it or whip it to death?"

"Eat it, of course. I appreciate the trouble you've gone to, thanks." I crunched bacon, followed by a spoonful of oatmeal, and then swallowed hard to get it down my throat. Jess rose from her seat as Bun raced into the room, slid to a stop, then ran toward the door and back again.

"Looks like Bunny has something on his mind. I'll be right back, finish your breakfast."

Rising from her chair, Jess headed for the door. "No, I'll go, you stay here and eat up."

Thank God. I wouldn't have to eat this slop.

Bun's voice came back to me as he and Jess went through the breezeway. *"You owe me, big-time."*

With a snort, I rushed to the sink, spooned oatmeal soup from the bowl into the food disposal system, and flipped the switch for a few seconds. I then ran back to the table. A few minutes passed before Jess returned.

"How was that oatmeal?"

"Truthfully, it was nice of you to make it for me. It isn't one of my favorites, though."

Her brows hiked a tad and her eyes held surprise. "You should have said so. You didn't eat it because I made it, did you?"

Ashamed to admit what I'd childishly done, I said, "Well, uh, I actually dumped it into the garbage disposal unit. I'm sorry, Jess, I don't mean to hurt your feelings, it's just that my mother made me eat it every day when I was a kid. I hated it then as much as I do now."

With a hoot of laughter, Jess shook her head. "I thought I heard the disposal running. It's very loud, you should have someone see if there's something wrong with it. The one my mom has isn't quite that noisy."

"Was there a problem in the barn?"

With a stern glance at Bun, Jess said, "Somehow, Bun escaped from the pen and the other rabbits followed suit. They had a great time running around the place. We should make the frame higher and add more wire to it. They're back in their cages, even Walkabout Willy."

I gave Bun a look of admonishment, but said nothing, nor did he. Instead, he blithely wandered off to his room and snuggled onto his fluffy pillow. This rabbit had a sweet life, for sure.

"Do you have clinical today?"

"Tonight. The only thing on my schedule now is the rabbits. Why?"

"I'm going out later and wanted to make sure I was back in time if you were on the schedule for your clinical work. I also want to show you the space I have in the barn that you might consider for your veterinarian use."

"Then let's get moving. Three rabbits need their morning checkups before we do anything else."

I tidied the kitchen while Jess went to the barn. In no time, the rabbit cages were cleaned and re-stocked with hay, food containers were filled with fresh veggies and a fruit mixture, and fresh water was added to their drip bottles. Jess followed me into the shop where I showed her the space off that area. She was thrilled at the length and width of it. We sketched out rooms and measured the sizes she thought would offer her the options of seeing and treating animals, not just the rabbits.

The clock chimed eleven as Lizzy popped through the door with her enthusiasm in full bloom. "How do you like my redecorating so far?"

Her infectious grin caused us to respond in kind.

I said, "It looks great. I haven't a decorative bone in my body, so have at it. How long will you be here today?"

Pointing to the jumbled supplies in the corner behind the counter, Lizzy said, "Those supplies have to be organized. I'll stay until four this after-noon, if that's all right with you?"

"Sure, I'll be out for a while, so if you need a hand, Jess will be here as will the high school kids after classes end for the day."

Jess joined in. "Just give a holler if you want me to help you."

We left her to organize the rabbit-care goods

she'd taken down to make the yarn displays. Jess
went back to the rabbits, and I went in search of
Bun.

"What are we waiting for, Jules? Let's get rolling."

I'd browsed the newspaper obituaries for Arty's
death notice. His address wasn't listed in the arti-
cle. After some consideration, I called a customer
Arty and I had worked for in the past and asked if
she knew where he lived.

"Funny you called, I was just putting my receipts
together and have one of Arty's in the bunch. You
must be very distressed over the poor man's death,
it's so sad," Melissa Reynolds said as she went
through her receipts.

I agreed it was a shame he was dead, and heard
paper rustling, then an "Aha!" came across the
phone line. "Yes, here it is. He lived out on Summers Road. Um, let me see, oh yes, at number fifty-
eight. Summers Road, that's a good distance from
town. If I remember correctly, it's a wooded neigh-
borhood with few homes on that road."

As his residence was off the beaten path, Bun
and I would be gone a good while. Thanking her
for the information, I was about to hang up when
Melissa reminded me of the birthday party she'd
booked me for in April.

"I'd never forget Alison's birthday, she's such a
sweet girl. I'll be in touch before then to finalize
everything."

"Wonderful, Alison adores your rabbits, and so do
her friends. You wouldn't happen to know of any-

one who could take Arty's place, would you? He'll be sorely missed by the children. And some of the parents, too."

Who could take Arty's place? No one I knew of. I said I'd give it some thought and rang off before Melissa came up with another request.

"You got it? Are we going now?"

"Look, before we go off on this adventure, we need a plan. We just can't drive up and park in the yard, then sneak around. What if he has neighbors? What if the sheriff has labeled the door with crime tape or something? Think, Bun, think!"

"I'm simply anxious to find the killer, is all."

"How about if we take a look around the grounds and if he hasn't any close neighbors, we'll go inside the house? No harm in that, right?"

"What if his door is locked? What then, huh?"

"Bun, you sound as if you're afraid. I thought you were anxious to check things out."

"I'm not afraid. I'm giving the whole idea some thought, just like you said. We could be walking into who knows what kind of mess. What if the killer is there, what about that, huh?"

"If you're that worried, I'll go by myself and save you from having a nervous breakdown over the various scenarios you'll come up with on our way there."

"Jules, I didn't mean it like that. I was only trying to offer the what-ifs of the situation. You know how brave I am. Gosh, I could be a superhero. I've come to your rescue in the past, haven't I?"

I smiled, trying to remember if that occurrence had ever taken place. An image of Bun in a superhero's cape nearly had me laughing out loud. I scooped him from the floor, tucked him into the sling I'd put on, and started our trip to Arty the Mime's house.

Bumping over the dirt road leading to Arty's, I listened to Bun complain about being jostled, the condition of the road, and that he feared we'd be caught.

The road in was nearly empty of other inhabitants. The long, winding road was bordered by overgrown trees that stuck out into the road, crowding any vehicle that traveled it. I counted three driveways with mailboxes at the edge of them, with no homes in sight. Dwellers must enjoy living deep into their land, sort of like I did. Granted, mine wasn't overrun with trees or overgrown foliage. It was my lucky day, for sure.

"You'll be fine. We're almost there." I parked my compact car out of sight behind a thick stand of tall arborvitaes at the rear of Arty's house. In stealth mode, Bun and I left the car and crept toward the side entrance, peeking in the cottage windows as we went. Still in his sling, Bun poked his head out and gawked to and fro, taking in all that he could see, smell, and hear.

"Anything unusual?" I asked as we drew closer to the door.

"Nope, all's clear. Try the doorknob."

It jiggled in my hand, but the door didn't open. I searched for a key and found none under the doormat, in the flowerpot, or underneath it. I looked up at the small pitched roof above the entry, with a concrete step up to the door, and saw a silver key protruding past the edge of the left eave. I reached up, took it, and fit the key into the lock. When I tried the door again, it soundlessly swung inward, into the kitchen.

Bun's ears twitched as he rocked his head back and forth. His sign of approval, since he usually acted in such a way when I'd done something correctly. For all his bragging, Bun gave credit where it was due. We entered the dead man's domain, and I set Bun free of the sling and began my search for whatever clue could lead to who wanted Arty dead.

Off on his own, Bun hunted for what he thought might be useful to us. He bounded onto the living room furniture, stuffed his nose into a stack of papers in Arty's rolltop desk, sneezed, and sat back bewildered as the pile fluttered to the floor.

"Now you've done it. We're not here to make a mess, we're here to search and not be found out." I picked the papers off the floor, rifled the lot before shuffling them into order, and put them back.

"I could smell his essence on those papers, and it bothered my nose. He had a distinct odor, like someone who's sick. Have you noticed Merry Bunny has a similar smell?"

"Merry is recovering from surgery. I don't find her smell any different because of it. You do have intense senses, though. What did he smell like, besides sick?"

"Sort of gross, like a rotten potato. Sickly. That's the best I can do, I'm not a doctor, I'm a rabbit."

Unwilling to let him see how humorous I found his comment, I rubbed his ears and gently scratched his nose. "You're right, you've done well, Bun. Let's keep looking, shall we? If you hear anything out of the ordinary, let me know, okay?"

"Sure will."

We separated. He poked around while I went into what appeared to be Arty's makeup den. Costumes hung on hangers on a rack, and a huge mirror was attached to the wall above a table covered with assorted jars of cosmetics. The table held a small drawer that caught my eye. I pulled it out and lifted notes from it. They didn't seem important, but I tucked them into my jacket pocket for a closer look later.

"Can I come in here?" Cautiously, Bun hopped across the threshold, his nose wiggling as he sniffed. His eyes squeezed shut, Bun let out a sneeze. He shook his head and backed away. His long ears flopped down and up again when he sneezed over and over.

"Are you all right?"

"More sickness in here, I'd say. The same smell lingers in this room as on the papers out there." He tipped his head toward the other room and left me alone.

It didn't take long to go through the pockets of the outfits. I found nothing of interest and returned to Bun, who stared out the window from atop a short bookcase.

"I'm going to see what's in his bedroom. Can you go into the kitchen and have another look around?"

His tail flipped up and down while his ears perked upward. Seconds later, Bun was in the kitchen. It's always better to keep Bun busy when I want to check things out alone. Otherwise, he pestered me with questions. Who knew how long we would be here? What if someone showed up out of nowhere and caught us?

The bedroom was quaint, as was the cottage. There might be two tiny rooms on the second floor, but that would be all. Arty had been neat as a pin for the most part. His bed was covered with a frayed, but spotless, star quilt. I wondered if it was a family heirloom he couldn't bear to part with. Neatly stacked decorative pillows lay in front of the ones he used for sleeping, his shoes were lined up along the wall next to an old oak dresser, and a Bible sat on a crocheted runner. I noticed a card next to the Bible. For a moment, I wondered if Arty had been ill but kept it to himself. Startled when I heard Bun's voice, I turned to him.

"Nothing of interest out there, Jules. Can I help you?"

"I think you should keep watch in case someone comes. Will you do that for me?"

"Okay, boss. I hope this will soon be fruitful for us. I'm getting hungry."

As Bun went off to perform his task, I fingered the Bible and lifted it off the dresser. It was worn, well used, and the idea that there'd be worthwhile information inside it pushed me to open the front cover. Inside, a family tree lay scrawled across a two-page spread. I wanted to study it, but Bun bounded into the room, his eyes wide with panic.

"We've gotta go, now, right now, come with me. Hurry up, we must leave the house. Come on, come on."

Taking one look at his wild eyes, his fur jittering as though he was electrified, I knew we had a visitor. "Okay, we'll go out the rear door. Climb in." I bent down, lowered the sling, and helped Bun inside. We scrammed from the bedroom, out the back door, and along the side of the house, away from the car's motor that I could hear running.

A stack of logs piled high sat not far from the door. Holding Bun close, I rushed past the wood-pile and hunkered down, trying to avoid falling on the wet ground. When Bun tried to stick his head out to see, I slipped in the mud and landed hard. Squishy muck soaked my jeans, then splashed my jacket, causing Bun to fall out of the sling.

"Oh dear, my paws are dirty. Get me off this disgusting ground."

His distress apparent, I lifted him up and held him close to my chest. I refrained from any attempt to rise for fear I'd upset the woodpile and we'd be spotted.

"Did you see who drove up?" I whispered.

"It looked like the sheriff's car, but I didn't see who was driving. Sorry, Jules."

"Not to worry, we're safe and hidden from view."

A couple pieces of odd-shaped logs offered a peephole with a restricted view of the backyard and included the door we'd left by. Was someone searching for the same things I had? Why hadn't they looked before now?

I squinted at the door and drew in a breath when Officer Bonnie Jones stepped outside. Bun's head was pressed against mine as he edged in and tried to see through the small opening. His head snapped back, and he hunkered into my arms, burying his nose into the crook of my elbow.

Leaning away from the woodpile, I smoothed his fur and scratched his head. The car door closed with a snap. I peeked through the small space again to find the area empty. Moments later, I heard the car engine rev. We seemed to wait forever for Bonnie to leave, yet I'm sure it was only a minute or so until the sound of the car was gone.

Slowly, I rose from the mud, looked over the top of the stacked wood, and viewed the property. "She's gone."

"Thank goodness. I was scared she'd find us."

"Why do you fear her, Bun? I know it's more than being here and breaking into Arty's house."

"Don't overreact because I was frightened. I doubt I'd look good in a jailbird's jumpsuit."

Laughing at the vision he presented, I murmured, "I don't think you have anything to worry about. Let's get out of here, before someone else comes along."

"Good idea, I'm really starving now. Could use a nap, too."

A towel sat on the floor behind the front seat. I used it to wipe away the now-dried mud on Bun's feet and then scrubbed the seat of my pants. I stamped my feet, and most of the muck came off. The rain certainly had done a good job of making the snow disappear, but left soggy ground in its wake. I sniffed the fresh air and wished for an early spring.

CHAPTER SIX

Slowly, we bounced over the road, taking our time to get to the main highway in case Bonnie lingered somewhere on the way back to town. I kept close watch for the cruiser lest she hid from view with a radar trap.

On the seat, Bun dozed in the sling, one dirty paw extended from within, sort of cupping his furry little chin. Why hadn't he shared his real reason for fear? I took a left onto Baily Schoolhouse Road. I'd taken this shortcut into town in the past, which cut off several miles of travel to the farm. The fuel tank read less than a quarter, and I turned into the nearest gas station. Leaving Bun and the sling on the front seat, I filled the tank and was screwing in the cap when Bonnie's cruiser came to a stop on the other side of the gas pumps from me.

"Hey there, Jules. Haven't seen you in town lately," she said as she washed the cruiser windows.

"I've been busy at the farm," I said while round-ing the trunk of my car. "What's going on with you?"

She chuckled. "Nothing much, just cruising around looking for bad guys."

"I see, do we have many of those hanging about?"

"Nah, but I did get a call that someone might be at Arty's house. I took a ride up, but didn't find anything out of the ordinary. What have you been up to?"

My dislike of lying is right up there with picking one's nose. But surely, this could be the exception to the rule?

"I had to meet a client. She had booked a birthday party for her daughter and wanted to discuss the arrangements."

With an even stare, Bonnie nodded and said she'd see me around sometime. I watched her cross the parking lot and enter the store. Nervously, I slipped behind the steering wheel and left for home, concerned that she'd known I lied.

Once we arrived home, I turned Bun loose in the kitchen, then replenished his food containers, before I scouted out the barn for Lizzy and Jess. I found them busily updating a shop that would, no doubt, please customers.

"Wow, you two have been busy."

Her attention centered on me, Jess said with a grin, "Where have you been? You're filthy."

I rubbed my hands on my jeans and looked down. Good thing Bonnie had been a good distance away, or she'd have asked how I'd gotten so grubby. Smears of dried mud stained the front of my pant legs, my shoes were brown rather than the shiny black they had been, and my hands were dirtier than the rest of me. I could only imagine what my backside looked like. Oh, my.

"I slipped and fell while we were out. The rain melted the snow, but left mud in some places."

"Only you would end up looking like you've been mud wrestling."

"That's what happens when there's soft, squishy muck." I turned to the racks and shelves. Neatly placed merchandise, organized to the nines, was delightful. Pleased with their work, I knew when customers came in to browse, they'd be drawn to the colors and feel of the yarn. How long would this tidiness last? I didn't dare ask.

Lizzy handed me two sheets of paper. "Here's your new inventory list. The second page contains the supplies you might want to order. We also began to clear the space Jess will use for her examination rooms. I hope you don't mind."

"Not at all. Show me what you've accomplished in there so far."

Furniture lined the barn wall waiting to be removed. Floors swept, several bins filled with debris sat near the door, and oddments my parents had left behind were packed and stored at the far end of the building.

"We didn't know what you wanted to do with all this stuff." Jess glanced at Lizzy, who agreed, and then she turned to the pieces. "Jules, there's a secondhand furniture shop in Windermere that would gladly buy all this."

"I'll have to clear that with my parents, it belongs to them, and I can't sell it without asking them first. I'll call my mother this evening. You've gotten a good start."

They were encouraged by my response. The next half hour was filled with suggestions and sketches that clearly showed Jess was serious about a veterinarian business. I listened in silence, didn't add my opinion to their excited explanations, but waited for them to stop talking.

Pensive for a moment, Jess said, "You look skeptical, Jules."

"There's one critical thing you've left out."

"What's that?" Lizzy asked.

"How do you expect to pay for the structural work that needs doing, the filing of applications necessary for your business, and order an inventory of supplies you'll need?"

By this time, we had entered the shop, closing the door to keep the chilly air from creeping in. I faced the two women from one side of the counter, while they stood on the other side. No way could I afford to take on the total construction expense.

"I've been in touch with the bank and my parents. The bank will give me a loan if my parents will guarantee it. My father wanted to know how much this endeavor would cost. I said you and I hadn't figured it out yet."

"Then the next step will be to contact Fred Costanza. He's a local builder my father had hired to make changes in the barn and the house over the past fifteen years. He's a fair man who won't take advantage of us. Shall I add him to my call list?"

Her smile lit up the room as she jumped up and down in glee. Jess's excitement sent Lizzy and me into a fit of laughter. "Don't think this won't be a lot of work, Jess, we've got a long way to go yet. But this is an undertaking that I look forward to."

The grandfather clock chimed five. Lizzy said she had to leave, Jess wanted to check the rabbits, and I needed a shower in the worst way. It was nearing six o'clock by the time we sat at the kitchen table for a light supper. Soup and sandwiches were the fare of the evening.

"Is this minestrone soup?"

I nodded. "Straight from a can. The sandwiches are an assemble-for-yourself kind of deal."

"Works for me."

We ate in silence for a bit. Bun sat in the doorway waiting to be filled in on the news since Jess still bristled with excitement.

"Is Jess okay?"

In answer to his query, I asked Jessica, "You're looking forward to opening a veterinarian business, aren't you?"

From the corner of my eye, I noticed Bun's ears twitch.

"Indeed, I am. I've dreamed of this for so long, it's the only thing that's kept me going. My classes have been difficult at times, and more than once I wanted to quit, but I refused to give up. All I need now is to finish this clinical rotation to graduate and then take my licensing exam."

"I'm glad you're willing to set up in the barn." I glanced at my watch and pulled my cell phone from my pocket. I dialed Fred's number.

"Fred Costanza."

"Fred, this is Juliette Bridge. Are you still in the construction business?"

"I am, what can I do for you, Juliette? How are your parents?"

"They're fine and loving life in Georgia. I'm interested in converting space in the barn into a vet clinic and wondered if you'd come out and give me an estimate on the job?"

"I can come by at ten on Saturday morning, if you'll be there."

"I look forward to seeing you, thanks, Fred." I hung up, filled Jess in, and then called my mother while Jess cleared away the remnants of supper.

Mom answered on the first ring.

I waited as she fumbled with the phone while saying, "Hello, hello?"

"Were you sitting next to the phone?"

"Juliette, it's so good to hear your voice. I was waiting for Annie to call, she's our neighbor. Her dog got loose and hasn't returned home yet. She's a nervous wreck."

"Oh, dear. I'm sure things will be fine. Dogs have a great sense of direction. Anyway, I have a favor to ask."

Hesitant, Mom didn't answer immediately. "What's the favor?"

"You sound wary, but don't be. I plan to use the storage space in the barn and would like to know if I can get rid of the odd pieces of furniture you left in there."

"Let me think, what did I leave behind?"

I listed the furnishings and waited.

"I can't think of any reason why you shouldn't do what you'd like with them. We took what we wanted and discarded the rest. Go ahead, dear, do what you think is best."

"Thanks. I hope Annie's dog comes home. I'll call you soon."

"Take care, dear."

My mother cut off anything I might add by disconnecting the call. I smiled, gave Jess the thumbs-up sign, and tucked the phone into my pocket. "We're good to go. After we're finished with our chores tomorrow morning, let's take a ride into town to the furniture store you mentioned this afternoon."

"I can hardly wait. If Fred offers a good estimate, I can get my bank loan underway."

"The store owner might be willing to buy the furniture. If so, I'll add the money to the construction funds. Every little bit helps."

Not long after we'd cared for the animals, we rode into Windermere and parked outside Ferguson's Fabulous Furnishings. The wide front windows displayed items found in brand-name stores. The difference being, the merchandise had a frayed-around-the-edges appearance. We glanced at each other, and I suggested we have Lizzy come down and shape the store up for Mel. Jess giggled and nodded in agreement.

We went inside, only to find the best furnishings were farther back in the store. Sofas, chairs, and tables were nestled in groupings, inviting lookers to seat themselves and feel the comfort. A man approached with an affable, used-car-salesman grin, and greeted us.

"Good morning, ladies, how can I, Mel Ferguson, owner and manager of this fine establishment, help you today?" If he'd been wearing suspenders, I swear he'd have snapped them.

We shook hands and I explained the situation. His brows furrowed, and his bottom lip curled outward as he listened. When I finished talking, his smile returned. "What I can do for you is to examine what you want to sell, before making an honest offer for the lot. How's that sound?" He rocked back and forth on the soft soles of his shoes.

"That would be good of you." I gave him the address to Fur Bridge Farm and made an appointment for the following day.

We left the store and walked to the corner coffee shop. We were discussing the possibilities of getting a fair deal from good old Mel when Sheriff Carver stepped up to the table and invited himself to take a seat.

"Glad to see you girls," he said as he peered under the table. "You left the rabbit home, huh?"

"I did."

"I heard you might have been up at Arty's house."

Not one to bluster very often, I calmly asked, "Where would you ever get that idea?"

"It wasn't mine, Bonnie thought you may have been out that way. Now why would you be poking around out there, I wonder?"

I shook my head and sighed. "Jump to conclusions much?"

"Not ever, so why don't you explain why you were out that way?"

"First off, I was fueling my car when Bonnie stopped to get gas. I have no idea why she'd think I was at Arty's house."

"She might be wrong, but I've never known that to happen. I do hope you're not probing Arty's death on your own, or with the rabbit in tow. Fat chance he could help if you ran into the killer, who, by the way, happens to still be on the loose."

"Don't you think I know that? I've been busy running my farm. Fred Costanza is coming to estimate a construction job for the barn, and then there's my shop to keep up with. How many things do you think I can handle on my own?"

"You do have staff to help you, which allows you to poke your nose where it doesn't belong." He shifted in the chair and said to Jess, "Keep an eye on her, will you? I can't watch her and find a killer at the same time."

Her eyes fixed on her coffee cup, Jess muttered, "Yes, sir, I will."

"Good, glad we've had this talk." The sheriff rose and meandered out the door.

I'd never seen him enter the room and wondered if he'd been here when we arrived. "Did you notice him when we came in?"

Jess shook her head. "Maybe he saw us and decided it was a good opportunity to have a few words. You haven't been poking around, have you?"

Like I said before, lies aren't my forte. I leaned forward and whispered, "I kind of went to see what Arty was about. His place is tiny, his yard neat, and yes, I almost got caught by Bonnie. If I hadn't parked behind his house and she'd seen my car, she'd have searched for me and Bun, and arrested us on the spot for trespassing."

Her elbows perched on the table, Jess rolled her eyes, took a deep breath, and let it out slowly. "Don't say anything else. I don't want to know what you were doing besides prowling Arty's property. Be careful, okay?"

With two fingers, I crossed my heart and then pretended to zip my lips. It was too much for her to deal with. "Yeah, right. Finish your coffee and let's get back to the farm."

The last vestiges of my coffee gone, I pushed back from the table. "Yes, let's. The students should be arriving in an hour or two. I don't know what I'll do once they've graduated. They're terrific with the rabbits and aren't afraid of hard work, either. Molly adores Petra. She grooms her long angora fur as if she's preparing Petra for a date." I stopped for a second to fasten my jacket and then joined Jess at the door. "Molly and Ray had a hay fight the other day. I guess their exams went well and they were in high spirits."

"Did you scold them?"

"Not really, I told them to clean up after themselves, which they did."

We'd reached the car and buckled in. Jess remarked on how soft I was on the help.

"I haven't any reason to be otherwise. The staff works as hard as I do, they're willing to take on extra duties if necessary, and I consider myself fortunate. What kind of boss would you have me be?"

"True. You do have great helpers, who carry their weight without question. Sometimes I worry about you being too easygoing with them. They aren't your friends, they're your employees."

"I realize that. Is all this because they had a hay throwing match? It was just a bit of fun, for goodness' sake."

"What if one of them was the culprit who broke into the barn? What then?"

I hit the brakes, pulled to the curb, and asked, "Is there something you're not telling me? You'd better speak up, if there is. Should I be worried about my help?"

"There's nothing to tell, I'm simply saying we never truly know the people we work with or employ as well as we think. Tell me, what do you know about your employees? Are they churchgoers, white knights in shining armor, school bullies, troublemakers, honest to the bone?"

"I know that each one is a good person, not some idiot trying to ruin my life and business. I'm even beginning to think this intruder has been using Arty and his death as a way to taunt me, rather than his performing Arty's last wishes. Where is all this coming from, anyway?"

"I've been thinking of all the possibilities, including how trustful you are. I mean no criticism, honest."

Mulling over the points she'd made, I pulled into traffic and drove away from the busy streets toward the farm.

"What if this concerns Rusty Cardiff? Maybe he's using someone to harass you instead of him doing it. So what if he had an alibi for the last break-in? He's covered his tracks by using someone else to do his dirty work. You can't discount him. Since I moved in, we haven't had one incident, what does that say?"

"Maybe you're right. It's possible the intruder knows it's now two against one, or maybe we're making silly assumptions. Any way you look at it, I must find out all I can about Arty. I'm sure that's where the connections and answers will be found."

I parked in my usual spot, got out of the car, and went into the barn with Jess close behind. At the door, I said, "We won't discuss this in front of anyone, understand?"

Jessica agreed as Lizzy pranced into view, her steps light and airy. All she needed was a tutu and ballet slippers to complete the picture.

CHAPTER SEVEN

"You're happy today. What's up?" I asked Lizzy, who acted like she had something to share but wanted us to ask about it first.

"You'll never guess who came by."

"I probably won't guess correctly, so tell me," I said encouragingly.

"Sheriff Carver's wife. She bought all the yarn that was on sale. Imagine? Her friend Carolyn was with her, and she bought a slew of supplies for her bunny, and then asked if we did shearing. I didn't know, so I took her number for you." She handed me a slip of paper.

"I guess I'd better add to the yarn order, then?"

"The best thing we did was put the old stock on sale. Mrs. Carver was funny, she kept touching the yarn, saying how soft and cuddly it was. I almost laughed, but knew better. Customers are interestingly odd where their hobby supplies are concerned."

I nodded and read Carolyn's phone number.

"Does Carolyn have any other rabbits or just the one?"

"I didn't think to ask."

"No problem."

Proud of her knack for merchandise display and sales ability, Lizzy showed me the changes she'd made to the stack. What yarn was left had been re-arranged to fill the gaps from what had sold. Knitting needles and such were still neatly arranged on pegs by needle sizes and styles.

Her excitement brimming over, she said, "I'm sure an open house would go over well, maybe when the new merchandise arrives. I'd be happy to handle the advertising for it, if you'd like. You could give a bunny tour and have your petting thingy set up for people to interact with the lovely furry creatures, especially those angora ones you have."

Apparent as it was that Lizzy knew less than anything about rabbits and their care, I mentioned we'd educate her on those subjects. I explained it would enable her to make better sales and suggestions to customers. Her head bobbed up and down like an apple in a water bucket the entire time I spoke.

"Great job, Lizzy. You're a blessing to the business." When the clock chimed the hour, I gave her a pat on the shoulder. "You've been here much longer than I expected. Get going, and enjoy the rest of the day."

Hurrying out the door, she turned and waved, got into her car, and drove off.

Jess watched her leave. "Have you ever seen such enthusiasm? I hoped she'd be beneficial to the farm."

"It's a relief to have her. Lizzy's talented and outgoing, I'm certain the customers will like her. I know I do."

Leaving the shop, Jess and I began the task of freshening up the cages, adding timothy hay and food pellets for the rabbits to eat. We were half finished with the task when Ray and Molly entered the barn. Hurriedly, they hung their coats, donned overalls, and took over the remaining workload.

Molly pointed to Petra's cage. "I'll take care of Petra. Her fur needs grooming and shearing as well. Do you have shears? I can trim her if you'd like."

"I don't know about trimming, have you had experience in that? I wouldn't want to hurt her."

"I watched some videos on YouTube last night. The hair needs to be gently lifted from her skin and snipped in small clusters, leaving about a half inch or so of fur on her body."

Surprised by her willingness to try her hand at shearing, I said, "I'll help you with that. If you do well, I have a customer who has at least one angora rabbit that needs a haircut. Let's get the rest of the chores done, and then we'll take care of Petra's fur."

From the other end of the barn, I could hear Jess and Ray rattle metal trays as they withdrew them from underneath the cages. Each tray had to be cleaned, sanitized, and returned to its proper cage. The two of them worked in unison, one person pulling and cleaning while the other sanitized it and put it back. A time-saving technique Jess had introduced the teenagers to.

By the time all was done, Molly and I had taken Petra from her hutch and laid her on the table.

Comfy in her position, she sprawled, stretching her legs a little farther. Used to having her fur sheared, she didn't bat an eyelash as we smoothed her coat. Molly began the process of blowing her fur with a hair dryer to lift it, allowing for ease in handling it.

We chuckled over Petra's love of being groomed. She lay still and calm, making the job go faster than I'd thought it would. But then, Petra was used to me and Molly. We used sharp scissors to snip the fur, starting with her back, on to her spinal area, and moved outward in a circular motion from there. Within an hour, we had a swath of angora fur that could be spun into yarn. Jess and Ray did other chores while we finished up with Petra.

"Have you been keeping track of the time between trimming Petra?" I always did, but wondered if Molly had.

"It's been about four months, and her fur was coming out in strands when I brushed her the other day. Her coat was a bit lackluster, too. It seemed like time, why do you ask?"

Her answer spot-on, I said she'd done well, and that I'd refer her to my customer. "Of course, I'll be there with you, just in case something goes haywire. It's easy to accidentally snip their skin."

The remaining hours for the two teens flew by. The barn was shipshape when they were ready to leave, and I handed their wages to them before they went home. I watched as they went down the driveway, past the farm sign, and started their trek into town. More than once I'd offered a ride, but they preferred to jog in good weather. Today was one of those days.

Having heard the tail end of my conversation with Molly, Jess asked, "Are you certain Molly can handle shearing on her own?"

"I'll work with her, she's quite good with the scissors and is very careful. We'll make a rabbit farmer out of her yet."

A snort of laughter came out. "I think she's going to college."

I grinned. "Me too. Let's have some supper, I'm starving and surely Bun is, too."

The next few days were busy. Other than Mel Ferguson arriving to look and then buy my parents' furniture and oddments, nothing out of the ordinary took place. Saturday finally arrived. At ten o'clock, Fred Costanza stepped through the barn entry door and greeted us. Jess was a bundle of anxiety and excitement combined.

Introductions made, we walked through the shop and into the rear barn. We followed Fred's lead as he studied the space, his face serious and demeanor businesslike. I wasn't certain of what he saw that might be different from what we saw, but then, I wasn't a carpenter, either. Bun had followed behind, offering his opinion.

"Good golly, it's cold in here. My toes are freezing. Give me a lift."

I picked him off the floor, held him against my chest, and gently kneaded his paws, which were very cold, indeed.

We walked as a group to the end of the open space and back, Fred asking questions as we went. I listened as Jess answered him.

"There should be at least three patient rooms and a waiting area for the overflow. A counter and shelf fixtures, and possibly cabinets. That should take care of the construction end of things." She gave him the dimensions of the rooms.

He'd nodded as she spoke, making mental notes, I guessed, since he didn't have a notebook handy.

"You've got enough room for that and storage for supplies, too. I'll work up the numbers and get back to you girls."

"Would you like a cup of coffee before you go, Fred?" I asked.

"No thanks, the wife has me on a low-carb-and-no-coffee diet these days." He shook his head. "Spoils all the fun in life, don't ya think?" With that he went on his way, leaving us gaping at each other. When the door closed behind him, we burst into laughter.

"I'm glad you don't treat me like that, Jules."

I gave Bun a slight squeeze.

Just then, Lizzy arrived. She rushed in, draped her coat and handbag over the hooks behind the register, and apologized for being tardy.

"Of all times for my battery to crap out, it had to be today!"

"We were here, not to worry, Lizzy."

"On top of that, my phone battery was dead, too. Do you mind if I charge it while I work today?"

I agreed and then asked what great plans she had for Fur Bridge Farm's Shop.

A list in her hand, Lizzy gave it a quick look and said, "First off, I heard you have angora that needs spinning. I can do that for you and handle customers who drop by. Yesterday, I worked up an open house ad for your approval. It can be altered to your specifications, but we do need a definite date. Tomorrow is the beginning of April, and we should have a two-week lead up to the event."

Her energy was daunting, her ideas knew no bounds, and every time Lizzy came to work, there were more promotions and orders to consider. Maybe I should make her the farm manager, and I'd be a simple worker. I trashed that thought in a fraction of a second and asked to see the ad.

She handed me the mock-up and waited while I looked it over, wringing her hands in the meantime.

"This isn't definite, if you want changes, we can shift stuff around. What do you think?"

Jess and I had our heads together while we went over the list Lizzy proposed. I wondered if she knew the amount of time and energy it would take to pull off an event like this.

"I know it's a lot of work, Juliette. Though I think we can manage it with your helpers and me there to give you a hand. You might have to pay them, but you could ask if they'd donate their time, even for an hour or so in shifts."

I hauled in a breath of air, thinking the whole time how this woman ran on high octane and wishing I did. "I want to think this over. You get started on your projects for today, Jess will bring you the angora, and I'll make lunch. Would you care for soup and a sandwich?"

Her eyes rounded, laughter bubbled over, and Lizzy gave me a huge smile. "That would be lovely, thank you, Juliette."

"It's Jules, and I'll let you know when the food is ready." I gave Jess a nod and went on my way, Bun in tow.

Could life get any crazier? If I had to organize an open house, how would I find time to investigate Arty's murder, let alone figure out who my intruder was? I shook my head, put Bun on the floor, and washed my hands before starting to cook.

Draped in an oversized apron, I took sandwich ingredients from the fridge and cans of Progresso soup from the cupboard. Bun hopped about until I nearly tripped over him.

"Hey, watch where you're going. You almost crushed me."

With a glance over my shoulder, I whispered, "If you would stay out from under my feet, you wouldn't get crushed."

He backed up a few feet and settled next to the counter. *"Okay, okay. You might have a point there. I was only interested in what people food you planned to serve. Geesh!"*

"Sorry about being snippy. I just can't think how we'll manage an open house, run this business, have Fred here constructing, investigate Arty's death, and find our intruder, who has been absent for some time now. I'm not complaining about his absence, I'm merely wondering where he's been and what he's up to."

"Are you talking to the rabbit again?" Jess laughed and shook her head. "Good thing I know you aren't crazy, Jules." She opened the cupboard door, took out plates and bowls, then got flatware from the drawer and set the table for three, adding glasses to each place setting.

"When I get overwhelmed, I talk to Bun about it. It makes me feel better to speak aloud in these situations."

"I understand. Lizzy has this agenda because she can see the possibilities, it's from the marketing talent she has. Her job was downsized due to the economy, not because she wasn't good at what she does. Don't worry, we'll work it all out. I think her plan is sound and would be a boost for business, too. We can offer so much to the public, and since you're well-known, we could easily be overrun with people, potential rabbit owners, yarn folks, and more."

There was a chance that it would take over my life if we were successful, and though I knew it was a worthy plan, I was undecided on the whole idea. "Lunch is ready, let Lizzy know, okay?"

Her expression puzzled, Jess said, "Will do."

Moments later, the two women strolled into the kitchen. Our meal was quiet for the most part. Lizzy spoke of her job at Windermere Marketing Consultants, Jess mentioned her clinical rotation, and then she asked Lizzy about spinning yarn. I was fascinated by handmaking yarn from animal fur and listened with interest.

When there was a lull in Lizzy's explanation, I asked, "Would you be willing to do a demonstration for the open house?" What was I thinking? I had no clue. It seemed to fit into the overall theme Lizzy had set out, so why not include it? I guess I'd made my decision on the venture, after all.

From the other room, I heard Bun comment, *"I knew you'd come around. It might even help us get a handle on who killed Arty. Just invite all those people you and he did parties for.*"

Ignoring his words, I asked Lizzy if she'd be interested in offering spinning classes. "It won't be every day, just once a week or every two weeks, depending on the number of students that sign up, and your availability, of course. Spinning, weaving, and fiber arts in general are quite popular now. What do you say? We could include the information in the ad and offer registration forms to our guests."

"Gosh, Jules, I think you should have taken up marketing."

"Don't even think about it, we have a murder to solve."

"I'm getting into the swing of things, is all," I said to both Lizzy and Bun. "I'll leave the marketing to you. Clearly, you know what you're doing."

The table was cleared. Jess and Lizzy returned to the shop to consider what else might be of interest to the public, while Bun and I readied for a trip outside. I hadn't gotten any real exercise in days and longed for a walk. I zipped my jacket, hung Bun's sling across my body, and tucked him inside.

He snuggled in until he was comfortable and said, *"You're getting really fluffy, Jules. I mean that in a good way. It's certainly comfortable in this sling, now that you're fluffier."*

Fluffier, huh? I heard Bun's light sigh and pondered a diet to go with my exercise and drove to the park.

CHAPTER EIGHT

I left the car near the ball field and took the walking and bike path. Bun relaxed in the sling, until I began to jog. I grinned at what I knew would be his response to being bounced around.

"Are you going to jog the entire path? My delicate bones are beginning to rattle."

"No need to whine about my jogging, Bun. I'm only trying to get my fluffiness under control." It had rankled that he'd made the remark. Rabbit or not, he should have known better. As an intelligent rabbit with a good command of language, who could speak, albeit by mental telepathy, Bun should have chosen his words carefully.

I slowed my pace, then lessened it again to a fast walk. Bun said nothing, but kept his head outside the sling to see where we were going. Having walked for a good hour, I noticed the sun had moved to the west. I turned to make our way back when Bun whispered, *"Beware, we're not alone."*

"Wha . . ." A sudden, intense pain in my upper

back knocked us sideways, off the path, and we went into a downhill slide.

I came to a stop. Bun moaned and then whispered, *"Act like you're dead, don't open your eyes, and hold your breath. He'll think we're dead or close to it."*

Head pounding, my back in the throes of a painful spasm, I took short breaths. Groggy, I was aware of Bun's advice and sucked in as deep a breath as I could and held it. Dry leaves left over from autumn covered the hillside. They crunched under the feet of our attacker as he came to view his handiwork. I let my mouth hang open, left my hand folded under at the wrist, and hoped my hair covered the rest of my face.

A deep grunt came from him as he stood beside us. Rabbits have an uncanny way of pretending they're dead to ward off those who would torture them until they died. Bun didn't move, I couldn't feel him breathing. The lower half of his body, still in the sling, was stuck under my armpit.

A heavy-booted foot nudged my shoulder. It moved, and I was relaxed enough to let it drop back in place. The full weight of the boot hit harder this time, flipping us on our side. Bun didn't flinch or move a hair, nor did I. As difficult as it was to maintain this act, my will to live had kicked in, forcing me to behave like Bun, as though we were no longer among the living.

"Huh, the nosy woman is dead, and so is her rabbit. Good riddance."

His voice was more of a growl than anything else. It chilled me to the bone to think someone would be glad we were lifeless. The footsteps receded as he climbed the hill. Bun and I had been left for dead. This was the second time in my life this had happened. I wondered if Bun had suffered the same experience in his lifetime.

We lay there for what seemed ages. Finally, Bun said, *"He's gone. Really gone. We can become undead now. Are you all right, Jules? I was nearly crushed by you. Thank goodness you're fluffy and not bony. I'd be a goner if you were."*

I opened my eyes to a mere slit, noticed how deep shadows filled the twilight, and peered at Bun. "I don't think my bones are broken, though my back hurts. How about you?"

He rubbed his sweet little nose against my hand and said he was fine. I ran my fingers over his head, allowing him to fully wiggle into the sling before I sat up. "We'd better get out of here before it's completely dark. Our first stop is the sheriff's office. I left my phone in the car, or I'd call and let the rescue people come get us. Are you ready?"

His head moved in agreement. I got to my knees, took stock of our surroundings, me and the sling, and realized I was filthy, yet again. What was it with me and dirt anyway? First at Arty's house and now here. On my feet once more, I staggered up the hill, pulling us up by grapevines that protruded from the underbrush. Some gave way, and some held fast. The journey up was harder than the one going down. I grimaced with back pain while we continued to the top of the path.

A cyclist, the beam of his headlight shining like a beacon, skidded to a stop next to us.

A look I took as astonishment covered his face. "Wow, you're a mess. Can I help you?"

"If you have a phone handy, I'd like to use it."

He fiddled around in the pack secured at his waist and handed me the phone.

I dialed the police station and asked to speak with Sheriff Carver. Two seconds later he came on the line.

"What can I do for you, Jules?"

"Bun and I were attacked on the bike path. Could you come get us?"

"Are you injured?"

"Somewhat. I'm able to walk but could use a hand."

"Be right there, stay put. Are you and the rabbit alone?"

"A cyclist is here with us."

"Let me speak to him."

Whatever the sheriff had to say was answered by several "yes, sirs" and nothing else. When the call ended, the man introduced himself to me as Frank Audet, and I told him who I was.

I wiped my hand on my pants and held it out to shake his. He dismounted and shook my hand, asking if I would like to try to walk with him, alongside the bike. I nodded and took a tentative step forward. The going was slow. We'd gone a few yards when a team of rescue personnel charged down the path, bright flashlights lighting the entire area. They stopped short when they saw me, then came forward at a lesser pace. Sheriff Carver caught up to them, looking as if he needed their help more than I did. He huffed and puffed, apparently short of breath.

I stared at him for a few moments. "Are you all right, Sheriff Carver?"

Having gotten his breathing under control, he

nodded and asked if I could walk to the end of the path. "It isn't far from here, Jules. The rescuers can bring a rolling gurney for you, if you can't make it on your own."

"No, I'm fine, I have to keep moving. We were struck, and I fell sideways down the hill. The man who attacked us kicked me in the back to make sure we were dead. It was scary, Jack."

"Left for dead again, were you?" Jack asked in a voice tinged with relief. Anger flashed in his eyes and stiffened his features.

"Seems that way. I was worried for a few minutes. Figured he might finish what he started."

"Any idea who it was?"

I shook my head. His body hidden from view, Bun's head appeared, reminding me of the Cheshire cat from *Alice in Wonderland*. Focused on the sheriff, his nose wriggled.

"Does he think we had time for that? Good gravy, it's likely nobody has time for that when they're being attacked."

My knees shaking, I remarked, "I didn't have the opportunity to do a meet and greet, Jack. He struck me from behind. Like I said, he knocked me off my feet, sending me down the hill. I lay there like a rag doll as he kicked me." That was when I fainted.

When I came to, Bun hung in Jack's grip. He handed him to another man in a jacket that had the letters *EMT* embroidered on it. I reached up and demanded, "Hand over the rabbit."

The man stared down at me. I was lying on the stretcher, draped in a blanket, and he shook his head.

"Don't make me get off this stretcher. Now give me the rabbit."

The EMT stood stock-still and slid a glance at Carver, who dipped his head a tad. Bun was instantly returned to me. I smoothed his coat as he crouched on my stomach.

"They didn't hurt me, Jules. It's nice to know you've got my back, though. You do realize I have yours, too, right?"

A lot of good that did me after he said we weren't alone and I was abruptly attacked.

"These people will take you to the emergency room. Would you like me to call Jess?" Carver asked.

"Please do. She'll come pick me up after the doctors are finished poking and prodding me. Thanks, Jack."

"I'll see you at the hospital." He walked away, leaving the EMTs to their job and him to do his. I watched as he questioned the cyclist. Within moments, Jack allowed the young man to leave. I thanked him as he rolled his bicycle past the stretcher. He gave me a smile and kept going.

Loaded into the rescue vehicle, I could feel every bump and turn. The truck had poor suspension as far as I was concerned. Bun was quiet, as was I. I assumed we were both thinking hard of who had tried to kill us. Maybe he only meant to maim us, even if he'd said he was glad that we were dead. Foolish man.

Behind closed eyelids, I relived the incident, focused on how it began, and why we were unaware of him until it was too late to fight back. Concerned that Bun's supercharged hearing had let us down in our time of trouble, I believed the man had lain in wait for us. How would he know we were on the path unless he'd seen my car?

The vehicle slowed, stopped, and we were unloaded. I refused to allow Bun to be taken from me until Jess stepped into view. "Thank goodness you're here. You can check Bun for any injuries he may have suffered when we fell."

"Always worried about the rabbit more than yourself." Jess sighed. "I'll take him to the car and examine him, then I'll join you in the ER. Be right back, Jules."

I wasn't sure if she sighed out of relief that I was alive and fine or if it was because I had put Bun's health ahead of my own. Either way, I wouldn't have to deal with that until later.

Dr. Swartz, the man who'd handled my accident years before, gave me a once-over, then sent me for X-rays. He stepped into the room after I was wheeled in again. "Things look fine, Juliette. You'll have soreness and some of those muscles may be strained from where you fell. Other than that, I'd advise a couple days of rest. If you have discomfort, take an over-the-counter pain reliever."

"I will, thanks. Can I leave now?" Hospitals have never been a favorite of mine, especially after the serious injuries I'd suffered in the past. The staff was great, the food sucked, and my mother kept telling me to cooperate. Easy for her to say, she wasn't being tortured on a regular basis by physical therapists.

The wheelchair ride was brief. Jess took a sudden turn into a small anteroom off the main corridor of the ER entrance. Sheriff Carver sipped coffee and waited for us at a table for two. Jess wheeled me close to the table and set the brakes.

"I'll make a cup of coffee for you," she said.

"How's Bun?"

She set the Keurig to brew and said he was perfectly fine. The coffee cup filled, she placed it on the table and leaned against the counter.

"Tell me again, what happened?" Jack Carver's voice held a no-nonsense tone.

"I thought back to the incident while on my way here. I was jogging back to the car and had slowed my pace to a fast walk when out of nowhere, I was struck across my upper back with something hard and sent flying downhill off the trail. I was lying there with my eyes closed, mentally assessing possible injuries, when I heard him approach. He kicked me twice, once to see if I was conscious. When I played dead, he kicked me again. Thankfully, he didn't check my pulse. He was probably sure he'd killed me. The fool left me and Bun lying there, saying he was glad I was dead."

His eyes narrowed, Jack leaned forward putting his elbows on the table. "He spoke? What kind of a voice did he have?"

"Gruff, like a growl, really. I wanted so badly to open my eyes a mere slit, but didn't dare. I was in no position to fight him off."

"It was definitely a man, then?"

"Had to be. I've never heard a woman's voice that deep before. I've never known a woman to wear boots that big, either. When he set his foot against my body, I knew he had to wear at least an eleven or twelve. Another thing, I think he was waiting for us. His attack was sudden, and I hadn't heard anyone else on the path."

"How about Bike Boy?"

It took me a second to realize he referred to the cyclist who'd helped me. "His name is Frank Audet, he was very helpful, and he's very slight in stature. I got the impression my attacker was big, don't ask me why."

"I'll run Audet's background and see for myself. I said I'd be in touch if need be." Carver slid his chair away from the table and rose. "If you come up with anything else, call me, even if I'm at home. Don't hesitate, Juliette. I want the person who's after you."

Sipping coffee after Carver left, Jess took the seat he'd vacated and gave me a long, hard look. "Someone has it in for you. I don't think you should go out alone."

That would put a crimp in my investigation, and Bun would have a fit if we couldn't complete the task we'd started.

"I refuse to fearfully hide from everyone and everything. Not happening."

"Why don't you listen to anyone's advice?"

Her pleading was wasted on me. I wouldn't be limited in my actions, not now, not ever. Cowering wasn't my way of life, nor would it ever be.

"What if I promise to be more aware of my surroundings and the people I come across? Will that be sufficient?"

She heaved a sigh. "I guess it will have to be. I can see your point. There's danger out there, real danger, and you might not be so lucky the next time, because there may very well be a next time."

"You're right. I won't take any chances."

With that promise in place, we went to the car. While Jess wheeled the chair into the ER, Bun hopped from the back seat into the front.

"I suppose you're in trouble with the sheriff and Jess?"

"Not trouble, they're concerned. I had to promise to not take any crazy chances. Why didn't you hear the guy earlier? I had no advance warning he was there."

"He must have been hiding in wait for us. When I warned you, he was right behind us. He wasn't on the path following us, Jules. I'd have known."

I soothed his fur, rubbed his ears, and was relieved we weren't dead.

Jess slid into the driver's seat. "Do you want Lizzy and me to pick up your car so you won't have to drive?"

"That's not necessary. Drop me and Bun off at the car park and follow us home."

CHAPTER NINE

Thankful we made the trip home without incident, I deposited Bun in his room and said I'd be in the barn. Happy to be there, he sprawled across the pillow.

"This has been an exhausting day. I think I'll nap awhile. We won't be going out again, will we?"

"Not that I know of. I'm going to check on Lizzy's progress, and then I'll be back."

On my way out the door, the phone rang. Fred Costanza was on the line.

"Hi, Juliette, I've got all the paperwork in order if you and Jess would like to get together tomorrow to go over it."

"That would be great. Jess can hardly wait to hear your thoughts and see the estimate. The bank is waiting to draw up the final paperwork. If she's amenable to the estimate, how soon could you start construction?"

"As soon as you'd like. I've completed my current project and have a few weeks before the next one begins. It shouldn't take more than that amount of time to complete Jess's clinic."

"I'll tell her, I'm sure she'll be happy to hear it. What time tomorrow?"

"I'll be by at ten, if that's okay?"

"Sure, see you then."

The two women were discussing the open house ad as I slowly stepped into the shop.

Hands on her hips, Jess asked, "What are you doing out here? I thought you were going to rest, Jules."

Before I could answer, Lizzy interjected, "You should take it easy. I'm so glad you're all right."

"Me too." I mentioned Fred's call to Jess. Her face lit up, and her eyes sparkled with excitement while Lizzy and I laughed when Jess danced around the room.

"You assume the estimate will be workable for us, right?"

Jess nodded and continued to swirl in place. Dizzy from all the whirling, she stopped and grinned. "I'm sure Fred won't take advantage of us. He appears to be a very honest man. Besides, your father wouldn't have had him work here if he wasn't, am I right?"

"Indeed. What have you there?" I asked Lizzy.

"The ad is ready to send out. If you approve, then I'll get it out to the newspaper and put it on-line in the morning. We can post it on Facebook, tweet it, and send postcard invitations to your customer list as well. If you have time to work out a promotional budget, it would give me a better idea of how many ads we can run."

I hadn't thought of an advertising budget, but

did have one for small ads in the local paper. "How much would you suggest?"

She tossed out a number and smiled when I agreed to it. Nothing astronomical, thank goodness.

The ad was perfect, and I said as much.

She slid the sheet of paper into a folder and tucked it into her leather bag. "I'll take care of this first thing tomorrow. I won't be in for a couple of days. The company is starting a major campaign, which means my time will be theirs."

"That's fine. You needn't be here every day. I can handle the store should customers stop in. I've placed an order for the merchandise you suggested, and it won't take but a few days to get here."

Gleeful at the prospect of our meet and greet, the promotion, and what the open house entailed, Lizzy readied to leave. "I'll see you midweek, then."

After she'd gone, Jess and I did the late-day chores at a slower pace than usual. The discomfort of my muscles and bruises was taking a toll. We chatted while working, then secured the barn. A walk-through at seven would end our workday.

Supper, a small affair of salad and a sandwich, was quick. Jess mentioned she was working rotation the following evening, but would be available during the day.

"What time do we expect Fred?"

"Ten o'clock. He's prompt so we'll need to get the rabbits squared away early. You don't mind, do you?"

"Not at all." She smiled and said, "I can hardly wait to see what he's come up with."

"Me too. It's rather exciting, isn't it?"

She nodded her head emphatically, and we turned to see Bun crouched at the opening of his room.

"What's happening with the big plans Lizzy has come up with? Why wasn't I consulted in regard to the goings-on that are on the agenda? And what's the date for it?" He sounded a bit whiny, and I wondered if he felt well after our day of excitement.

"Does Bun look a bit out of sorts to you, Jess?" It was my way of asking him if he felt well.

Her brows puckered as she picked him up. Smoothing his coat and rubbing his ears, she felt his nose, then said he seemed fine. He hadn't struggled to get away from her, which I took as a good sign.

"For your information, I am perfectly healthy. I merely want to be kept updated on what's happening."

I reached over and rubbed the fur on his nose and said to Jess, "I think he'll be happy when there's a petting pen on the day of our affair. What was the date Lizzy set for it? I can't remember."

"I think she said it will be on the second or third Saturday in April. You know, I'm a bit fuzzy on the date, myself. Must be due to everything we've got coming up."

Now Bun knew as much as we did, and he'd have to be satisfied with it. I gave him a sweet smile.

"Let's get the rabbits settled for the night."

Going through the breezeway, I glanced back and saw Bun on our heels. No way would he leave us to our work, in case we mentioned a tidbit of news he was unaware of. I considered the rabbit a nosybody.

Our chores didn't take long. The rabbits were set for the night, as was I. My downhill tumble had stiffened my muscles, leaving them sore. I could only imagine what the next few days would be like.

"You look tired. Why don't you go ahead in. I want to make a list of supplies for delivery this week."

I nodded, grateful Jess was willing to take the reins for the moment. I trudged back to the house. Bun had elected to remain with Jess. Having kicked off my shoes, I tossed them onto the boot tray and wiggled my toes. There was nothing better than letting my feet breathe.

The teakettle whistled shortly after I'd set it to boil. The tea would soon be ready, and I longed for a strong cup of it. While it steeped, I started up the stairs, and then Bun rushed in. His eyes were wild, and his whiskers jittered up and down.

"Come with me, come on, Jules, hurry up. Jess was attacked in the barn by a madman. Hurry, hurry."

Having delivered the news, he abruptly raced back toward the barn. I wasn't far behind and stopped short at the doorway, nearly tripping over Bun. Knowing I should call the police, I was about to do so when Bun said, *"He's still here, hiding somewhere. Can you feel him?"*

Afraid I'd alert the man, I decided to make sure Jess was safe first. Foolish, I know, but thinking clearly at times like this isn't my forte. I crouched close to Bun's ear and whispered softly, "I don't have that capability. Where is he, do you know? Did you get a look at him?"

*"I'll tell you later. Let's go get him, he's behind Walka-
bout Willy's cage. You go left, and I'll take the right.
We'll trap him that way."*

"Where's Jess?"

*"Over near Petra's cage. I can't see her, but she's there.
I think he knocked her out when she put up a fight."*

"You're sure he didn't kill her?"

*"When I ran away, she was still breathing. Let's go,
time's a-wasting."*

He moved in stealth mode, which is unusual for
a rabbit. With steps that were slow and small, unlike his usual hopping about, Bun reminded me of
a cat hunting its prey. It was odd, yet tickled my
funny bone. I fought to hold back a chuckle. In
the pale light cast from the main barn area where
we stored supplies, I crept along the left aisle, one
row away from Willy's cage. Other than rabbits
moving in the cages, there was no sign of the man.
Bun and I had almost reached the end of our re-
spective rows when I heard a voice.

"You hope to find me, don't you, Jules? You and
your little hare. Be careful of what you seek, you
might get more than you bargained for."

His voice, as taunting as his words, gave me
pause. What would I do if I met him face-to-face?
Uncertain of my combat skills when it came to im-
plementing what I'd learned into action, I hesitated.

*"Don't go all girlie now, Jules. We need to get this
bloke out of our lives. You know it, and so do I."*

To speak out loud would be certain folly. I crept
closer, caught my foot on a corner of the hutch
next to me, and stumbled.

The man was on me in a flash. I'd had enough

time to catch my balance, which was advantageous as far as I was concerned. Better than being flat on my face, at any rate. I struggled against his strength until he caught me around the neck and applied a choke hold. Bun must have been at his ankle, for he kicked his leg outward, yelling for Bun to get off him. While he focused on Bun's attempts to bite him, I grasped his thumb and peeled it backward. Nothing hurts like having your thumb or fingers pried as far back as they could go, until they snapped like his thumb did, that is. A howl of pain accompanied a hefty shove that sent me flying across the floor and into the leg of a rabbit cage. Though I was unharmed, this landing-hard thing was becoming tiresome.

Heavy footsteps pounded down the aisle, away from us, toward the rear door. How did this man keep getting in? Bun and I vied for first place as we raced after him. I heard the door slam shut, before all went silent.

"He's gone. I can't feel or hear him any longer."

Disappointment filled his voice as he sat back on his haunches.

A soft moan sounded from the next aisle over.

"Don't be sad, Bun. We'll catch this guy the next time around. Let's check on Jess."

We'd reached Jess to find blood trickling down her face. She sat up, rubbed her head, and mumbled, "Did you catch this guy or what?"

"Not this time, but we will. I think I either sprained or broke his thumb when I tried to get free of him. He was some ticked off, I can tell you that. Stay right where you are, I'll call Jack and the emergency services to come check you out."

"That's not necessary, I'll be okay."

"Stay put, you're bleeding, for heaven's sake." I dashed down the aisle, made the call to Jack, and then called the rescue people. Before I knew it, sirens blared and they all arrived together.

The emergency crew flowed into the barn like lava from a volcano. Jack followed behind, as I directed them to Jess, who impatiently awaited them. Bun sat next to her until the men drew near. He joined me and sat at my feet.

"I see you have the rabbit to protect you," Jack said with a dip of his head in Bun's direction.

"If you must know, he was instrumental in my not getting strangled. Bun attacked the man, and I think I might have broken his thumb when I peeled it back. He was more focused on Bun than choking me to death. Bun can be very fearsome, you know."

Incredulous, Jack coughed lightly and said, "I'm sure. Besides being the most sought after by attackers, you certainly never have a dull moment."

I agreed. "I guess you're right. I could do with a bit of the mundane in my life. I've had enough of this breaking-in nonsense. It needs to stop."

"Did the man say anything to you?"

I'd explained what took place and watched rescuers wheel Jess out the door to their vehicle. Loaded and ready to roll, I called out, "I'll be right behind you, Jess."

"No, we'll be right behind her. I want her side of this since she was the first person attacked. Get your coat, we'll ride together. And, uh, the rabbit stays here."

"I don't know why he doesn't appreciate me, Jules," Bun whined when we entered the house.

I nuzzled his head and gave him a smooch. "I appreciate you."

He rubbed his head against my cheek and sighed. I said I'd be back soon and that he was in charge of the farm.

Chapter Ten

In near silence, we rode to the hospital. I refrained from speaking lest Jack ask too many questions concerning Bun's attack on the man. At the traffic light, a block from the hospital, Jack asked, "How did you know there was an intruder if Jess was unconscious?"

This was what I had feared, him asking indirectly about Bun. Weighing my words, I said, "She was supposed to come into the house not long after I did. When she didn't, I got worried and went to see what was keeping her."

"What did the rabbit have to do with this whole situation?"

"What do you mean?"

"It's a simple question. I want you to explain how the rabbit came to be involved. If he broke the man's skin when he bit him, I might have to put him down. You realize that, don't you?"

Shocked at his words, I couldn't believe I'd been stupid enough to have admitted Bun had been involved. "I'm sure Bun didn't hurt him, but merely startled the guy. Must you make an issue out of it if he did come to harm? Bun was only trying to protect me."

"We'll worry about that problem when we find this guy. You should have called me first before going after him."

"I know that, but it's a moot point now, isn't it?"

"Don't do that again. Call me first, not last."

"Okay, okay."

Our arrival at the emergency room saved any further discussion of the matter. Once inside, we were told to be seated in the waiting area until the doctor could speak with us. I knew the routine, as did Jack. He grimaced and walked with me into the room. In his professional capacity, Jack didn't like being ordered around. I hid a smirk and settled in.

A half hour later, a short, balding doctor walked into the half-filled room and called my name. I got out of the chair and approached him.

"I'm Juliette Bridge. How is Jess?" By this time, Jack was next to me.

A kind look in his eyes, the doctor said, "She's doing very well. No serious injuries. Miss Plain has a headache from being struck and a possible concussion. You should be prepared to keep an eye on her for the next few days."

Relieved her skull hadn't been fractured, I thanked the doctor and waited for Jess to be released.

"She was very fortunate," Jack murmured.

"You've got that right. I was quite worried."

"Have you ever wondered how your intruder

keeps gaining access to the barn? You lock up when no one is in the barn, don't you?"

"Yes, whenever we're not present. I've wondered about that, too. Anything come to mind other than this person is a great lock picker?"

"It's obvious he's either that, or he has a key. How much do you know about your workers?"

"Not long ago, Jess and I discussed that at length. I can't imagine one of my helpers doing this. It doesn't make sense. First off, I'd have recognized one of my workers. Secondly, they all enjoy working with the rabbits. They're aware these animals couldn't fend for themselves on their own."

"Do they have keys to get in? If so, one of your people may have had their key taken, used, and then returned without their knowledge."

"The high school kids, Ray Blackstone and Molly Perkins, don't have keys. They work a few hours after daily classes end and on weekends. My college student, Peter Lambert, has a key, but rarely uses it. He, too, works weekends, but occasionally comes in during the week, if he is free. I've also given Lizzy Fraser a key. She now runs the shop."

"Ah, yes, my wife has spoken of her. Quite the salesperson, too. Meredith came home with shopping bags filled with yarn I'm sure she didn't need. But who am I to complain? At least she isn't at the mall spending hundreds of dollars on clothing that would sit in the closet."

Wheelchair bound, Jess was rolled to a stop by an orderly. A square bandage covered her laceration. Her face no longer covered with blood, she gave me a crooked smile and said, "Get me out of here."

Sheriff Carver drove us home and came in for a chat. I rolled my eyes when he invited himself in, but I remained courteous. Bun hopped to the kitchen door and asked, *"Is Jess all right?"*

"How are you feeling, Jess? Can I make a cup of tea for you? How about you, Jack, a cup of tea, or coffee, perhaps?"

Jack waved away the offer. "I'm all set, thanks."

Jess said tea would be great and sat opposite Jack, awaiting his questions. They went over what happened, he took her statement and then sat back while she sipped tea.

"You never saw his face?" Jack asked for the third time.

"Not once. He knocked me to the floor from behind, then hit me with something. It was lights out from then on."

"Did you hear the scuffle between Jules, the rabbit, and the man?"

With a slight shake of her head, she took another sip from her cup and asked if I had seen him. I said I hadn't.

"You should go to bed, it's been quite an evening," I urged.

Jack agreed. "I'll stop by tomorrow to check in on you." He gave us each a serious look. "If anything happens, call me or the station immediately." His emphasis on *immediately* hit home and we both promised we would.

The three of us stood at the door as Jack drove away. When his car taillights disappeared, I recommended Jess go straight to bed. "Bun and I will check on the rabbits, then we'll call it a night."

Her nod was brief as she turned to climb the stairs. A few minutes later, I heard her bedroom door close.

Walking into the barn, Bun and I chatted softly. Tuned in to who might be lurking in the softly lit barn, we made the rounds, checked all the cage doors, and said good night to everyone.

"That went well. Better than earlier tonight."

"You're right, when did you sense something amiss?"

"Jess wrote her list, while I went through the barn. I'd gotten about halfway down Petra's aisle when I heard a scraping noise. That's how I knew we had company. It's my fault Jess was injured. I ran back and hounded her until she followed me to the back of the barn. That's when she and the bad guy fought. I think he was trying to let Walkabout Willy out. None of the other doors were open. Not that I can remember, anyway."

"He didn't have enough time to free Willy. You and I interrupted him. Were you scared?"

"Not scared, mad mostly. He has no idea what would happen to the rabbits if he turned them loose, or maybe he knows and doesn't care. It makes me sad to think of the consequences his actions would bring when they couldn't fend for themselves. After all, we are domesticated. I have pondered what living in the wild would be like."

"Let me be frank, you'd be hunted by man and beast, have to forage for your own food, and there'd be no warm, snug housing provided for you. Those are the most important things to consider."

His ears twitched as he craned his neck to look

up at me. *"As always, you make a good point. It's too bad Sheriff Carver doesn't understand my strengths and abilities."*

Except for our coffee, breakfast was finished. Jessica didn't look any worse for wear. The only sign of discomfort was the look in her eyes.

"The next time someone breaks into the barn, run like hell, okay? How's the headache?"

Her shrug was half-hearted.

"I'll be fine, I took a pain reliever when I got up. Just waiting for it to work."

"Take it easy today. I'll do the work, you study or something. You can deal with Fred when he arrives. No heavy lifting, and no work for you. Got that?"

"With the way I feel, I don't think I could manage much. What did you and Sheriff Carver discuss last night?"

"We both agree with your assumption that one of my employees might be at the bottom of our problems. I can't imagine who it could be. Any idea?"

She shook her head and winced. "I better not do that again."

Our coffee cups were empty. Jess went out to the shop while I finished the house chores and started the ones in the barn. It took longer than usual to clean cages, refresh the rabbits' hay, and refill their feeders and water trays, but by ten o'clock, I'd finished up. Just in time for Fred Costanza's arrival.

His hearty laugh echoed through the empty side of the barn as Jessica filled him in on what she had decided to do with the space. I followed behind, noting what they agreed upon as we went. I figured the costs would come to a tidy sum, but between Jessica's loan and what I could contribute, we'd manage.

After measurements were taken, the three of us returned to the warmth of the shop and sat before the fireplace. Fred finalized his figures and handed the contract to Jessica. I leaned toward her, we read it over and then signed on the lines provided. His estimate was more than fair, and even if he ran a bit over budget, we could still handle the cost.

When all was agreed to, Fred said he'd get started by midweek. Her delight apparent, Jess nearly hugged him as he went out the door. I laughed when she turned back to me.

"Sounds like you'll be ready to start your business right after you get your license."

With a squeal of happiness, she said, "I'm thrilled, but you know that, right?"

Her smile was contagious. I put my problems aside for a while and enjoyed Jessica's future success until the delivery truck arrived with rabbit supplies.

The driver, Ron Hurley, gave me a hand unloading and stacking bales of hay and bags of feed after I explained I was working alone for the day. I signed the bill of lading and thanked him for his help.

"Where's your vet girl today?"

"She's a bit under the weather. I'm sure she'll be fine tomorrow."

Ron sidled up to me and murmured, "She's very nice. Does she have a boyfriend?"

"Not that I know of. Why, are you interested?"

He stared down at the ground for a second and then shrugged.

"You should attend our open house this month. Jess won't realize you like her if you don't let her know. Keep an eye on the newspaper, we'll be running an ad."

"I'll give it some thought. Thanks." He walked off whistling a happy tune.

I snickered and returned to the shop. I'd put in a call to the local locksmith, to set up an appointment to have the locks changed, just as the sheriff arrived. I hung up the phone, heaved a sigh, and wondered what he would put me through today. Hopefully, Bun would stay in the house rather than get underfoot while Jack was here. There was no doubt that he didn't care for Bun. It was also becoming clear that Bun had begun to resent him in return.

The patrol car came to a stop and the door slammed. Sheriff Carver walked toward the barn. I opened the shop door and summoned him inside. He veered to his left, stopping just inside the door to wipe his feet.

"You two doing all right today?"

"We are. Jess is resting, her headache is severe. Even if she hasn't said as much, I'm sure she has bruises and discomfort from last night's altercation. What can I do for you, Jack?"

"One of my patrolmen kept an eye on this place last night. He'll be around for the next few nights, too. You should get a watchdog to prevent break-ins, Jules. I could recommend a couple breeders, if you'd be interested. Old Mort Franklin has a two-year-old Rottweiler he's looking to find a home for."

I shook my head. "I'm having the locks changed later today. Only Jessica and I will have keys. Everyone else will work during their scheduled time slots. Nobody will be alone, have a key, or otherwise have access to this building. I'm fed up with what's been happening."

"If you're sure, then I won't push you to get a watchdog."

"I have Bun, that's enough to deal with."

His snort was instantaneous. "As if he could protect you from the likes of a killer. I've yet to hear of a perpetrator who feared a rabbit."

I tipped my head up a tad and looked down my nose at him. "There's a first time for everything. Are you and Meredith attending our open house event?"

"I imagine so. It'll be a good opportunity to put plainclothes officers in place to listen and watch those who might show up with more than festivities in mind."

"Great idea. You don't think they'll be recognized by the locals?"

"I have two men and a woman who are from out of town that work the graveyard shift. They don't have much to contend with during those hours, and have little to do with townspeople. Their job consists of patrol and stopping drunk drivers. Occasionally, we have a domestic situation, but they tend to take place before midnight."

"If that will help, please feel free to send them

along." Informing Jack of the date and time Lizzy had designated, I watched him scribble the information on his notepad before he went on his way.

An hour later, the locksmith showed up, installed new padlocks, slide bolts, and door locks on every door in the barn and shop. I declined his offer to install a window alarm system, should someone try to get in that way.

"I think the new additions to the doors will be enough. Thanks for the recommendation, though." I paid him, took the receipt, the keys, and waited until he drove away before returning to the house.

Bun was in the kitchen with Jessica, who was having tea, and I joined her in a cup of brew. "Feeling better?"

"I am, that nap did the job, along with the pain reliever. I think I'll do my rotation tonight, after all. I need those hours to graduate."

"If you think you can get there and back all right, go ahead."

"What have you been doing while I rested?"

"I handled Sheriff Carver's insistence that I get a Rottweiler to protect the grounds and us. Then the locksmith arrived to change all the locks and add more. I think we're on par with Fort Knox."

She chuckled. "Glad to hear it."

"Carver is sending plainclothes officers to our event. He said they can listen to and watch what's going on. It might be a good way to figure out who's after the rabbits."

"True. Do you have a new key for me?"

I slid it across the table. She added it to her key ring and handed me the old key.

"Have you time to address invitations to your

customers? I'm supposed to see Lizzy tonight before I leave for my shift. She called earlier to ask if I'd bring them to you."

"That was fast, I thought they'd go to a printer to be done. Gosh, I must be behind the times."

She snickered. "You are. Lizzy designed the card on her computer, sent the file to the office supply store, and they're now ready. Because we didn't need a ton of them, it was a quick job."

CHAPTER ELEVEN

While Jessica studied, Bun and I walked the farm grounds, sharing our thoughts on whether one of my employees was the culprit or helping the person who was. Fresh, crisp air smelled of a mix of cool and dry late winter that meshed with the fragrances of a promise of early spring. A breeze that chilled and signs of new beginnings abounded.

Snow had melted, mud was now hard dirt, and buds were beginning to form on trees and shrubs. In a few weeks, if the weather held, grass would push out of the ground as would the daffodils and tulips my mother had planted some years ago.

I sniffed appreciatively, took a deep breath, and listened to Bun ramble on about his candidate for our bad guy, before moving on to who should be invited to our festivities.

"I refuse to believe one of the staff is involved in these shenanigans. They all seem to understand why domestic rabbits need care. The only person I can think of would be Peter. He's very quiet, and you know what is said

*about the quiet ones, right? Still water runs deep and all
that. He hasn't ever been mean or spiteful to any of the
other helpers or to us rabbits, so maybe I'm off the mark.
What do you think?"*

"I'm not sure what I think. It may have nothing
to do with our employees, and I refuse to start sus-
pecting them, or watching for telltale signs of re-
sentment toward me. It could be someone with no
ties to Fur Bridge Farm, but who is trying to throw
suspicion on my farmhands rather than have the
sheriff start nosing around Arty and my clients.
I'm certain Peter has no part in any of it."

*"Jessica and the sheriff are grasping at straws, then?
On another note, are you serving food and drink? Who's
catering? Will I have to stay in the petting pen the entire
time? I would be of greater use if I was free to wander. I
could be an undercover sleuth, like Carver's people. I'm
good at being a gumshoe."*

As imaginative as Bun could be, a picture of him
as a sleuth was just too much for me. I started to
chuckle, then broke into laughter that soon became a sidesplitting turn of events.

"You don't have to be rude, Jules." His emphasis on
my name cut my humor short. I'd hurt his feelings
and swiftly apologized for doing so.

"I pictured you in a Sherlock Holmes hat, with a
spyglass and pipe. The pipe did me in. I'm sorry,
Bun."

Ears upright and twitching, Bun wiggled his nose
as though he were a hound hot on the trail of who-
knows-what.

"What's wrong? What do you smell?"

*"Move to your left, very carefully. There's an odd
scent, and it isn't you."*

Doing as he advised, I tiptoed toward a small copse of trees. Thick and dense with brush, the trees easily blocked our view. We drew closer, until we'd reached the edge of the tree cluster. Not seeing what bothered Bun, I edged farther to the left to catch sight of what lay in the clearing beyond.

"Stop, stop now. Crouch down, and, uh, don't squash me."

I lifted Bun's leather riding pouch outward and let it hang over my knees as I bent them. His usual sling needed laundering and this pouch, though supple, was heavier. It was difficult to get a clear look at what had Bun on guard. I stretched my neck forward, then to the side, and back again. Bun leaped from the pouch, bounding into the dense brush. He was too fast and slipped through my grasp.

Bun never liked getting his feet wet or muddy. While the ground was dry and hard, he'd still get his feet dirty, so why had he taken off? About to make my way through the brush, I waited for a second or two in hope of his return.

"Bun," I whispered in the direction he'd taken. "Where are you? Get back here right now."

He popped up in front of me so quickly, I lost my balance and fell back onto the hard ground. "Where did you go? You scared the bejeepers out of me."

"You won't believe this. There's a tent over there. Come on, let's take a gander." He turned to hop into the brush again when I caught him by the scruff of his neck and hauled him to me.

"Get into your pouch. If things go wrong, I don't want to worry about you being left on your own." I held out the leather opening, tucked him in, and waited until he snugged his way to comfort. He complained the entire time.

"You take the fun out of things, don't you? I can handle myself and protect you at the same time. Look how I jumped that guy in the barn, huh? He got what was coming to him."

"Yes, he did, and you are a superhero. But until we see what the tent holds, it's best not to tempt fate. Now stay calm and we'll go in as though we have every right to, which we do because this is my land."

"We should have done a property search before today. We might already have solved the mystery and caught Arty's killer."

"Shoulda, coulda, woulda gets you nowhere. Be still and let me take the lead if someone is in the tent." We'd reached a small clearing on the other side of the trees. A bunch of small, broken branches lay stacked near a makeshift firepit. Rocks formed a round border, used to keep the fire in check. A stump sat close by, and a half-baked spit, consisting of two crudely cut, thick branches that forked and had been jammed into the ground. Wire went from side to side and held a dented old teakettle.

Approaching the tent, I moved with caution, making no sound. Bun began to quiver. I shook from the inside out, and then summoned enough gumption to whip the front tent cover aside. I hadn't realized I'd held my breath. I let it out on a sigh of relief when I saw the tent was empty.

"Aww, that's disappointing."

"Really? What if this person had been waiting

with a bat, or a gun, or another dangerous weapon, huh? Would you still be whining about disappointment then?" I reached into the pile of men's clothing, strewn haphazardly on the ground. There was no identification to be had, nor any indication of who camped on my land.

Twisting his head to see me, Bun said, *"I hadn't thought of that. I didn't expect to find danger. Sorry."*

"I understand, it is disappointing to find the place empty. The problem is, we aren't prepared for a confrontation. We'll go back to the house and call Sheriff Carver. He can find who's been residing here and make them talk."

Our trip back to the farmhouse was quicker than when we'd left. Within twenty minutes, I hurried through the door, dialed up the sheriff's office, and told him of our find.

"We'll be there shortly. Stay put, no heroic stuff, you hear me? Let us take over from here. Any idea who might be living there?"

"None, I checked the clothes in the tent, but found nothing. I didn't linger, I wasn't about to be caught by the squatter."

"Smart move. Stay put." The line went dead. While we waited, I freed Bun and made a cup of tea.

It wasn't long before Sheriff Carver's cruiser pulled into the yard followed by two other police cars. Four officers followed Carver to the front door. I stepped aside and let them in.

Only Carver spoke.

"You were smart not to hang around the campsite. Was there any sign of recent activity?"

"The fire ashes weren't that old, the wind hadn't taken them from their bed, and the teakettle was dust free. Other than that, I couldn't tell when the place was last inhabited. The clothes were men's, a tall guy by the look of them. Could it have been the same man who attacked me on the bike path?"

"I don't know, anything's possible at this stage. Where exactly is the tent and how long will it take us to get there?"

"It was a good half-hour to forty-five-minute trek to get there. I wasn't looking for anything, just taking a walk. The tent sits in a clearing behind a copse of trees. I can show you the way if you'd like."

"Since I don't know the layout of this property, you'd better come along." He slanted his head toward Bun. "The rabbit stays here."

"Sure thing, I'll get my jacket."

Bun stiffened and turned away while I donned my jacket. He refused to look at me and hopped into his room without a word. Oh, yeah, I would hear about this later.

We walked in silent pairs, with Carver and me in the lead. A half hour later, I recognized the cluster of trees and stopped, indicating the tent just past them.

Carver nodded and murmured, "You'll be safe here with Adam. He'll keep an eye out for strangers while we check the site." He gave Adam a look, meaning what, I had no idea. I stood next to Adam, watching the officers head for the clearing.

"The sheriff says you have a nose for news, is that true?" Adam asked softly as he gazed off into the trees and the surrounding land.

"I wouldn't go that far, I merely happened to find Arty dead. I didn't plan to end up in this situation. Has Carver made any progress on the injury to our intruder's leg?"

He gave a shrug. "I couldn't say. He doesn't keep me in the loop."

"For a cop, you're a really bad liar. Cough it up, the truth, come on. Carver found the man had been treated locally for an animal bite, didn't he?"

"All I'll say is that he came across the fact that somebody had been treated at one of those walk-in clinics that have popped up everywhere. Don't ask me anything else, because that's all I know."

"Sure it is. I'll have to settle for that much, I guess." I heaved a weary sigh, heard the crunch of underbrush at the same moment Adam heard it, and stepped behind him for my own protection.

Adam whispered, "Slowly step back into the trees, Jules." He put his fingertip on the microphone attached to a tab on his shoulder and said in a low tone, "He's coming your way."

No sooner had we melted into the copse of trees and hunkered down than a man sauntered past. He didn't look our way, and we didn't move a muscle. I don't even think I blinked. Good thing Bun wasn't here. He might have jumped from his pouch and scrambled off to who knows where. On second thought, he would have been trembling too hard to move an inch.

A few minutes later there were sounds of a scuffle mixed with a lot of grunting. Adam and I rushed from the trees to join the fray. Two of Carver's men were holding a man face down on the ground, while another handcuffed him.

Adam placed his hand on my arm and ordered me to stay where I was while he went toward the other officers. I wrung my hands and watched their actions closely as their prisoner gave them a hard time. Sheriff Carver turned to me as Adam leaned forward and murmured something to him. Curious, I walked over, staring at the man in handcuffs the entire time.

I needed to speak with the stranger about why he was camping on my property, and who he was. Before I could reach him, Sheriff Carver cut me off.

"Stay right where you are," he said. "We'll take things from here." He turned and nodded to his men. Together we watched them walk away. The stranger turned his gaze to me, but never said a word. His shaggy brown hair danced in the wind, and his blue eyes were cold and as angry as his expression. A tad more than average in height, this man had worn, but not shabby clothes on. I wondered if he was a bum or just down on his luck. How long he had been here was certainly a mystery. Why I had never noticed smoke rising from the trees must have been because I hadn't paid attention. There was too much going on in my life lately, and I didn't like it one bit.

Once he'd been marched past us, I turned on Carver. "I have every right to question this man. I need to know why he's on my property and how long he's been here. It would also be nice to know if he's the one who's continuously entering my barn and lying in wait."

"I understand. You need to give us time to do

our job. Let's go back to your house, then after I've questioned him, I'll let you know what he said. He could simply be a homeless squatter."

I slanted a look of disbelief in his direction. "Do you think that's the case? He does look disheveled."

We walked through the woods and across a field, before arriving at the house. Carver walked in behind me and asked, "How many acres do you own?"

"Twenty or so, I believe." I wiped my feet on the mat and waited for his response.

"I'll be in touch with you as soon as I know anything. Until then, remain vigilant. This might not be our man, Jules, so let's not get our hopes up." With that, he left the farm behind the other cops.

Twilight was on its way as I prepared supper. Jessica scooted down the stairs. Her face was filled with what I took as concern.

"Was that Carver? Did he have a bunch of other officers with him? I saw them rush across the yard surrounding another man. Is that our guy?"

I held up a hand. "It was Carver and four of his men. We—Bun and I—came across a tent pitched way out on the property. We came back and called Carver. Wouldn't you know, I left my cell phone on the charger?"

"Who is he?"

"No clue. Nobody would let me get close enough to question him."

"There's more to this, isn't there?"

Bun came forward from his spot at the threshold of his room and said, *"Of course there is, but I wasn't allowed to go with you, was I? You didn't even in-*

sist. Some friend you are, Juliette Bridge." He went to Jessica, sat at her feet, and stared at me just like she did.

Ignoring his snippy attitude, I picked up the pasta box and poured the shells into a pot of boiling water. I emptied a leftover bowl of sauce into another pot, turned the heat level to low, and set the lid on it. "If you give me a minute, I'll tell you what happened."

By this time, Jessica had begun to set places at the table, urging me to give her the lowdown while she did so. Bun had moved aside to give us space to walk, but never uttered a word. It didn't take long to relate the entire story once I stopped Jess from interrupting every other second or so.

Bewildered, Jess gave me a stern look that included Bun. "You can't help yourselves, can you?"

His whiskers jittered. *"Excuse me? I wasn't in on the second half of that adventure."*

I cleared my throat and opened my mouth to answer Jess. Bun made a clicking sound with his front teeth, then rudely interrupted what I'd been about to say.

"Right, I forgot, she can't hear me. Well, go on, then."

"We were merely walking the property. I wasn't looking for anything or anyone, we just happened upon this man's campsite. Nervy of him to squat on my property like that. Carver's going to question him and then give me a call."

I drained the pasta, dumped it into a bowl, and poured the sauce over it. I set it on the table as Jess added a salad to our fare. We chatted about how she was feeling. I asked if she was working her rotation tonight, and she nodded.

"If you'll be okay by yourself, I'll go. If not, I'll have to make up the clinical work I'll miss."

Waving away her concern, I said I'd be fine, after all, Bun was here to keep me company.

With a shake of her head, she grinned. "A lot of good that would do you if there was trouble."

I glanced at Bun, who turned his face away from Jess and peered at me. "He's been very good company and I can read his signs when there's a problem. His whiskers jitter, his ears stand up straight, and he's like a pointer when someone's around that shouldn't be. I couldn't ask for more." I leaned sideways and scratched his head.

"If you say so, then I'll go. When I can take a break, I'll give you a call. If you don't answer, I'll call the police. You'd better answer the phone, Jules. I mean what I said."

"Guess she doesn't have faith in me either. Good thing you do, Jules. I take back what I said about not being a good friend."

We stood at the door watching as Jessica drove away. I took a breath and let it out slowly.

"What a day."

"You can say that again. On second thought, don't bother. Was the camper familiar to you? I wish I'd seen him, I might have known him from somewhere. That old biddy I lived with before coming here had lots of company and not all of it good."

"You never mentioned that before. What kind of company, and what were they like?"

"Some were quite disreputable, others just everyday

folks. I tried to stay out of the way so I wasn't abused, you know? One time I made a remark about one of them, and the old biddy gave me a kick."

Picking him off the floor, I hugged him to me and rubbed my face against his cheek. "I'd never let anyone hurt you, Bun. Not ever. I promise."

CHAPTER TWELVE

After a night of tossing and turning, I gave up the idea of a good night's sleep and got out of bed. Jess had called when her class took a break, I'd said all was well and that I hadn't heard from Carver. Her voice seemed disappointed, but she said Carver must not have anything to tell us yet. I considered our phone conversation while the coffee perked, and I filled Bun's feeder.

It was early when Bun and I shuffled into the barn to check the rabbits and ready them for the day. "You take one side of the barn and I'll take the other side. We'll meet in the middle. If anyone's been about, you let me know, okay?"

Bun tipped his head to the side, twitched his ears, and jumped into action. I walked the other side of the barn's aisles, checking for food, water, and waste trays. I met Bun in the middle aisle. No one had entered during the night, which meant the newly installed locks had held so far, or we hadn't had an unsuccessful invasion attempt. I double-checked that the slide bolts were still secured, and all the window locks. That done, I added hay and replenished water bins before filling rabbit feeders. I saved cleaning the waste pans for last.

While I wondered why Carver hadn't called the night before, I assumed I'd hear from him today. Jessica had arrived home later than usual and was still asleep. Caring for the rabbits and doing what was needed, I had nearly finished when the phone rang.

Discarding my work gloves, I answered the call. "Fur Bridge Farm."

"Sheriff Carver here. I hope I didn't wake you, I thought you might be doing chores. If you have some free time, could you swing by the station this morning? I want to fill you in on the man we arrested yesterday."

"I'm always up early. Is something wrong?"

"No, not at all. I think it would be better if we spoke in person. What time can you come by?"

"How about eight thirty? I'll have time to clean up and drive to your office." After chores, I liked to take a quick shower.

"Eight thirty it is."

After I set the phone on the charger, Bun and I went into the house. My mind buzzed with questions that had no answers. Bun had asked many of the same questions I mulled over.

"I have no idea what Carver wants," I murmured. I poured a cup of tepid coffee, reheated it in the microwave, and made a slice of toast. Slathering it with jam, I munched away while Bun went on and on over my visit to the police station.

"Watch what you say, this might be a trap. Sheriff

Carver is up to no good. Otherwise, he'd have told you over the phone what he learned from his prisoner. Mark my words, he's up to something."

I could hear Jessica walking the upstairs hallway. Before she came downstairs, I whispered, "You only say that because he doesn't think highly of you like I do."

I tilted my head as Jess came into view. "Good morning."

She smiled, flipped her hair out of her eyes, and mumbled the same greeting.

"Is there any coffee?"

"Just what's left in the pot. You'll have to reheat it. I'll make more toast, if you want some."

She agreed and set about pouring herself a cup of coffee. A piece of toast hanging from her mouth, Jessica brought it to the table and slid into her usual chair.

"I have those invitations. They're more like fancy postcards. There are great pictures on the front. Lizzy did four sections, with a picture of the farm, the rabbits, the shop, and one of you and Bun she got from your website." She shuffled over to the coatrack and rummaged through her book bag.

She handed me a stack of large postcards that were perfect for what we wanted to get across to our customers and the public.

"I can drop some of these off at various shops in town and address the rest for mailing. The rabbits are all set for the morning. Fred will show up any-time now, but you're in charge of that. I have to stop in to see Carver when I'm in town."

Her eyes widened a tad. "What's that all about?"

"He said he wanted to talk about the squatter. I haven't any other information. He was being secretive by saying he thought it would be better if we spoke in person. Who knows what theory he's come up with now."

"I take it we didn't have any visitors last night?"

"The new locks did the trick, and everyone was safe and sound. No keys are to be given to anyone, okay?"

"Sure, I'm all for that if it means we'll no longer have barn invasions. I wonder why the guy never came into the house, but stayed in the barn?"

"Could be he was only interested in setting the rabbits free like he said, or didn't have a key to the house. There's no money in the barn and nothing of great value either, other than the rabbits, that is." I glanced at my watch and calculated how much time it would take to shower and get to the police station now that I'd procrastinated. Making the eight thirty appointment would be a close call, but I could do it. I left the chair and my mess on the table.

"Can you tidy up things this morning? If I don't get going, I won't be on time, and you know how Sheriff Carver can be when it comes to that."

Her laughter followed me up the stairs as she said she'd be happy to take over for the day.

Hot water pulsed against my skin as I lathered my body and hair. The heat relaxed the tense muscle and nerves in my neck and shoulders. I'd rinsed and dried myself off when it occurred to me that I had nothing to be nervous over. I'd committed no crime, other than breaking into Arty's house, of course. I had no reason to be anxious, either.

Then why was I? I shook my head, finished dressing, and tied my sneakers.

The blow dryer left my hair wild. Without time to primp in front of the mirror, I dabbed lipstick on my lips and scooted downstairs. I grabbed a bundle of the postcards and rushed out the door.

The public parking lot behind the police station was nearly full. Slowly, I searched for a parking spot. Many of the vehicles belonged to officers. I recognized some of them. Others might be owned by people who had business to take care of at the station. Nearly filled to the brink, only two empty slots remained. I parked in the one closest to the door and hurried into the station.

I stated my business to the officer at the front desk, who directed me through the security scanner. When the alarm didn't sound, the officer showed me to Carver's office. I already knew my way but let the man do his job.

I knocked on Carver's office door and entered when he bid me to do so. He greeted me, motioned to a chair, and picked up the phone. After instructing the person on the other end of the phone to bring the prisoner into interrogation room one, he hung up and sat facing me.

"Don't pussyfoot around, Jack, just tell me what you found out."

His bushy brows hiked a tad as his eyes narrowed. It seemed he didn't like my being forthright, but my nerves were stretched to the max as was my sense of humor over this new situation. Maybe Bun was right, maybe Jack was playing a game, maybe I was being paranoid, and maybe I needed to calm down.

He sat back in his leather chair and teetered a bit. Resting his elbows on the chair arms, Jack pressed the tips of his fingers together, reminding me of a pitched tent. I took an even breath, held it to the count of ten, and let it out slowly.

"Are you having a rough day?"

"Not at all. I have a lot to do, and I'd like to get this over with. After all, you called me. I hadn't planned on this visit."

He looked down at his fingertips, his brows drew together, and I wondered if the feeling of doom that hung at the edge of my horizon was about to become a full-blown event.

"I see. The man on your property has been squatting since your difficulties began at the farm. He refuses to admit he's the one who broke in time and again, that he's been trying to intimidate you, or that he even knew Arty. He also mentioned he doesn't know you or that you own the land."

I snorted. "What did he think, nobody owned it? Every piece of property is owned by someone. Is he of sound mind?"

"He seems to be. My gut says he's not our guy. Any ideas?"

"None. I was surprised to find that campsite, and was even more so at his anger for having been arrested. Surely, if you're a squatter, you might expect to be arrested when you'd been caught out, wouldn't you?"

"You'd think so." He stood and summoned me to follow him.

Entering a hallway, we climbed a flight of stairs to the second floor and came to a row of glassed-in rooms. All but one was empty. An officer stood inside the room with a lone man seated at a table, while another man stood guard outside the door. Inwardly, I quaked and hoped to never be in such a position.

The officers stood at attention. The one in the hallway opened the door for us to enter and tried to take my handbag as I walked in. I gave him a look, but he held tight, so I let go.

"Sit there." Carver pointed at one of the chairs opposite the prisoner.

Once I was seated, I folded my hands in my lap and remained silent. Clearly, I was out of my depth. The man across from us had startling blue eyes, short, shaggy brown hair, and a scar that rode from his left eye to his jawline, which I hadn't noticed the day before. Lean and lanky was how I remembered him. His shoulders weren't wide, but bony, as though he hadn't eaten a decent meal in ages. Empathy for his plight set in. I fought it off, knowing I'd be a fool to let his concerns move me.

Sheriff Carver asked, "Your name is?"

"Like I've said before, Andrew Stone." The man's voice, soft and even, didn't hold the gravelly or sharp sound of my intruder.

"Where are you from?"

"Berkeley, California."

"What are you doing in New Hampshire?"

"Nothing much, just camping on her land." His chin jutted toward me.

"Why?"

"I had nowhere else to go, and it seemed a perfect spot," he said, centering his attention on me. "I thought the land I camped on was state owned. A wildlife sanctuary, maybe."

I said nothing. My need to ask him a thousand questions had instantly vanished. He was not the man we sought. Instead, he was homeless, in need of help, a job, a decent haircut, and fattening up.

Carver shifted in his chair. "What brought you east?"

"There was nothing for me out there, so I thought I'd head this way. Why am I locked up for camping? Is it against the law in New Hampshire?"

I sat up and said, "It is when you're squatting on someone else's land. If you had asked permission, I wouldn't have cared, but you didn't."

"Is that what this is all about? I thought . . ." Andrew's voice drifted off. He clamped his mouth shut and refused to answer any more questions.

I jumped at the chance that he'd seen someone hanging about on the property. "What did you think? Have you seen or heard something you'd like to share, Mr. Stone?"

"Why would I tell you if I did?"

"Because I've been having problems at the farm with an intruder. Now, if you have information, I'd be grateful if you'd share it with me."

"I'm not your man. I don't intrude, I guess I squat, but I don't invade people's homes or whatever this person has been doing at your farm."

"Have you seen or heard anything that might help us find this man?" I sounded pathetic, like I was pleading, and I considered it a sign of weakness. Apparently, Mr. Stone didn't feel the same way.

"I wasn't aware of your farm when I first camped out. It's some distance from my campsite, and I keep to myself. One night, I heard feet running across the hard ground. A man, breathing hard, raced past without noticing me or my setup. It seemed odd, but again, I mind my own business. I wasn't willing to follow him and ask questions."

As if we were in the room alone, I asked, "Why didn't you come to the farm?"

"I had no reason to. I live off the land, eat what I can catch, and forage for what I need to stay dry and warm. I'm quite adept at that."

I'd been about to ask another question when Carver interrupted. "Where did you learn your survival skills?"

"It doesn't matter, I just know how to take care of myself."

"Were you in the military?"

He fell silent, looked away, and then offered a half-hearted shrug.

Carver said, "Juliette, do you wish to press charges against Mr. Stone?"

"No. Mr. Stone can keep camping on my property, if he wishes to do so." I slid my chair back and left the room, collecting my handbag from the guard. Soon, Carver was walking alongside me.

"You'll allow this tramp to stay on your property? You don't know anything about him, for goodness' sake. What if he's a killer? What if he hasn't been honest with us? I'll run a check on him to see if he's a military man. I must say, you got more out of him than we did, and we took turns all night trying to get him to open up." Carver smirked. "I should have called you in to handle the questioning."

"He could use some help, a haircut, and a decent meal. Don't you see that? I'm not saying he's harmless, I think he has other issues."

"Oh?"

I stopped on the stairs and looked up at him. "I'm no doctor or psychologist, but just from what he said and how he's malnourished, it's plain to see he's got problems. I'm surprised you didn't notice, being a cop and all. Aren't you folks trained to see past the norm? Isn't there a homeless shelter in town or a parish that could help him out, even temporarily?"

Carver raised his hands defensively. "There are. I'm not a social worker, Jules, but I'll point him in that direction. Maybe he'll take advantage of their help. If not, there's nothing I can do about it. When I get word from the military, I'll let you know. Until then, I have to release him."

We'd reached the main corridor leading to his office. I lingered at the door. "Thanks, Jack, I appreciate you taking this seriously. Tell Mr. Stone to stop at the farm before returning to his campsite." I glanced at my watch, left the station, and drove to the supermarket. I hadn't shopped lately, so my food supplies had dwindled, especially now that Jessica had moved in.

I left postcards at the service desk inside the market. The clerk, Bette Pringle, immediately read both sides and said, "You've never had an affair like this at the farm. Are you branching out? I heard Jessica Plain is opening a vet clinic in your barn. Is it true?"

Her curly red hair bobbed up and down as she

spoke. The freckles on her face stood out, reminding me of a bad case of the measles, but her grin
was infectious. I responded with a smile and told
her we were finally inviting the public in to see
how we care for the rabbits.

"Is that because of the person who keeps causing you trouble?"

"Not really. I want the public to be aware of how
well we care for the rabbits, and the services we
offer. Lizzy Fraser has taken on the publicity job
and these postcards are her design."

"Great job, bright and bold, eye-catching. I
think you're onto something, Jules." She looked
past me. I turned to see a line had formed behind
me, and stepped aside.

"Bette, let me know if you need more postcards,
okay?"

She gave me a nod and greeted the next person.

The market bustled with activity. Shoppers
whizzed up and down the aisles as fast as I did, taking goods from shelves and filling carts. Little
tykes sat in carriage seats pointing to this and that
as their moms shopped. I was greeted by many,
asked about the vet clinic, and a few shoppers in-
quired about the open house. Gossip ran rampant,
and several people expressed interest in attending
the open house after I mentioned the cards for
the event were at the service desk. Maybe a dozen
cards hadn't been enough.

The checkout lines weren't too long. Waiting
my turn, I flipped through a magazine in the hope
that I'd get out of the store before anyone could
ask questions concerning our invasions. I didn't

want to discuss the issue, mostly due to what would then be twisted into something altogether different and spread around like wildfire.

Next in line, I set my goods onto the conveyor belt and paid the bill. After packing the bags into the carriage for transport to the car, I reached out to take my change from the cashier when I heard a familiar voice behind me.

Her voice low, but nasty as ever, Margery Shaw's eyes gleamed with spite when I turned to look at her. "Where's your creepy little rabbit, you know, Satan's spawn? I bet you even dance on a pentagram with him right beside you."

Stepping away from my carriage, I moved up to her, close and personal. "I've had enough of your crap. You should really see a psychiatrist for your paranoia, Margery Shaw. The rabbit does not talk, it's all in your wicked little mind. Now leave me alone or I'll call the police and tell them you're harassing me."

Her features had changed from cruel to shocked that I had the nerve to step into her space and tell her off. Until now, I'd scurried away from her, hoping to evade her meanness. After all I'd been through lately, my attitude had taken a turn, and I no longer let things slide. She moved back while I glared at her, then slammed her groceries onto the conveyor.

Angry, yet satisfied to have had the last word with the mean witch, I rolled the cart to the car. The groceries lay piled on the back seat as I headed to the library. I parked at the side of the building and went in.

Mary Brickworth stood behind the counter, eyeing me as I crossed the floor. Her five-foot ten-inch, reed-thin body was draped in clothing that looked as though it belonged to someone larger.

At one time, Mary had weighed in at a hefty 250 pounds. When her doctor advised her to lose weight or else, she decided she'd had enough of dragging the extra weight around. Now she resembled a wraith, but claimed to be healthier than ever. She was a good soul, strict when people were noisy in the library, but outgoing outside of work. I gave her what I hoped was a cheerful smile and murmured a greeting.

Her soft-spoken hello was accompanied by the repetitive question of what could she do for me today. I think librarians are trained to say that first thing when people step up to their counter.

"I wondered if I could leave these postcards here. I'm doing an educational open house at the farm on caring for and raising rabbits. I thought you might allow me to drop these off for anyone who would be interested in attending this free event."

After I handed Mary the short stack of cards, I watched her read the front and back. There was no attendance fee listed, nor were there any merchandise sale ads. Her head bobbed up and down and she took the stack, gathered them neatly, and set them on the counter in plain view.

"These are very nice cards. You do such great public service programs, Juliette. I'm sure families with children will flock to the event. If I need more cards, I'll call you."

"Thanks, Mary. Oh, I wanted to tell you how wonderful you're looking." I smiled, bid her good-bye, and scooted to the next stop on my mental list, the corner coffee shop Jessica and I had stopped at after going to Ferguson's Fabulous Furnishings. I'd never gotten the name of the coffee shop, but did so now and chortled as I pulled up to the curb and read the sign above the door.

Cassi's Café au Lait had few customers this late in the day. I'd spent a lot of time with Carver and then the market, and though my stop at the library had been brief, I'd eaten up the morning hours.

With postcards stuffed in my purse, I ordered a coffee to go. The waitress rang up the sale, and I foraged in my purse for money, setting the cards on the counter to dig through the mound of junk I carried before finding my change pouch. The waitress, who chewed gum, had shocking green hair clipped on top of her head, and a nervous tic in one eye, snatched one of the cards and read it.

"You that woman who's been having police problems at yer farm?"

"There haven't been any police problems, I've had an intruder." I handed her the correct change. "Could I speak to the owner, please?"

Her eyes widened. "I didn't mean nothin' by that question." She leaned toward me and whispered, "If you complain to Cassi, she'll fire me. Please don't make me lose my job." She spit the wad of gum into the trash and looked at me with pleading eyes.

"I have no intention of making a complaint. I simply want to ask if I can leave these cards for your patrons."

She shook her head. "I don't think we have any patrons. We only have customers."

Though I was sure of her sincerity in the matter, I nearly chuckled. Since she wouldn't have known what I was laughing about, it would have been more than rude to do so. "In that case, why don't you ask Cassi if I could speak to her about leaving these cards for the customers."

"Sure thing. Wait right there." She went through the swinging doors to the kitchen and called to Cassi.

Truth be told, this young girl had no idea how to present herself to customers or to her boss. I gazed around the small café and wondered how much business she did. The place had been quite busy when Jessica and I had come in. Swinging doors banged against the wall as Cassi walked through the opening. They swung closed behind her and she gave me a curious look.

"Has that girl been rude to you?" Cassi had a no-nonsense attitude that reminded me of my grandmother's. Big-boned and well-muscled, Cassi was probably daunting to some.

"Not at all. She's a sweet girl, just young."

"Well, she doesn't have a shut-off button when it comes to speaking out of turn. That's why I asked."

"I'm the owner of Fur Bridge Farm, located out in the valley? I'm hosting an educational event at the farm and am distributing informational postcards to various businesses in Windermere. I want to ask if it would be all right to leave some for your customers."

She glanced at the cards and nodded. "Sure, that'd be fine. If you're having it catered, we could supply coffee and tea for you if you want. I also make dainty pastries." She reached back and took one of these delightful little gems from the glass case behind her and handed it to me. "Go ahead, eat it. I make the best pastries in Windermere. I'll give you a good price, too. Not like those fancy bakeries on High Street, who charge you eight dollars for a cupcake. No sirree. Just so you know, I studied culinary arts with a minor in pastry creation at Josephson's College over in Radford."

Familiar with the college and encouraged by her enthusiasm, I asked, "Would you have a list of what you offer? A menu of sorts?"

Her smile wide, Cassi rummaged under the counter and handed me a thin binder. "Let's sit at a table and talk this over."

We discussed what she would make, how much it would cost, and if she could deliver to the farm. Happy with her answers to my questions, and her promise to be early for setup, I placed an order and paid a deposit.

The remainder of my stops were uneventful. Eventually I turned toward home, excited over the prospect of having gotten so much accomplished. Parking the car, I went into the barn before going to the house. The lights were on in the shop. Fred's truck sat alongside Jessica's, and I wondered how the construction was coming along.

CHAPTER THIRTEEN

Voices, followed by laughter, echoed from be-yond the shop. Walking through the open space toward the rear of the barn, I stopped short when I saw what Fred had been up to. The area was clean, two-by-four stud framing was in place, and insula-tion had been stapled over it. This room was ready for the next step.

"You don't waste any time, do you?" I asked Fred while taking stock of his handiwork.

Jessica and Fred turned to me and grinned. The happiness in Jessica's face could have generated enough electricity to light the room.

"I didn't do this alone. My helper, Billy Ogden, was here for a few hours and after he left, Jessica was good enough to lend a hand." He turned to her. "Are you sure you want to have a vet business? You could always work for me as my handy helper."

She chuckled, as did I. No way would Jess leave her dream behind to become a construction worker.

"Sorry, but no."

"At this rate, it won't take long to finish the job, then?" I asked while considering the room. There was no doubt in my mind the construction would pass the town's required inspection if all the rooms came out this way. Our illustrious inspector took his job seriously. Fred had gotten the construction permits required before he'd begun to work. If the work wasn't correct, there'd be no certificate of occupancy issued, and nobody wanted that to happen.

"It shouldn't. I'd planned on a week, two at most. If I have help, the job will go faster. I'm not sure if Billy can work for me every day, and I know you girls have things to do. Not to worry, the job will be finished in time for your soiree."

I hid my smile at the term *soiree*. Our open house would be far from it. "I'll let you get back to work. Did you have lunch? Just wondering since it's after two o'clock."

Jess checked her watch. "We were so busy we didn't think about it. At least, I didn't. I could use a sandwich, how about you, Fred?"

"Sure thing, that's kind of you." He dipped his head and smiled before picking up his nail gun and returning to work.

Jess remained with Fred as I went into the house. Hurriedly, I put together three sandwiches consisting of roast beef, lettuce, and tomato. I added gobs of mayonnaise to the hearty wheat bread and slapped the food onto plates. I added potato chips and bottles of water to the fare, then carried the loaded tray to the table.

I let the two workers know lunch was ready in the kitchen. While I had assembled lunch, Bun hopped from his room, stood near my feet, and asked questions.

"How did it go with Carver?"

"We spoke with the camper. Seems he's from California, is homeless, and didn't realize he'd camped on my land. His name is Andrew Stone. He's not our guy."

"You're sure?"

"I am. He saw someone running past his tent on the same night as our intruder was here, though."

"He might be making that story up, you know."

"My gut says he's telling the truth."

"Right."

Footsteps and chatter echoed through the breezeway. Bun returned to his room and huddled by his door in silence. The two workers washed their hands in the sink and sat down to eat. Conversation was nil until we'd had our fill.

"Anything you want to share about this morning?" Jess asked.

"The squatter isn't our intruder, but thinks he saw a guy running past his campsite one night." I crunched a chip and then filled her in on the rest of the conversation with Stone. "He might be lying, but I really don't think so. I got the feeling he's just down and out, not dangerous."

"He's not going to stay out there in his tent, is he?"

I shrugged. "I don't care if he does, as long as he doesn't destroy the area, and isn't a bother to us. Why?"

"We could use another hand in the barn once the kids graduate from school. They'll be done in the middle of May, and that'll be the end of our help, other than Peter Lambert. Have you asked Peter if he'll be working for you throughout the summer? Classes end for him in May, you know."

Fred sat silently fiddling with his water bottle while Jess and I talked. His eyes switched from one to the other of us as we spoke.

"I had planned to ask him about that when he arrived for work this weekend. Jess, do you think it's a good idea to have Andrew Stone work for us?"

When she hesitated, Fred leaned forward, perched his elbows on the edge of the table, and said, "If you trust him like you said, then I don't see what harm it would do to have an extra hand here at the farm, Jules. He might need the help more than you do."

A police cruiser drove into the yard and parked next to my car. With a nod to the driver, Andrew Stone left the passenger's seat and watched the officer drive away. He studied his surroundings for a moment or two before he climbed the steps to the front door.

I'd watched from the window and waited at the door to let him in. Jess and Fred turned to see the tall, thin man. They gave each other a quick glance and then welcomed him, beckoning him to take a seat.

Stone took the empty chair between Fred and Jessica. Once he was comfortable, I made introductions and asked if he'd like a cup of coffee.

"Sure, thanks."

While he didn't seem uncomfortable, he did appear a tad wary. I poured the brew for him and brought it to the table with a milk pitcher and sugar bowl. He waved them away and drank the coffee.

"He's kind of ragtag, don't you think?"

I set the coffee carafe on a trivet and offered Bun a raised-brow look.

"So, Mr. Stone, will you be staying at the campsite, or do you plan to move on?" I asked.

"If you don't mind, I'll stay for a while. It's peaceful back there and I like that."

Bun took a step forward and stopped. *"More like what he needs. Something is bugging him, I can smell it."*

Jessica pushed her plate aside. She looked Stone in the eyes and asked, "I'm not judging you, I'm simply curious. How do you survive living like that?"

"I manage. I have no responsibility to anyone but myself, and that makes life easier for me. Haven't you ever wished you could be free of everyday worries?"

The man had a point. I had so many things going on, my life was overflowing. Though, I couldn't see myself living in his circumstances. I liked comfort too much to live rough.

Fred excused himself by saying he would be in the barn. As he walked toward the breezeway, Jessica said nearly the same and followed Fred. That left me, Bun, and Stone alone.

"I didn't scare them away, did I?"

I smiled. "They have work to do and a schedule to follow, so no, you didn't scare them."

"You're sure you don't mind my staying at the site?"

"Not at all."

"I don't make you nervous? I am, after all, a stranger."

I shook my head. "Not nervous at all. Besides, the sheriff would have let me know if you were a danger to us, and you wouldn't be here right now." I reached for the lunch plates and began to clear the table.

His gaze steady and watchful, Bun grumbled, *"I think you shouldn't offer him a job. You know next to nothing about him, and he's troubled. I can smell it, I tell you."*

Knowing full well that animals have keen senses, I was certain Bun was onto something. What it was, I didn't know, but my curiosity was at an all-time high due to his insistence. Stacking the dishes in the sink, I gave Bun a wink and then turned to Stone.

"Do you have enough blankets and such? The nights still get rather cold."

"I'm all right, thanks. If I find I could use an extra one, I'll come by, if that's all right?"

"Sure."

"I do have one, maybe two questions for you, though. Why would you allow me to stay on your land?"

"You're not bothering anyone, so why not? What's your other question?"

"Why would someone want to break into your farm?"

"That's a long story that I'm not really sure is the real one. Mostly theory on my part."

Though he was idle and now relaxed, his interest gave his face an animated appearance.

"Tell me."

Willing to talk to someone who might offer a different aspect of the situation, I gave him a quick summary of what had happened at the farm. I added the discovery of Arty the Mime's body, and left it at that. He listened without interruption.

"Any ideas or thoughts on these issues?"

With a shrug, he pushed his chair away from the table and stood up.

"That's quite a mystery. You have taken precautions though, haven't you? More security for the barn?"

"After the last time, I put all that in place. I've never had to worry about security before, but I guess I should have."

Stone readied to leave, zipped his jacket, and walked to the door.

"With all you've been experiencing, I wouldn't blame you if you had pressed charges against me. I appreciate that you didn't."

Stone opened the door and walked out without a good-bye or even a glance over his shoulder. He veered toward the wooded land past the barn. I watched him until he was out of sight.

"I think he's a survivalist kind of guy. Something bad in his life, too, that makes him a loner. Aren't you glad I'm not a loner?"

With a roll of my eyes, I chuckled. "You could never be a loner. Where would you get that yummy tasting food I give you every day?"

"Mm, you're probably right. I'm used to being treated like the prince I am." With that, Bun scooted from the kitchen into the breezeway, with me not far behind.

I'd reached the shop just as Jess walked in from

the back section where Fred was working. I heard the *ca-chink* sound of his nail gun and looked at Jessica.

"Well, what do you think?"

"Mr. Stone is strange, for certain. You didn't offer him a job, did you?"

I shook my head. "If he likes his life the way it is, why would I interfere with that?"

"I thought the same thing. Now tell me, what else happened in town? You were gone forever."

I withdrew the sheet of paper from my pocket that held the fare to be served at the upcoming open house. Jess snatched it from my hand, gave it the once-over and handed it back.

"You were busy."

"I also put postcard invites out for people to take. I'll take care of the rabbits now and then fill out the invitations for the mailman to take. What are you up to?"

"I've done all I can to help Fred. My clinical rotation is on for tonight, then I'll give what I've learned a final review. The professor said this won't be a final exam, but he'll be in there when I do my final rotation." She grinned and went on her way.

Bun hopped back and forth across the room, sniffed the air, and twitched his ears every time the nail gun sounded. Eventually, he stopped in front of me. *"Can we take a walk now? I haven't had any fresh air today."*

I knelt and smoothed his coat. "I've got to check the rabbits first, and then we can go out for a while."

He followed me into the barn, then scurried

through the aisles. I went in the opposite direction, took stock of which rabbits could use more water or hay, and met Bun in the middle row.

He told me which rabbits were low on supplies. I cared for those who had little or none.

I checked on Fred and asked, "Could you lock up if I'm not back before you leave?"

"Certainly, I'll be at this for another hour, then I'll head for home. You just go about your business, I'll be back tomorrow."

I thanked him, got my jacket, and tucked Bun into his sling.

The phone rang as I opened the door. Carver was on the line.

"Hi, Sheriff, what's up?" A sense of dread instantly weighed me down.

"The government wasn't of much help when I contacted them about Andrew Stone. They said he had been in the military, nothing more. My lieutenant then Googled him, and come to find out, Stone is a decorated veteran. That's all we could find on the man."

"That's better than nothing, I suppose. Thanks for calling." I hung up, told Bun what Carver said, and closed the door behind us before anyone else could interrupt our plans.

Walking the path along the side of the road, we veered off the track toward the lake where we'd found Arty the Mime.

Bun poked his head out of the sling and kept up a one-sided conversation. He seemed to be working something out, but his voice droned on and on in my brain. At the water's edge, I came to an abrupt halt and gazed out over the now ice-free water. Strange how the seasons can change the look of one's surroundings.

"Why are we here?"

"I'm admiring the landscape and the view of the lake. It's nice now the snow has melted, and the ice is gone. Do you remember exactly where we found Arty?" I hesitated at the fence where we'd first stopped that cold, wintry day. Headed in that direction, I stopped at the gate that blocked the road and peered out toward the beach. Sunshine sparkled and danced across the water, waves lapped the shoreline, and a heady breeze ruffled my hair. Bun's ears twitched.

"Down to your right, I think. Let's look, maybe there's evidence left in the grasses."

Moving in the direction he'd indicated, I said, "I'd be surprised if there was. It's rained buckets since we were here last. Besides, I'm sure Carver has given the area a thorough going-over."

Grasses lay mashed flat in this section. It was the only spot that might have held Arty's body. All the rest of the tall grass waved in the breeze. Focused on the ground, both of us were intent on finding a remnant of Arty's demise that might have been overlooked.

"Looks like you're right. I think Carver has given it the attention Arty deserved. Nobody should be left in the cold like that poor man was, even though he was miserable to you."

"I agree." As I turned away, a flash of light caught my eye. "Did you see that?"

"See what?"

"There's something over there." I pointed to where the sun sparkled off something shiny.

"Well, don't just stand here, let's see what it is."

His excitement was obvious, yet his voice doubtful. Bun liked to be the one who made discoveries. I stepped to the right, then moved a foot or two closer to the edge of the flattened grass when sunlight bounced off the item again.

Opening the sling, I waited until Bun jumped to the ground, and together we foraged for what had caught my attention. Parting the grass, I gently pulled the shreds aside and crouched down on my knees.

"Looks like an old-fashioned key."

I lifted the key that had been jabbed tip down into the ground, and wiped it on my jeans. Digging into my jacket pocket, I found an old tissue that I used to wipe the grime from the carved details where it would fit into a lock. Studying it closely, I turned it over in my hand and then showed it to Bun, who began to shiver. His eyes widened, his whiskers jittered, and he backed several steps away from me.

"What's wrong?"

"I've seen that somewhere. I don't remember where, but it wasn't a good place. I know that for certain. Get it away from me."

His eyes were a tad wild looking. I knew Bun well enough to know he was terrified of the key, but why? Quickly, I tucked it into my jeans pocket, lifted Bun off the ground, and secured him in the sling. He shook until the heat from my body calmed him.

"Are you all right?"

"I don't want to talk right now. Can we go home?"

"We can." I set off at a fast-paced walk and then

jogged awhile until Bun made it clear I jostled his fine bones and demanded I quit doing so. Bun had recovered from his fear and was his usual self. Smiling, I slowed to a walk, commented on the beauty of our surroundings, and mentioned how anxious I was for the open house to be over.

"It will be successful, everyone likes you and, of course, us bunnies. We draw them like moths to light. Have no fear, you'll be famous before you know it."

"I'm not in search of fame, I simply want to expand the business a bit and help Jessica become established as the best vet in Windermere."

"Did Lizzy's car just fly past us?"

"It looks like her car. She's slowing down for the turn into the farm. I wasn't expecting her today, I hope nothing untoward has happened. She's quite an asset to the business."

Hurrying along the driveway, I stopped in at the gift shop. A huge pile of bagged yarn lay stacked haphazardly on the counter. Several large empty cardboard boxes lay in a jumbled heap on the floor. Lizzy was nowhere to be seen.

"Hello? Lizzy?"

She popped up from behind bags of yarn, a wide grin filled her face. "I saw you and Bun walking. I apologize for not stopping to give you a ride, but I wanted to get this yarn unpacked right away."

Blends of silk, soft wool, angora, and mohair skeins were gorgeous, soft, and luxurious. The luscious colors made me think of strawberry, pistachio, and creamy vanilla ice cream. I reached out and played my hands over the skeins, enjoying the softness of each. Lizzy snickered. Together, we separated and stacked the yarns before placing them in diamond-shaped bins that hung on the wall.

Delighted at the cheerful colors and brightness they added to the shop, I regarded the skeins, asking if there were any new knitting and crochet supplies to accompany these beauties.

After digging through another box, Lizzy spread a heap of circular bamboo knitting needles across the open space on the counter. She added crochet hooks, in a myriad of colors, ranging from thin, to fat, to enormous.

Lifting a few crochet hooks, I gave each a good look. "Where did you get the idea for buying these?"

"YouTube."

"Where?"

"My niece stopped by for supper the other night and we got to talking about the shop. She had her iPad with her and opened the YouTube channel. She showed me a variety of projects made with different-sized needles and hooks, so I thought we should have some for sale. You don't mind, do you?"

I shook my head. "Not at all, it's just that we should have a few display projects to create interest, and time is running short."

"Not to worry on that count, I have a couple friends who are making shawls, bags, and hats to place beside the yarn. They knit and crochet quite fast."

Bun, who had remained quiet until now, entered the conversation. *Is there any angora to be used for a project?*

In answer to his question, I said, "I'd especially like to have something made from angora."

Lizzy nodded. "I'd considered that and gave one of the girls a skein to knit a cloche. It's going to be gorgeous."

"Isn't she brilliant?"

I nodded. "Wonderful, I think you're on top of things, more so than I."

"Thanks. Now let's get the rest of this merchandise on display so I can go home. I'm exhausted. Thank goodness the promo we're doing at the office is nearly over. The boss has us running around like crazy people."

"You will be available next weekend, though, won't you?"

"That's the plan. Have you gotten any responses from the cards you put out and invitations sent?"

"Not unless there are messages waiting for me in the house. I've only just put out the cards, which are very well done, thank you. I spent part of a day taking care of that end of things and doing chores here as well. I figure word will spread pretty quickly."

I mentioned Fred's construction of Jessica's vet clinic and showed the progress he'd made in just one day.

Thrilled to see how quickly the project was coming along, I watched when Lizzy whirled in place to see all and everything that had been accomplished.

"He's amazing. Where is Jess, by the way?"

"Her car is gone, so she's left for her clinical rotation. Jess has worked so hard, and with her own vet clinic project underway, she's somewhat stressed."

"Don't worry, she'll be just fine." With a glance at her watch, Lizzy exclaimed she had to leave and rushed out the door with a promise to come back the next day.

I waved as she backed out of her parking place and drove helter-skelter down the drive and onto the road. Bun stood at my feet, staring out the door, and then said, *"All that fresh air and hard work has left me hungry. Can I have something to eat?"*

After locking up and shutting lights off in the clinic and the shop, we walked into the barn, double-checked the rabbits should any of them need anything, and then went on through the breezeway into the house.

Having settled in for the evening, I listened to my phone messages and then opened the laptop to check my email, wondering if there'd been any responses to the postcards I'd spread around town. I thought it unlikely, but was pleasantly surprised to hear from people I knew who had gotten cards from the various stores where I'd left them. They were mostly curious over what was planned for the open house. Eager to read the number of queries there were, I set about answering the questions.

CHAPTER FOURTEEN

Asleep in the comfortable armchair facing the fireplace, I abruptly awoke when I heard the shuffle of feet. I sprang from the chair, ready for battle when I heard Jessica speaking softly to Bun. The pounding of my heart slowed, and my nerves stopped jittering when I realized nothing was amiss.

Sunshine filled the room with its brilliance, and awareness of the beginning of another day's dawning gave me pause. I entered the kitchen as Jessica set the coffee to perk.

"What are you doing up so early?"

She gave me a smile and said, "It's nearly eight o'clock. You must have been exhausted to fall asleep in the chair. When you never stirred when I came in last night, I didn't have the heart to wake you."

I rubbed the sleepiness from my eyes and face, then brushed my hair back and stretched. "I thought I heard someone walking around in here, and that's what woke me just now."

"I've just come in from feeding the rabbits. Sit down, I'll make breakfast."

"I need a shower, then I'll eat. Thanks, Jess." I took the stairs two at a time and rushed through a shower, dressed in a fresh set of work clothes, and joined Jess at the table.

"Bun's all set for the morning. I cleaned his room and set him up with his favorite hay. Fred will be here shortly. I'll give him a hand for a while if you don't need help finishing up with the rabbits."

"Do what you need to do. I'll be fine. Oh, Lizzy came by yesterday with a load of yarn and oddments to go with it. The yarn is fabulous, you should see it. Honestly, I can't imagine how we managed without her. She said she'll be by after she leaves work tonight."

"I can't wait until I'm finished with my rotation schedule. Then I'll be ready to take my state board exam. It's been a long haul to get through all of this."

"You've worked hard to achieve your goals." I bit into a slice of toast and caught sight of Fred's truck coming up the drive. "Fred's here. You go on, I'll take care of this." I waved my hand at the breakfast dishes.

"Okay, see you later, then." Jessica was gone in a flash.

"She's quite happy, isn't she?"

"Yes, and rightfully so. It's amazing how you feel when your dreams are realized. That's how I feel about this farm, you, and the other rabbits."

"I knew I'd make you happy the moment we met. It was the best day of my life when you rescued me from that

horrid witch." Bun gave a slight shudder and then asked, *"Did you have a chance to look at that key you found yesterday?"*

I shook my head, swallowed a mouthful of coffee, and said, "You don't seem so frightened this morning. Have you given the key some consideration? You were very distraught yesterday, and I didn't want to mention your reaction to it."

"It scared me, badly. I can't remember what brought on the fear, but just seeing the shape of it made me quake inside. Can you show it to me again? Just set it on the floor so I can get a close look at it, and smell it, too."

"Sure." I stuck my hand in my pocket and pulled the key out. I'd taken it from yesterday's jeans pocket and tucked it in this pair to give it a closer inspection. I set the key in a brilliant patch of sunlight on the floor and watched as Bun slowly came near. His whiskers fluttered up and down, and his nose worked overtime as he sniffed the metal before he carefully withdrew from it.

"Any ideas what it goes to?"

"Not one. It seems familiar, though. There's something bad connected to this key, I can feel it in my bones. What it is, I can't say. Quite the quandary, wouldn't you say?"

"You don't know, or you refuse to remember, what your association with the key is?"

Bun moved a shoulder that resembled a shrug. I hid my smile, as it was such a human action. He hopped toward his room and mumbled that he needed to sleep on it awhile and maybe then he'd remember.

"Bun, are you feeling okay?"

"Of course, I'm merely trying to bring forth a reluctant memory." He hesitated and then asked, *"Haven't you*

ever had a memory bother you, especially when it refuses to come out on its own?"

Instantly, I was back in a hospital bed where I'd woken up after having been run off the road and left for dead. I'd had no immediate recollection of what had taken place. That terrifying memory had come later, after much urging from a trauma specialist.

"Don't force it, Bun. It'll present itself when your brain thinks it can handle what you've forgotten." I slipped my boots on, plucked a clean pair of work gloves from the bottom drawer in the cabinet, and said I'd be in the barn if he needed me. When there was no reply, I stopped to observe Bun slowly enter his room. It was so unlike him, I began to worry.

I left him to his own thoughts and went to work. Entering the barn, I heard the phone ring and saw Sheriff Carver's cell phone number on the caller ID.

"Good morning, what can I do for you, Sheriff?"

"You sound chipper this morning. I hope this news doesn't spoil your day, Jules. The coroner's final report from Manchester arrived. It shows Arty suffered from brain cancer, which could have contributed to his irrational behavior. I've given it some thought, and Arty's actions make sense."

Shocked over the coroner's findings, my mind harked back to the start of my work relationship with Arty.

"Are you still there, Jules?"

"Yes, I am. Thanks for letting me know, Jack. I appreciate the call." I hung up, remembering when Arty and I had entertained at social events. Arty had been interesting, amusing, even. Tuned in to his audience, his professionalism never slipped for a second. He'd never remarked on the rabbits, other than saying they always appeared happy and calm. It wasn't until the previous summer that I'd noticed Arty started to act oddly. Not having known the man outside of parties and town fairs, I'd been unable to get a sense of when those actions had initially begun.

Heaving a sigh, I went to work, which can be very therapeutic. After I'd been released from the hospital and my physical therapy was completed, I had thrown my energy into raising rabbits, and all that came with the responsibility of it. When asked to help with Bun, I knew I'd found my calling. During my early days, I'd been part of a team that rescued mistreated rabbits and nursed them back to health. Satisfied that I'd made a difference in the life of an animal made a huge difference in my recovery after having been nearly killed by Rusty Cardiff.

I mused over how far my rabbit farm had come, the way it had developed, and the fun the rabbits and I shared in the petting pen at family gatherings, school education classes, and at other events. I was happier than ever over having an opportunity to share the rabbits and my farm with others.

With two and a half weeks to go before the open house took place, I was certain the affair would be a success. While wondering how many people would actually attend, I emptied bunny poop from trays. It was the least enjoyable job on the Rabbit To-Do work list, but it was fulfilling to know the rabbits were well taken care of.

Glad to be wearing a mask that helped diminish the smell of fecal matter, I carried litter trays to the hopper, scraped them clean, then sanitized and dried each one, before sliding them under their rightful cages. Earlier, Jessica had taken care of the food and watering end of things. I swept all the doors open and let the warm breeze flow in and out of the barn, while figuring out how and where the petting pen would be set up.

The rabbits would need constant attention in case a child got out of control and tried to carry one off. As calm and friendly as my bunnies were, I wouldn't tolerate any harm coming to them. While children didn't often realize how rough they were being, it paid to be attentive when they were involved with the animals.

Once I was finished with chores, my thoughts turned to my earlier conversation with Sheriff Carver.

"The report is same as it was, except when Dr. Radmore finished examining Arty's brain, he realized the man had brain cancer, stage four," the sheriff had remarked. "How Arty managed to function as long as he did is a mystery as far as Radmore is concerned. Were you aware he was ill?"

"No, all I knew was he was irrational. He became violent and hysterical over things he felt were wrong, and that needed fixing. Nothing more. Why?"

"I thought you might have had some insight into what was going on with him."

"Oh. I knew something wasn't right, but it never occurred to me he had brain cancer. Sorry to hear that, the man had nobody to care for him, and that's just plain sad."

It was just as I was ready to hang up that he'd dropped the second part of his news, which didn't come as too much of a surprise since the sheriff's lieutenant had Googled Andrew Stone.

Carver's friend, a major in Washington, DC, had gotten back to him about Stone upon his return from vacation. Andrew had an impressive service record and had been honorably discharged. The information ended on that note. When Carver had asked if Andrew had stopped in for a visit or two, I said no and that I had better things to do than mind his business.

The following week, filled with hard work, preparations for the open house and all that entailed passed without incident. Grateful for that, Jessica, Lizzy, and I worked tirelessly to iron out the final details, along with completion of the clinic. Bun, of no help whatsoever, acted as the boss of all and everything. When I'd lost my patience, I picked him off the floor and marched into the house.

"There's no need to manhandle me, you know."

"Bun, you aren't helping me by giving orders," I whispered. "It's time for you to stay out of the way and give us all a rest. Do you think you can do that?"

Bun's ears drooped and lay flat against his head and down over his shoulders, giving his features a sad look. Guilt-ridden over having hurt his feelings, I smoothed his coat and explained the amount of stress we were under to be ready for our grand adventure. At the mention of adventure, he perked up.

"If I have been bossy, it's only because I want this to be a great day for all of us. I'm sorry, Jules."

"Just relax and stay here where we won't trip over you, okay? I know you're only trying to help, and while I appreciate that, you can do me a favor by staying put for a few hours."

Rubbing his head against the palm of my hand, Bun said, *"I will. I think I need a nap anyway."*

I left him on his own, lounging on a floor pillow and snacking on a bit of timothy hay. While he rested, I returned to the barn to find Lizzy and Jessica setting up the rabbit pen. A box filled with the rabbits' favorite chew blocks, untreated willow baskets, and willow balls sat alongside a basket made of untreated apple twigs containing balls with bells inside.

"How is it going?" I grabbed the fourth corner of the pen and tugged the wall out until it snapped in place.

Lizzy, breathing hard from the exertion of the setup, groaned. "How do you manage this by yourself when you do kids' parties? By golly, this is hard work."

Jessica and I laughed and kept working. "Why don't you make sure the shop is all set for the onslaught of people we'll have stopping and hopefully shopping this weekend. Jess and I can finish up in here."

Wiping her brow, Lizzy nodded and walked away. Leaving the door open, she finished sorting a few odds and ends she'd mentioned adding to the sale table. Her friends had donated their time and prowess to knit and crochet luxurious scarves, shawls, cloches, and had even made a few knit bracelets with beads threaded onto the yarn. It was my guess that these little darlings would be the hit of the show.

I'd written letters of thanks for the handiwork to Lizzy's friends and included a gift card for discounted merchandise the day of our affair. Lizzy had delivered them and reported back on how excited these three women were.

I gave the shop a last look, then thanked Lizzy and Jessica for their patience and hard work to make this day a success for all of us. "Shall we take a break? I know I could use one."

Lizzy looked around, peered into corners, and then asked, "Where's Bun?"

"He's on a time-out. I tripped over him one too many times, so he's in his room. He was happily eating hay and lounging on his bed when I left. Not to worry, he's content."

"I wondered where he'd gotten to. He's such a little busybody, isn't he? Poking his nose into everything," Lizzy noted.

I glanced at Jess and we both agreed. The phone rang. I answered the call and listened to Cassi ask if all was set up for the open house.

"We're as ready as we can be. You're still bringing the food, aren't you?"

"I'll have everything ready to go. I'll be at the farm by seven thirty that morning if it's all right with you. That way the coffee urns and punch jugs will be ready for your guests. You must be excited."

"I am, we all are. I'm hoping for a good turn-out."

"I've heard lots of talk about your farm and what you're doing. I don't think you have anything to worry about. I'll see you then." Cassi hung up, as did I.

The two women hovered near the door, listening.

"That was the caterer. We're good to go on that account. She's bringing what's needed, so I won't worry about food, beverages, and paper goods."

"Then let's take that break you talked about, because we're ready for tomorrow's crowd," Lizzy said. "I think it's going to be a splendid day, don't you, Jessica?"

Jess nodded, and we headed into the house. On our way through the breezeway, I glanced out of the glass enclosure and saw Andrew Stone lingering at the edge of the woods near the field. I waved and beckoned him to join us. He stared for a few seconds and turned away, then melted into the trees. For a mere second, I thought I had imagined his sudden appearance. I shook my head, followed the girls into the house, and closed the door behind us.

"Did you see Andrew Stone out there?" I asked, pointing to the far end of the grounds, which turned shrubby and treed.

Jessica's eyes widened, while Lizzy looked confused. "Who is Andrew Stone?"

"He's the man who was arrested for squatting on Juliette's property a while back. Jules decided he should be allowed to stay because Sheriff Carver said he's harmless. He hasn't been around since then, has he, Jules?"

"I haven't seen him, have you?"

Jess shook her head. Startled at the news, Lizzy asked if he was indeed harmless.

"So far as I can tell, he is. He doesn't bother us, and we return the favor by staying clear of him. I'm curious, though, as to why he was staring at the house. I motioned for him to join us, but he just went back into the woods."

With a small shudder, Lizzy exclaimed, "You mean he's been here for a long time and nobody told me? It's creepy to have a stranger lurking around your place, Jules. Just creepy."

I put my hand on her shoulder and gave it a squeeze. "There's nothing to worry about. As a matter of fact, since we found him squatting and agreed to let him stay, there hasn't been one incident at the barn. Maybe he's our lucky charm. What do you think, Jessica?"

"You're probably right. Besides, it's your property, and you make the rules. I'm okay with him being around since the sheriff is undoubtedly keeping his eye on things. I noticed a cruiser going by around the same time every night when I return from class."

I gaped at her while the teakettle filled with water. "You never said a word."

"I thought you knew."

"Well, I do now. Tea anyone? I have a box of Tastykakes to go with it?"

Lizzy and Jess agreed to the idea. We went into the living room and made ourselves comfortable.

Lizzy moaned, while Jess and I groaned over our aching backs. It had been a long week of preparation for the crowd I expected to attend our event. If no one showed, I'd be as devastated as the other two women would be. I stopped that line of thinking and turned it into a positive instead. If no one showed, there'd be enough food for an army, and I wouldn't have to cook for a week or so.

A tray filled with teacups, a teapot, and various Tastykakes sat between us on the coffee table. We'd sipped, snacked, and chatted for an hour before Jessica asked if I'd give her a hand in the clinic. Lizzy remarked she'd be on my doorstep at the crack of dawn to make sure every detail had been tended to, and then she left for the day.

In the clinic, Jessica and I set out clipboards with forms for those who might be interested in filling them out and bringing their pets in for a checkup after Jessica graduated and opened the clinic. Molly Perkins, nearly finished with high school, had generously offered to monitor the clinic while the open house was in full swing.

While we set about closing the clinic and the shop, Jessica asked if Ray Blackstone and Peter Lambert would be in attendance.

"They both offered to come in and give us a hand to get the rabbits squared away for the day. Pens and hutches still need their usual maintenance and bunnies have to be fed. I was happy to hear they'd be able to help. Fred did an astonishing job building the clinic and doing extra painting and whatnot to make it ready for tomorrow. I thought for sure you and I would be burning the midnight candle to get the walls painted and the stock put away."

A furtive movement to my left caught my eye as we entered the barn. In slow motion, I reached out and tapped Jessica's arm, slightly tilting my head in that direction when she looked at me. Instantly, we split up and each took a side of the barn, moving as quietly as possible. The rabbits weren't nervous, which left me to wonder if I had been mistaken to think someone had entered the barn while we were in the clinic.

We'd reached the end of the rows and found Andrew Stone lounging against a stack of hay bales. He nonchalantly watched us approach and then stood up straight.

"You left the doors open, Juliette."

"I know."

"Anyone could have entered and done harm to your animals."

Jess watched him in silence, then asked, "What are you doing here?"

"Checking the place out. I saw someone hanging about last night and wanted to make sure the place was safe."

"Have you been watching over the farm?" I asked.

"Not at first. I'd been fishing at the lake about two weeks ago and saw someone messing about in the place where that dead body was found. They were hunting for something, but apparently didn't find it. Another time, I noticed you and the rabbit were there, searching the grass. That's when I became suspicious of the other person and figured he might be the one who broke in here on occasion. It's none of my business, but you've been fair to me, so I thought I'd return the favor by keeping an eye out."

My heart pounded, my pulse raced, and my anxiety started to grow. Who had been searching

Arty's deathbed besides Bun and me? Why hang about? Again.

"When I motioned to you earlier, you didn't acknowledge you'd seen me. Is there a reason for that?"

"I'm not looking for friends. Like I said, I wanted to return the favor since you've done right by me. Nothing more."

"Good to know. Thanks. Did you recognize who scoped out the place where Arty was found?"

"I have no idea who it was. I haven't met anyone in town, and don't care to."

"I see, well, thanks for looking out for us. I appreciate it."

He gave me a brief nod and left the barn. I locked the door behind him and said to Jess, "Let's give the place a once-over."

We set off in opposite directions once more, took our time, and walked each aisle. We checked window locks, hutch clasps, and took stock of the rabbits before we met at the front of the barn where the double doors were already latched and secure. There was nothing left but to feed the animals again before the day ended.

CHAPTER FIFTEEN

The caterer arrived on time. Lizzy had flown up the driveway as though riding a broom instead of driving a car, and Jessica directed my two helpers on the rabbits' needs. Bun stood at my heels and insisted the day would be splendid. The sun was bright, and all would be well at Fur Bridge Farm, as far as Bun was concerned.

I leaned down, snatched him up into my arms, and nuzzled his ears. Enthusiasm among the crew was on the rise, the air filled with excitement. We all seemed in tune with one another. This event would move on greased wheels, I was sure of it. All was ready when the first few cars arrived.

Peter Lambert was the parking guru for the day, waving people into spots for their cars, which reminded me of parking at Disney. Satisfied with how he handled the traffic, I focused on welcoming everyone and asked them to sign the guest register set up at the double doors.

A warm current of air filtered in and warmed

the barn. It promised to be a splendid time. I crossed my fingers and continued my role as hostess. Many of my former customers arrived with children in tow. Playing with their bell toys, and having a grand time, the rabbits entertained the children. Ray Blackstone handled the kids and rabbits as well as I did, leaving me impressed. When Sheriff and Mrs. Carver walked in, Meredith immediately stepped into the yarn shop. I grinned when I heard her squeals of joy over the luscious colored yarns. Standing next to me, Jack shook his head and crossed his fingers.

"Hoping this isn't going to cost you too much, Jack?"

"If only," he replied before being drawn into a conversation with a man from the city council.

On it went until I thought my feet would give out, my face would crack if I had to smile one more time or redirect shoppers to the yarn shop and recommend the clinic tour. The response to my open house was so much more than I had imagined it would be.

I felt a yank at my skirt and looked down to see Emmy Sounder, a third-grader at the local elementary school.

"What can I do for you, Emmy?"

She leaned in close and whispered, "There's a strange man in there. He's kind of glaring at the rabbits, Miss Bridge."

The smile on my face froze. "Thank you, Emmy. Why don't you go play with the rabbits while I go see this person?"

She nodded and went to the rabbit pen where Ray showed her our angora rabbit. It took a second or two for me to figure out the man had disappeared. The back door stood open, gently swaying in the breeze. I knew for certain it had been closed and locked when we'd opened for business. I glanced up and down each aisle, took stock of the rabbits, and realized their hutch doors were secure except for those who were in the pen.

Seconds later, Peter Lambert was at my side. "Is everything okay, Jules? You're looking a bit frantic."

"Everything is fine. Emmy Sounder told me she saw a man lurking over here. I think he made her nervous. Could you and Ray keep your eye on the aisles, so the kids don't wander unaccompanied by an adult?"

"Sure thing. We'll stay vigilant. This affair is going too well to allow anyone to spoil it."

I gave him a nod and moved toward the breezeway entrance where Bun hovered.

"Are you okay?"

I plucked the rabbit off the floor and turned my back to the crowd. "All is well," I whispered. The last thing I needed was for Bun to scamper off and incite the children. I placed him in the pen and removed one of the other rabbits.

Handing her to Ray, I asked that he take her to her cage. She'd been out for quite a while, and I didn't like to have the rabbits become too excited. Some stimulation was fine, but they responded in kind when kids became boisterous.

I leaned toward Peter and murmured, "Keep the kids under control, okay? I don't want the rabbits overwhelmed by them."

"Will do. Why don't you take a break and go into the shop for a while?"

With a smile, I walked toward the door, glanced back, and saw Peter charming the children by holding Bun so they could pet him. Of course, Bun would love the attention and most likely deny the fact later.

The shop was half filled with shoppers and lookers. Those who wanted to see the clinic were going in that direction. Jessica waved as I made my way toward her. Molly Perkins held a registration book to collect names and information from those who were interested in being contacted when the clinic was ready for business. She then handed out information packets on services that would be available.

"How's it going in here?"

"We've taken names of those who would like appointments or house calls when the clinic is up and running and I have my license. I'm astonished at the interest we've gotten. This was a great idea." Jess stepped close and whispered, "I'll be glad when it's over. I'm dead on my feet."

"That's a given. Have you had a snack or beverage?"

She shook her head.

"I'll bring you two something, I'm sure Molly could use refreshments right about now."

"Thanks, that would be great." Jess turned to a woman who had stepped up beside me.

"Hi, Mrs. Colleri, how are you and Oscar doing?"

I'd walked away and didn't hear Mrs. Colleri's comment. Upon reaching the refreshments table set up to the left of the fireplace, I loaded a plate with finger sandwiches and slices of fruit, and then poured two glasses of punch. On my way back to the clinic, I noticed a couple in the farthest corner of the room having a heated discussion.

Wondering what it was about, I deposited the food and drinks into Molly's capable hands and made my way through the line of customers waiting to pay for their goods, and went toward Mary Parker and her husband Bill.

"I'm so glad to see you, Mary, and of course, you too, Bill. How long have you been here?"

Her face flushed, Mary swiftly nodded her greeting.

Diplomatically, Bill said, "Not long. This is quite a party you've got going. Great idea, Juliette."

They'd switched from cranky behavior to being amiable so quickly, I was almost caught off guard. But then, I had approached the married couple with a welcoming attitude. "Have you seen the clinic? Jessica has done a wonderful job setting up her business, and this entire affair has been a great success."

Bill nodded. "We took the tour, albeit briefly. I'd have thought Jessica would want a larger space for her business. So many people in the area have pets and farm animals."

"She'll be making house calls for cows and horses, you know, large animals that won't fit in an exam room."

Mary piped up. "We've made an appointment for our son Jackson to come in and possibly give her a hand. He has a year to complete his school project before graduation next spring and this would be a perfect venue for him."

Hoping I'd hidden my surprise, I asked, "He's interested in veterinary medicine?"

"Oh, no, he just wants something easy to fulfill his volunteering obligation for a year."

"How nice." Not. Jess would see through him in a minute, but I would stay out of it, no matter what. We made the job look easy, though it was far from that.

"Our daughter, Ginger, will be six years old in two weeks. I wondered if you'd like to bring your rabbits to her party?" Mary asked.

I gave Bill a quick look and told Mary that I'd be happy to call her on Monday to make arrangements.

"It's not going to be the same without Arty the Mime, is it, Juliette?" Bill asked with an odd expression on his face.

Curious, I said graciously, "He will be missed by many, I'm sure. His was a grand act and children liked him. It's too bad he's gone."

Warming to the subject of Arty the Mime, Bill laid his hand on my shoulder. "You found his body, didn't you? You poor thing, what a shock that must have been for you."

I inclined my head and agreed. "Quite shocking."

"Have the police made any headway investigating his death?"

I shrugged. "I have no idea, but Sheriff Carver is here, you might ask him."

"Mm, I might just do that." Bill craned his neck

and scanned the crowd. When his gaze settled on Carver, I watched him walk off without saying a word to Mary or me.

Looking tense, Mary waved a hand toward the refreshment table. "I haven't had a thing since we arrived and would enjoy some of that punch."

"As would I, let's have some, shall we?" It was an opportunity to dig into their knowledge of Arty. Why would I miss that?

A bit taken aback that she couldn't get rid of me, Mary recovered quickly and walked toward the table.

"Have you thought of getting a rabbit for Ginger? They make wonderful house pets."

"I can't imagine cleaning up bunny poop. We don't have animals, Bill doesn't think people should have pets. He's of the opinion all animals should live in the wild."

"He and Arty must have agreed wholeheartedly on that. It was Arty's favorite subject, toward the end of his life, that is," I remarked, and handed Mary a glass of punch.

Her eyes widened. "I didn't know that. He certainly wasn't his usual self the last few times we met."

"When was that exactly?"

Wariness filtered into her eyes and she sipped her punch.

"I only ask because Arty was very ill. Did you realize that?"

"N-no, maybe Bill did, but I never thought for a moment he was unwell." Thinking for a moment, Mary said, "Now that you mention it, he was oddly out of sorts and ranted a bit about, uh, things."

"What sort of things?"

Seemingly embarrassed, she looked away from me, then back and murmured, "He'd rant about your farm and the rabbits. I never heard him mention them until two months ago. Was that when he became sick? What was he suffering from?"

"He had brain cancer. Sheriff Carver told me the other day. Sad, really. Arty was a great entertainer."

"Bill was friendly with him, more so than I. I have enough to keep up with between Jackson, Ginger, and my job at the park."

"That can be stressful. So, when did you last see Arty?" Like a dog with a bone, I wasn't about to give up the chance to find out as much about Arty's personal life as I could.

Nibbling a sandwich, Mary moved toward the pastry end of the long table. Cassi had refilled plates with goodies and had poured more punch into the huge urn. I turned the spigot and refilled our glasses.

"I can't remember for sure, but I believe we saw him a week before he died. I was at the supermarket. Bill had gone into the hardware store across the parking lot. When I brought out the groceries, he and Arty stood near our car in conversation."

"About what, do you remember?"

Her discomfort apparent, she set her glass and plate on the table. I figured any moment Mary would take flight.

Gazing across the room, she shook her head. "I have no idea what it was about. Bill seemed put out, and Arty was angry. That's all I can tell you." Checking her wristwatch, she said, "I must be going,

Jackson has a baseball game later that I must attend. You've done a great job, Juliette. I look forward to having you and the rabbits at Ginger's birthday party. If you happen to know of anyone else who might take Arty's place to help entertain the children, let me know when you call me."

I nodded and watched the woman rush across the room. Furtively, she leaned close to Bill and said a few words. Then the couple left abruptly without a backward glance. Their behavior intrigued me. When I called to discuss Mary's plans for her daughter's party, I would try to get her to tell me more. If she had nothing to hide, why would she be so nervous?

The crowd began to dwindle within the next hour or two. Our success boosted my spirits. While Carver and his wife chatted with Lizzy, Jess glanced toward me. I crooked a finger to summon her from the other room and we joined the small group at Lizzy's counter. Carver and Meredith greeted us with smiles and congratulations on our function before they took their leave.

As they reached the door, Lizzy called to them. "Mrs. Carver, you've forgotten a bag."

Meredith hurried forward while I walked over to Jack.

"Did you know Bill Parker was a friend of Arty's?"

He nodded.

"His wife had the jitters when I asked her about the last time they'd seen him."

"You just can't help yourself, can you, Jules?"

His wife returned to his side.

"My deputies will remain until all the guests depart. Feel free to tell them whatever you, or your help, heard or saw that seemed off."

His words were more of an order than a request. I agreed that we'd include his officers in our conversation.

The last couple bid us farewell as they left the farm with their little tykes in hand. The rabbits were soon in their cages, fed and watered, and given timothy hay as an extra treat. It wasn't long before Bun was at my feet, yammering on and on. What he had gleaned when eavesdropping would be a matter for a later conversation. I couldn't very well talk to him now, and knew he was aware of it. He stopped his monologue when I offered a narrow-eyed look, pointed directly at him.

The regular coffeepot perked, and water boiled in an electric teapot, though the food and punch were gone. I invited my employees to have a cuppa of their choice and brought bottled water from the small refrigerator in the main barn, before requesting the deputies join us. Coffee was handed out, tea was steeped and poured, and everyone found a place to relax.

Our beverages were nearly gone before anyone spoke up. I'd waited, not wanting to push them into saying things they weren't comfortable with. Ray Blackstone was the first to say he'd enjoyed the day.

"The kids were kind to the bunnies and interested to learn about them, too. This was a good idea, Jules."

"I think so, too," I said. "Did you hear any gossip or complaints?"

"Just one family seemed a little out of sorts," Ray

answered with a shrug. "I don't know what their problem was, other than the kid's mother being negative about rabbits being unsanitary. I schooled her on how clean they are and said we have only their best interests at heart."

I smiled, as did Jessica. Ray was a huge fan of the rabbits, and I was sorry he'd be leaving. "Thanks, Ray, we're going to miss having you work here with us."

Embarrassed by my admission, Ray finished his water in silence. Lizzy jumped in to offer her take on what had happened in the shop. "I'm dead on my feet, honestly. Customers were quite willing to wait in line, and the sheriff's wife bought a ton of stuff."

That said, Lizzy giggled and then became serious. "There was one episode that left me a little unnerved. A woman came up to the counter demanding to see Bun, she was determined to see him for some reason. Cranky bird, that one. Fearful she'd make a scene, but not knowing why, I said he wasn't available."

"Can you describe her?" Deputy Printer asked, and made notes when she did.

It was then I realized the woman in question was Margery.

I felt a soft body quiver near my feet and picked Bun off the floor.

"I love Lizzy for saving me from the likes of that miserable woman."

"Thanks so much, Lizzy, for not telling her where Bun was. Even though he spent most of his time in the barn, Bun wasn't always in the pen with the other rabbits."

"Her attitude was terrible. She gave me the willies, but I refused to let her near Bunny." Lizzy reached out and smoothed the fur on the top of his head.

His tiny sigh tickled my sense of humor. This rabbit was just too human for words. I glanced at the others and asked if they wanted to share their impressions of the day. Each person, other than the cops, gave their opinions.

Noticing the help was ready to leave, I said, "I appreciate everyone's assistance with this event, it couldn't have been done without you. Thanks."

Before long, only Jessica and I remained. Lizzy had willingly scooted out the door on the heels of the others, including the deputies. I mentioned Bill and Mary's conversation to one of the officers before he left. He said he'd give the information to Jack.

Jess insisted on helping me clear away the tablecloths. She cleaned the coffeepot, while I washed the punch urn and swept the floors. It's surprising how much debris is tracked in on people's shoes. Bun watched us from the doorway.

"I'm getting hungry. How long before you're finished, Jules?"

As Jessica locked the clinic door, I went about checking all else and then scooped Bun up in my arms. "I'll be in the house feeding Bun. Supper should be ready soon, I started dinner in the Crock-Pot this morning," I called over my shoulder.

"I'm coming," Jess answered, running to catch up with us. She set the table while I tended to Bun.

Ready to serve supper, I heard a knock on the door. I set the Crock-Pot lid in place and opened the door. Andrew Stone stood on the doorstep.

I invited him in and asked if he'd eaten. He shook his head. "I'll eat when I get back to camp."

Jess piped up. "Nonsense, Jules always cooks more than we can eat. Take a seat while I get your place setting."

After he'd washed his hands, Andrew took the chair Jess indicated.

The smell of pot roast, potatoes, onions, and carrots made my mouth water. I'd not had a decent thing to eat all day, nor had the help, including Jess. I figured Andrew's usual menu wasn't as good as this fare, either.

Jess chewed the tender roasted meat, rolled her eyes, and swallowed. "This is delicious. I hadn't realized I was so hungry." She leaned back in the chair. "It's been a long day."

"Sure has." I chuckled and refilled my plate with a second helping. Andrew looked at us in turn and nodded in agreement. I handed him the platter when I'd finished with it. Our plates heaped with food, we took time eating our second helpings. Jessica nibbled a roll and waited until Andrew had swallowed a mouthful of potatoes.

"How are things going at the campsite? The nights must get chilly."

"It's not bad. I have enough blankets and the tent is treated to keep the wind out, for the most part, anyway."

Done with supper, I set the coffeepot to perk and brought a plate of cookies to the table.

"Sorry about the dessert, I didn't have enough time to make anything today."

Andrew didn't comment, but Jess chuckled and pulled the plate toward her. "These will be fine." She took two oatmeal raisin cookies and set them on her napkin after sliding her dish aside.

I noticed Andrew had eaten the last of his dinner and contemplated the cookies, but shook his head when I offered the plate. "No, thanks. I'll have some coffee though, if you don't mind."

"Sure thing." I filled cups and brought them to the table with sugar and cream.

CHAPTER SIXTEEN

Aware of Jessica's interest in Andrew and his past life, I waited for her to pry. Surprised when she didn't, I heard Bun say, *"I think Jessica is curious about this guy. He's an odd duck, and she should stay away from him, for her own sake, if not for ours."*

Jolted from my own thoughts, it was as though Bun had read my mind. I'd been witness to Andrew's reluctance to discuss his background. He insisted on privacy, and I willingly honored that, even if others didn't. Sheriff Carver and Jessica were determined to dig into Andrew's life.

"You should have a talk with her later. Jess ought to mind her business and not badger him. He has problems to work through, I can feel it in my bones."

I pushed my chair back from the table and turned to Bun, who backed into his room. I scooped him off the floor and whispered, "We'll take a walk later. Until then, eat your dinner, Bun." I set him in front of his hay.

I closed his door and returned to Jess and Andrew. Seated again, I asked, "Andrew, what brought you by?"

"I guess you realize it wasn't for a hot meal, although, it was tasty. I noticed a man hanging about the farm a few nights ago. He was focused on the comings and goings."

Startled, Jessica jumped into the conversation. "And you waited until now to tell us this?"

I raised a hand a bit to stop her from speaking. She got the message.

"Is there more to this?" I asked.

"I'd gone to the lake to fish, and saw the same man poking through the grass in search of something. He didn't realize I was there. He kicked at the ground, ripped some of the grass out, and swore out loud. In the end, he came away empty-handed."

My elbows on the table, I cupped my hands around my coffee mug and stared into the vestiges of the brew. When I looked up, his stare held a glint of interest. At least, that's what it looked like. I wasn't aware of anyone lurking about the farm, nor was the staff. If they had been, surely, I'd have heard about it.

I gave Jess a keen look and asked if she'd known about someone surveying us.

"No, I've been too busy to pay much attention to the farm's surroundings, sorry."

It had been a long day. I wanted to walk with Bun, but with this news, I was tempted to stay home and lock the doors. Foolish, I know. Fear never served any purpose, other than making one into a victim, that is.

"Can you describe this guy?" My nerves jangled

with anticipation as he gave his impression of the man's height and weight. Disappointment struck deep when Andrew said he hadn't seen the man's face. He'd been wearing a hooded jacket, with the hood concealing his head and face.

"What color and make was the jacket?"

"Black. I'm not fashion conscious. I have no idea what brand the jacket was. Could have been any kind, I wasn't close enough to see if there was a brand name on it."

"Could he be the same person who ran past your campsite not long ago?"

He shrugged. "I didn't get a look at him then. Because you've treated me fairly, I wanted to let you know you're being observed. Don't ask me to become involved in your troubles, though."

"I didn't, I haven't, and I won't. You needn't worry about that."

I knew my retort was sharp, sharper than I'd meant it to be. There was no reason for him to get tangled up in my problems. The last thing on my agenda was to enlist his help.

With that settled, Andrew made a hasty exit. Jessica, surprised at my response to him, gawked at me in silence. From the other room, I heard Bun remark, "*I guess you burned that bridge. If he had considered helping you, he certainly won't now.*"

"Do you mind cleaning up? I'd like to take Bun for a walk before dark."

Agreeing to the request, Jessica got started. I grabbed the sling from its hanger and opened the door to Bun's room. He scampered into my arms and patiently waited for me to help get him into the sling.

"I'm so happy we're going out. Some fresh air will get rid of your foul mood."

My foul mood? When had that happened? Because I was testy with Andrew, I was in a foul mood?

Outside the front door, I broke into a run. Not the usual jog; a full-on run. Bun never liked it when I ran flat-out. This time, he wisely kept his annoyance to himself. I slowed a bit and then eventually jogged, decreasing my speed until I had worked off my aggravation.

"Feeling better now?"

"I guess."

"Where are we going?"

"To the lake if it doesn't get dark too soon. I don't want to return in the pitch-black of night, my flashlight is at home."

His head protruding from the sling, Bun craned his neck to see me. *"What's the plan once we get there? Are you going to see if you can find what that man sought?"*

"Exactly. I'm sure Jack has had a crew of forensic people down here searching the grounds. He's thorough when it comes to that. When I was run off the road and left for dead, the crime scene crew went over my car inside and out looking for clues. They found fingerprints on the passenger-door handle that turned out to belong to Rusty Cardiff. It was an important piece of evidence that helped put Cardiff behind bars."

We'd reached the road leading to Lake Plantain. We veered off onto the beach, then made our way to the spot where the ground was matted with crushed and uprooted clumps of grass. Gouges in the ground showed where someone had dug deep and kicked bits of earth away. I set Bun on the ground.

"You look over there and I'll start on this side. Maybe we'll have better luck finding what this guy wanted, unless he was after what we found. It sure is messy here."

"That it is. My paws are getting dirty, you know I don't like that."

"Don't worry, I'll wash your feet later. Now, get moving." I waited until Bun went off on his hunt before starting my own.

Within a half hour, the sun had begun to set, and the sky grew dim. Darkness would soon be upon us. We'd found nothing, and began the trek home. A tad disappointed, I didn't say so. If the searcher hadn't found what he was looking for, then maybe the sheriff's team or Bun and I had. Carver would never tell me if they had come up with any evidence, though it wouldn't hurt to ask.

"At least we've enjoyed the fresh air, and it is peaceful. After the crowd at the barn today, I relish this."

"Me too. I thought I'd be trampled a couple of times and had to hide under Lizzy's counter. She has very nice legs, you know."

Too much for me to handle, I burst into laughter and started a slow jog home. Sheriff Carver's empty car idled in the driveway. I peered at the window and saw Jess talking with him.

"Looks like we have company. I wonder what he wants? Could be he needs our help after all. What do you think?"

"I think we should dig into Arty's life a bit more.

Carter's visit presents a perfect opportunity." I glanced down at Bun. "Do me a favor and keep your words of wisdom to yourself until we're alone, okay? I can't answer your questions and keep a civil conversation going with anyone when you interrupt."

His body stiffened, and he gave me a haughty glance. *"If you insist. I'll be in my room, all alone, with no one for company, and will keep my brilliance to myself."*

Not giving in to his attempt at emotional blackmail, I gave him a gentle squeeze and thanked him.

In the kitchen, I released Bun, wiped his paws free of mud, and watched him scamper into his room. Carter sipped coffee, while Jess drummed her fingernails on the table. I flopped into the nearest chair.

"Good evening, Jack. Guess you didn't get enough of our company today, huh?"

"Everything okay out here?"

"Yes, why?"

"Thought you might be having difficulties after the minor upset you had earlier."

I took the coffee Jessica poured for me and sipped it while trying to figure out if she had called him about the man Andrew saw watching us. Before I could come up with an answer, Jessica spoke up.

"I called him. Don't be angry, Jules. It's important that we're all on the same page where this intruder is concerned. The man Andrew saw could very well be the same one who's been giving us a hard time."

I glanced from her to Carver. "There was no upset. Andrew mentioned someone has been watching what we're doing. That is disconcerting, but I expect it under the circumstances. I don't believe for one moment that our intruder is coming by on a whim. I'm certain he plans his visits."

"I see you've given this some thought. Just so we get things straight, it wouldn't be a good idea for you to take this person on by yourselves. It's a police matter, just like the murder of Arthur is. Don't take chances, either of you." His eyes flicked to Jess and then to me.

"Where did you get that idea?"

"I know you better than you think I do, Jules. As for Jessica, she did the right thing by calling me. It's imperative that you two are careful. While you might want to take this intruder on, I recommend you don't. Remember what happened the last time you two scuffled with him."

The moment had come to ask if any evidence had been found after Arty's body had been removed. I nodded in agreement to his warning and placed my cup aside.

"Okay, if we're being frank, I have a question for you. When your crime scene people searched the ground where Arty was found, did they find anything of value in your investigation?"

His hands resting on the table, Sheriff Carver appeared taken aback. Why? I had no idea, but I wanted to know more now than ever. "Well?"

"Why do you want to know?"

"I went walking earlier and ended up at the lake. I noticed the ground was torn up and clusters of grass had been ripped out. I wondered if it was your people who did it."

"We didn't, but the area was well searched by the SOC team."

"They're very efficient, so I wondered, is all. Did anything come to light that would help in the case?"

He shook his head slowly, never taking his gaze from mine. "Do you want to tell me if you found anything? I'm sure you and the rabbit gave it a good going-over."

"We did, but found nothing. Have you made headway in the murder case?"

"We're considering a few suspects, but so far, there's no progress." He heaved his plump body out of the chair and donned his hat. "If you have anything else to share, or the intruder returns, give me a call." He walked toward the door, wished us good night, and left.

Waiting until he'd driven away, I took in Jessica's sullen face without saying a word. Though it rankled me to no end, she'd been looking out for us by calling Jack.

"I know you're thinking I ratted you out. You had no plans to tell Sheriff Carver what Andrew shared, I know you didn't. I was only trying to help. . . ."

"I'm not upset. You did what you thought best, let's leave it at that." I left the table and added our empty cups to the dishwasher. There was no sense in being aggravated by what Jessica had done, and it had given me a chance to question Carver.

The hours had flown. My trip to the lake had

taken longer than I'd thought, topped by Carter's visit. That meant the rabbits hadn't been checked for the night. On my way through the breezeway and into the barn, I flicked light switches as I went. All was quiet, and the rabbits snoozed. Jess had followed behind to check one half of the barn while I did the other. We met at the shop door and went inside to find it neat as usual.

Our trip through the clinic was also brief. Relieved to find things quiet, we turned toward the house, chatting softly. Jessica bid me good night and climbed the stairs to her bedroom. Tired, but thinking over the day's and evening's events, I opened Bun's door. He came forward, rubbed his head on my ankle, and followed me into the living room.

Sprawled across the sofa, I tucked an arm behind my head.

"You heard?"

"Of course. You aren't angry with Jess, are you?"

"A little put out, but not angry. Her heart dictated her actions, what more can I say?"

"Not everyone is as brave and strong-willed as we are. I'd be surprised if she stays with us much longer. Things sure have been crazy lately."

"True, and she does have her own apartment. I think you're right, though. You were mindful of Carter's conversation?"

"Indeed. He's befuddled by the lack of evidence in Arty's murder, don't you agree?"

"Mm, at the moment, he's also aware that Andrew Stone is keeping an eye on us. He must be wondering why. I know I am. Andrew did say we'd treated him fairly. Could be he truly wanted to return the favor."

"Or, he could have his own agenda. Don't take him at face value just yet. I've told you before he has problems to work through. Let's not put him on a pedestal just because he said we're being watched. How do we know he isn't the watcher?"

"Valid point. I'll keep all that in mind as we move forward." I thought for a moment and then said, "It just occurred to me that I have Arty's notes to read. Are you all set for the night?"

"I am, I'll just sit with you while you see if there's anything important in them. I promise not to bother you, but I'll listen if you want to talk about what he wrote."

Bun sprawled on the rug near the sofa, saying nothing else. On tiptoes, I went upstairs to retrieve the papers from my dresser drawer. I returned to the living room and nestled under the afghan to read them. Bun lay quiet as a button.

One line jumped out at me. Startled, I read it again. Surprised by Arty's words scrawled across the page, I nudged Bun with my toe. Sleepy-eyed, he looked up at me. I said, "Listen to this. 'I've finally confessed that I'm his father, though he thinks I lie.' Imagine that? Arty does have a family. At least, a son. Who could it be?"

"Is that it? Nothing more? You woke me for that?"

Clearly, Bun wasn't the least bit impressed. Disheartened by his response, I slumped farther into the cushiony sofa. "Maybe I need to go to bed."

"Good idea, we'll talk in the morning."

Bun went into his room, snuggled in for the night, and I went upstairs. I'd nearly passed Jessica's door when she flung it wide and asked, "What's going on? I heard you go by my room earlier and then return downstairs."

Offering her the paper, I yawned and waited until she'd read what Arty wrote. Her eyes round and wide, she handed it back to me.

"Arty has a son?"

"Unfortunately for me, I didn't take the family Bible when I searched his house. A deputy came by and almost caught me. That was the day I returned home filthy, remember?"

She nodded, then laughed.

"So, you wish you'd stolen the Bible along with this note?"

Abashed by my behavior, I stared at the floor and then looked up with a grin. "That about covers it. I should have taken the darned thing. I'll try again and hope I'm not caught this time, either. I'm afraid I'm not much of a burglar."

"True. I'll tell you what, I'll help by going with you."

"Impossible. What if we were both caught? Then who'd take care of the rabbits? Certainly not Lizzy."

Her laughter matched mine over the visual Lizzy and the rabbits presented. Lizzy would never be able to handle poop duty, let alone lift bales of hay. "Come on, I need a break from work and all that's been happening. A little intrigue is good for the soul, is it not?"

"I'd rather you didn't take a risk like that. And, by the way, don't let the sheriff know."

With two fingers, Jessica crossed her heart. "Not one word, I promise."

I said I'd see her later and went on my way. Considering how and when I'd tempt fate with this half-baked idea, I worried that someone else had already taken the Bible. Maybe Arty's son? Was he even local? Who was this man? Like an itch, the need to know irritated me.

CHAPTER SEVENTEEN

Two days later, Jessica drove into town for supplies and to pick up our teenage workers. Alone at the farm, the pleasant solitude didn't last long. I heard a knock on the barn door and found Andrew standing outside. Wind whipped his shaggy hair to and fro, buffeted his jacket, and accentuated his lean body.

Though wary of what he wanted, I invited him in. The man rarely showed his face, yet in the last few days, he'd been around quite often. Why? For what purpose? I bit back a sigh at how suspicious I'd become of everyone and everything that happened. My paranoia was becoming an issue, one that I wasn't happy about.

I closed the door after he'd come in.

"I'm surprised to see you, is everything okay at the campsite?"

Before answering, he scanned the barn, which was more a study of the entire layout, as if he hadn't experienced the place. "Taking good care of these animals must be hard work."

I shrugged. "Worthwhile. Some of the rabbits have been abused by past owners. I took them in and have brought them back to health with Jessica's help. They're wonderful, all of them."

"I can see that. Your eyes light up when you speak of them. This must be your calling, if you will."

I dipped my head in agreement. "I guess you could say that. I found them soothing after I was injured, it was as if we needed each other. Are you here for a reason or is this a social call?"

"Has the sheriff offered an update on the murder investigation?"

"Have you been watching us?"

"I saw his car parked here, that's all."

My disbelief must have shown.

"It's true. I was walking through the trees up the road when I saw his car turn into your driveway. You weren't having trouble, were you?"

"Not at all. It was a check-in on his part."

"You didn't answer my question. Is there any progress?"

"He says no, and for the life of me, I can't come up with one single suspect for Arty's death, either." I lied, not because I wanted to, but because I wondered if he'd known Arty.

"Why the sudden interest?" I leaned against a beam and waited.

"I can't help but think your intruder and Arty's demise are linked to a greater degree than someone merely out to make your life miserable by using the man as a reason to taunt you."

"That makes sense, but what does it have to do with you?"

Pensive for a moment, he looked me squarely in the face and said, "Not a thing." Idly, he wandered the aisles of cages, his focus on the rabbits, with me not far behind.

He turned to me. "They are quite calming, aren't they?"

I nodded, then walked alongside him. We'd come full circle, standing at the end of a row facing the barn door, when Bun scampered in. He skidded to a halt. *"What the heck is he doing here now?"*

"Is there anything else you wanted to know other than information on the sheriff's investigation?"

Bun sidled up against my ankle. I couldn't tell why, though he might have thought Andrew could become aggressive. Again, I had no idea why he'd think that, but there are times when Bun gets weird vibes from people and his imagination takes over.

"Are you sure that's all he wants?"

I glanced down at him, raised a brow, and then turned back to Andrew, who said, "It occurred to me that you have quite a stake in Arty's death. How far are you willing to go to find his killer?"

His words gave me pause. Was he aware of my intrusion into Arty's home? Did he know more than what he'd heard from me and Jessica? If so, how did he come by that knowledge?

Bun thumped the floor with one foot, and I looked down.

"Take care, Jules. The man is riddled with discontent. I have no clue why."

Andrew's words disturbed me to no end. "Why

would you ask me that? I can't put myself or the farm at risk."

"You've been brave enough to take on an intruder." He shrugged. "I thought you might be willing to search out the people who have been after you and have tried to harm the rabbits. It only makes sense, especially since you've already done some sleuthing on your own. From what I saw at the lake the other day, you were eager to find evidence that could lead to the killer."

"I suppose you're right. I believe there's more than one person involved. The intruder is average in build, even on the slim side. The man who assaulted Bun and me at the park was larger, heavier. Then there was the truck that followed me home one night, he tailgated my car all the way. Made me jumpy, too. I'm not in any hurry to have the same type of accident I had a few years ago."

"So, we're in agreement on more than one man, then? You're not safe, you know that, don't you?"

I stepped away from the cages. "If you think for one minute that I'll scurry for cover like a frightened mouse, think again. I won't, even if it's dangerous for me. While I'm not stupid enough to take on someone bigger than I am, I'm not fearful of doing so, if need be."

His grin slight, Andrew nodded.

By this time, Bun was flustered. He hopped erratically about the open space, until I plucked him off the floor and tucked him under my arm. "Calm down, Bun," I whispered against his fur.

Did it ever come to mind that this man might be the killer? He could be trying to trap you into saying some-

thing stupid, like he could be the killer. We are alone, ya know."

I smoothed his coat and hoped he'd shut up, but refrained from saying so. As much as I adore Bun, he can get on my nerves by pointing out what might be obvious to others, but not to me. It was possible that Andrew had more at stake than I did. He was lean and tall like the intruder, but did he have anyone to help him? Nah, I was being silly. Surely the man had no connection to what had taken place last year and more recently. I put Bun on the floor and did a mental eye roll at the turn my thoughts had taken.

"While I mind my own affairs and refrain from interfering with other people's problems, I'm willing to help you bring the man to justice. If you want, that is. Otherwise, be careful, very careful. With the frequency of his visits, I'd say this person is obsessed with you, the farm, and is intent on getting even for something. Anyone with a reason come to mind?"

"Not readily, no. I've got to get back to work, if you don't mind. Thanks for the offer to help figure out who's doing all this to us, though. I appreciate it and will give it some consideration." Not.

"Sure. Let me know if you want to look at Arty's house. A fresh pair of eyes is always a good thing. You have been there, haven't you?" He smiled, offered a farewell nod, and walked out the door without waiting for an answer.

Was it obvious to everyone that I'd searched Arty's house? My confidence took a sudden nose-dive when I remembered how I'd nearly been caught. Were the police watching me? Was I certifiably paranoid? I shook my head in disgust.

"I think he's got our number, Jules. He knows way more than I'm comfortable with, how about you?"

"I'm certain he's been watching us closely. I wonder why?"

"Me too."

"This is probably a crazy idea, but do you think Andrew is Arty's kinfolk? He's never offered to assist in any way before, so why now? How would he know we'd been at Arty's house, unless it was a wild guess on his part, of course?"

"It's possible, but why hide it from everyone? He is a conflicted guy, which is why he has withheld that information. It would also make him a suspect, don't you think? After all, he'd have been estranged from Arty, so why show up now?"

"Those are all good questions, Bun. Nothing quite adds up when you take it all under consideration. I'm certain everything is somehow connected, I just don't know how. We'll take a ride up to Arty's again, what do you say?"

"I'm in. When are we going?"

From the window, I saw Jessica arrive with Ray and Molly in the car. Knowing the teens would help Jess with the remaining chores, as well as unload the supplies, I said, "Now is as good a time as ever."

We scurried into the house. I grabbed Bun's sling and a spring jacket from their hooks and met Jessica at the barn entrance.

"Bun and I have an errand to run, you'll be all set here, won't you?"

Suspicion crossed her face. "You're going to Arty's, aren't you?" Jess whispered after she'd glanced over her shoulder to see where Ray and Molly were.

I nodded, stepped past her, and murmured, "We'll be back soon. If not, you might need to bring bail money to the police station."

"See you later, then. Be careful."

I greeted the kids with a smile, thanking them for working with Jessica today. Bun popped his head out of the sling and told me to get a move on.

Traffic was heavy. Schools were closed for the day for teacher education meetings, and kids with cars took advantage of their freedom. Impatient with the busy streets, Bun groused about the time it took to reach Arty's road. He grew calm as we passed his driveway and drove a bit farther around a sharp curve. Edging the car onto a grassy shoulder, I shut down the motor and locked the doors before we got started on yet another home invasion.

Anxious for freedom, Bun wiggled around and stuck his head out of the sling to view our surroundings. *"All is quiet, let's go."*

His senses keener than mine, I set off down the slope into the wooded area. Minutes later, we hurried toward Arty's house. Bun had jumped from the sling and bounded across the yard ahead of me. I reached the side entrance where he anxiously awaited me.

"Honestly, you need to be faster than that. What if someone saw you?"

This from the rabbit who complained about how fast I ran, and how he was bounced around like a sack of potatoes.

"Relax, will ya?" I reached up, found the key on the eave ledge, and let us into the house, once again.

"I'll look down here, you check upstairs. If you hear a car or footsteps, let me know."

Bun turned toward the staircase and then was gone. I gave the kitchen a quick once-over, moved on into the living room, and found nothing of use there. I finally entered Arty's bedroom. The dresser had one thing missing, the one thing I was after. The Bible was gone. Who had it, and why? Miffed over my stupidity in not having taken it on my previous visit, I grumbled over it.

"Jules, Jules, I found something."

I took the steps two at a time, reaching the landing to find Bun excitedly hopping about.

I chuckled at the sight of him. "It must be something good, because you only act this way when you've hit the jackpot. Show me."

Racing into the room on my right, Bun called for me to follow. When I stepped inside, I saw his stance being close to that of a pointer when finding a flock of birds. I leaned down to see what was so important.

Underneath the bed, sitting in a fine layer of dust, was a hand-painted tin document box. I dragged the rectangular-shaped, beautifully painted box from its hiding place. The box was locked. After digging into my jeans pocket for the key we'd found at the lake, I stuck the key into the lock and gave it a turn. One click, then two, and then three clicks. The spring-loaded lock popped open. I was careful to be gentle when I lifted the lid. The box appeared very old and frail. The other option was that it was booby-trapped, and who knew what that would produce?

The lid leaned back, nearly flat, and offered up nothing. Other than dust that showed something oblong had lain in a spot at the back side of the interior, the box held nothing. Disappointment fell over me as would a heavy cloak. I sat back on my knees and closed the lid.

Scrambling around under the bed, Bun sneezed and then returned with an envelope hanging from his mouth. He tried to release the letter, but his sharp front teeth had pierced the paper, causing it to dangle. I worked it free, gave a cursory glance, and tucked it into my pocket, then told Bun of my fruitless search of the box and for the Bible.

"Have you given the other rooms a look?"

I nodded. "Come on, let's get out of here before somebody finds us."

On the first floor, we took a second look around. Satisfied we'd given it our best search, Bun and I trekked back the way we'd come. Nearing the slope, Bun stopped short, and his ears twitched as madly as his whiskers.

I scooched next to him, my nerves grew tense as a taut wire. "What's wrong?"

"Somebody is at the car. What are we gonna do now? We can't sit here forever, I'm getting hungry."

I touched his fur, ran my fingers over the softness of it, and smoothed his coat. His tension released, Bun snuggled against me. I whispered, "Stay here, I'll find a place for us to hide."

"Uh, okay. Don't be long. Whoever's up there might come this way and catch me for his supper."

In an instant, his anxiety had returned. Dang, Bun becomes unpredictable when that happens, which is annoying at best. I tiptoed away from the slope, toward a cluster of scrubby bushes that would barely give us cover, yet allow me to see who was on the road above. Crouched to the ground as close as I could get, I beckoned Bun and watched until he reached the safety of our hideaway.

A man's angry voice was audible. I held my breath and listened, then gently parted a cluster of bush branches a little to peer at a man dressed in a hooded sweatshirt and jeans. The sweatshirt hood shrouded his entire head. His back was turned toward us while he spoke on his cell phone. Plainly he was slim and tall, very much like our intruder.

His argument ended, he slipped the phone into his jeans pocket and raised his hands, then peered through my car windows. Finished with scrutinizing the car, he studied the road in both directions, but still, his complete face was hidden from view. Hastily, I withdrew my hands from the parted bushes, allowing them to hide us from his view.

A few seconds later, he stumbled down the slope, no more than thirty feet away from us. Frozen in place, I held my breath and hugged Bun close, not moving a muscle. Eager to get a look at the hooded face, I watched his descent. Once he was gone, Bun and I scrambled up the slope, into the car, and sped away. If the man had heard the engine, I didn't know or care. Frustrated because I hadn't been able to see his face, I wanted to get as far from him, as fast as I could.

Our trip home was quicker than the length of time it had taken us to get to Arty's. I wasted no time in traffic, took a few shortcuts, and arrived safely. The chores finished, the students were gone, and lunch was on the table. How Jess knew we'd be back so soon was a good guess on her part.

"What did you find?" Jess demanded as she sliced bread.

With Bun in his room eating hay and nibbling pellets, I washed my hands and joined her at the table.

I withdrew the letter from my pocket and waved it about. "I haven't had time to look at this, but I can feel it in my bones that it's important." I slipped it back into my pocket. "I'm starving, what are we having?"

"Ham sandwiches and salad." Jess leaned back in her chair and said, "You're bristling with excitement, tell me what happened. Out with it, now."

I filled her in on the man who snooped around my car and his argument on the phone. "I have no idea how he knew it was there, or if he had simply come across my car by accident. I wasn't followed. Anyway, he went through the woods, the same way I did, headed toward Arty's house. Oh, crap, I forgot to leave the key."

"Did you hear what he said? As to the key, I'm sure if he knew it was available, he'll know who took it. You better watch your back, Jules. If this guy doesn't know what you were doing out there, he's certain to become curious. Maybe he'll even cause trouble for you with the sheriff by saying he saw someone on the property."

"I doubt he'd do that. After all, he'd have to explain his own actions, wouldn't he?"

"Good point. Let's hope nothing comes of it, then. By the way, my clinical rotation is over today. I'll be back around five. Would you answer any calls that come in? I've had several requests for information and questions on when my clinic will be opening."

"I'll do what I can. Before I left, I thought I heard Molly offer her help."

"It's a gorgeous day, I didn't have the heart to keep her here. All she talked about was going to the park, then the mall, and meeting up with some friends later. Ray had to leave by noontime, so he's already gone. Remember what it was like to be their age? Not that we're ancient, well, maybe we are to them."

"Right, twenty-five is old when you're still a teenager."

Plucking at a loose string on the cuff of my shirt, I said, "Andrew came by while you were gone. He asked about the investigation into Arty's death. Wanted an update, I guess. I told him I didn't know any more than he did." I shrugged. "I don't think he believed me. Though, he did offer to help me find Arty's killer and was willing to go to the house with me. I blew him off by saying I'd consider the offer. I think he's got his eye on us and our doings."

Her eyes widened as she gasped. "Why would he do that? He has no reason to be interested in us, does he?"

"He's keeping watch for our safety would be my guess." I washed the last bite of sandwich down with a gulp of water and started to clear the table. "Get going."

Jess went on her way. I rushed through my house tasks and then returned to the barn to handle the rest of the day on my own.

Chapter Eighteen

The hours flew by. I shuffled one rabbit after another into the bunny playground in between answering Jessica's phone. If this was a measure, the clinic would do well. Thrilled as I was for Jessica, I worried over how she would manage alone while I took care of my own business. I knew I couldn't do both.

The last rabbit returned to his cage, I leaned against the counter and rolled my shoulders to relax.

I went into the yarn shop and slid up on the stool. I propped my elbows on the counter surface, and cupped my chin in my hands in thought. I couldn't handle this alone every day, and I wouldn't ask Jess to help me after her clinic business got rolling. Peter would be leaving soon, Molly might want the summer off before heading off to college, and Ray Blackstone had already said he couldn't work for me too much longer.

The door opened, and Molly walked in. I opened my mouth to ask why she was here.

"Don't tell me you've worked all day by your-self?" Molly asked. "I know how busy you are with the rabbits, entertaining at birthday parties, and doing whatever else that comes along, but you have to have help, Jules."

"You're right. I was just considering my loss of workers before you came in. Are you taking the summer off?"

"Not if you need me. I could use the extra money, besides, I would miss you and the rabbits."

I agreed that she was a great help and said the rabbits responded to her quite well.

She tossed her coat on the counter and said, "I can give you a hand right now to tend to the rab-bits."

"You are wonderful. Thanks."

We gave each rabbit an extra cluster of timothy hay and squared them away for the rest of the day. The only thing left to do was make my rounds later on in case any of the furry critters were in need of something.

Molly slung her coat over her arm and promised to work for me when I needed her. As she walked out, Jessica arrived.

"Hey, I finished early and stopped by my apart-ment to get my mail. Has anything happened?"

"Nothing. You had quite a few calls, I did my best to answer questions and made a list of people who want brochures. Are you planning to move back to your place?"

"Not until this guy who's been causing you trouble is in jail. Then, and only then, will I move out. Unless you want me to go now?"

"Not at all, just asking."

Her coat still on, Jess went into the clinic to get the list I left her.

"Jess seems quite happy. Her vet business is going to do well, I think." Bun sat back on his haunches and asked, *"Wanna share what's on your mind?"*

"There are two suspects for Arty's death and our break-ins. I think they're somehow connected, but I can't figure out how."

"Who's your number one culprit?"

"The first person would be the guy from today. I'm certain he's our intruder. I recognized the timbre of his voice when he spoke on the phone, though I couldn't make out what he said. The second would be Andrew."

"I understand your reasoning for the first suspect. I heard what he said, but it didn't make a whole lot of sense to me. But then, I'm just a rabbit, so there you have it. Why Andrew, why is he a suspect?"

My jaw must have dropped, leaving my mouth as open as a fly catcher, because Bun gawked and said, *"Is there a problem? You're not having a stroke, are you?"*

He drew closer, but stopped about a foot away.

"You didn't tell me you heard what he said. For goodness' sake, Bun, why not?"

"Uh, well, I guess I didn't think it worthwhile. I was rather hungry, tired, and had been nervous when that guy passed by so close. I could also smell his scent."

"You smelled his scent and didn't tell me? How can I solve this mystery without your input? Good gracious, Bun, stop thinking of how you feel. Think about Arty's killer, and help me identify who is causing us problems."

Okay, so I was in a snit, and close to losing my temper big-time. I paced the kitchen a few times, took a pad of paper and a pencil from a kitchen drawer, and then dropped into a chair with a huff of irritation.

"I'm sorry, I guess it was unthinking of me to hold back. It wasn't intentional, it really wasn't. I'll tell you what I heard and about his scent, okay? Don't be mad at me, Jules, I get scared when people get angry."

Knowing he played me like a concertina, I fell for his trap anyway. It was true, Bun didn't like anger of any kind, he couldn't deal with it very well, not even his own. His former owner and her family were to blame for that. He'd reaped the unsatisfactory rewards of their displeasure one too many times, leaving him on edge whenever things went awry, and someone became hostile.

I lifted him off the floor, hugged him, and whispered in his ear, saying how loved he was and would always be. "I'm not upset with you, not really. I'm mostly frustrated when it comes to getting a line on the intruder. I have Andrew almost figured out, and that has taken some doing. I couldn't have managed any of this without you, Bun. We're partners, after all."

He squirmed a bit to get comfortable in my lap, then jittered his whiskers. I chuckled, smoothed his coat, and rubbed his ears. Once again, all was well with Bun.

"Tell me."

"The guy in the woods argued with someone called

Sids or Sims, something like that. His voice was rather muffled, but still angry. It's hard to be certain. His side of the conversation was limited, but he did say one thing that bugs me."

The rabbit had become solemn and quiet. When he wasn't forthcoming, I asked, "Well, do I have to drag the words out of your mouth, or what?"

He sniffed, and then continued. *"Patience is a virtue, Jules. I was giving this a little more thought, is all. He said Arty had gotten what was coming to him, and so would the rest. I'm sure he killed Arty, but he didn't say as much. I'm also certain the rest of us means you and me, the other rabbits, and maybe even Jessica. Creepy, huh?"*

I shivered and gave him a nod. "Sure is. What else did you hear?"

"Not much, he was calmer by the end of the conversation. He agreed with something the other person said and put the phone away. Do you think it was his partner he was talking to?"

"You know, Bun, I've always wondered if this intruder was working with someone else, but who? Andrew? He's such a loner, it's difficult to see how that would work out. Then there's the big brute from the walking path at the park." Shaking my head, I set Bun on the floor and pulled the paper and pencil toward me. Fiddling with the pencil, I wove it out of my fingers like a baton and thought hard.

"Before I forget, his scent smelled peppery and strong. You must not have a decent sense of smell, it was very bold. I nearly coughed, it choked me up. What are you doing now?"

"I'm putting my facts and suspicions on paper. Then I'll take what I come up with to Carver. He knows more than I do about this whole thing, and he isn't sharing. This could be my chance to get him to open up. At the house, I searched for the Bible. It had been on the top of Arty's dresser when I saw it last. Now it's nowhere in the house."

"Do you need my help with getting your thoughts together?"

I could hear the hopefulness in his voice. "Not now, but when I'm done, I will read them to you, and you can see if they make sense. You're brilliant when it comes to that." Who was playing whom now?

Preening over the praise, Bun didn't seem disappointed by my not taking his offer to help.

"I'll sit right here, then, and wait until you've finished."

I scribbled words onto the paper as fast as my thoughts presented themselves, well, almost as fast. After Bun interrupted one too many times, I slanted him a look that quelled any other questions or input he might have. Not wanting to miss writing one single thing I'd learned, I kept going until my hand became cramped. I dropped the pencil, stretched my fingers, and sat back, reading the scrawled words.

Andrew was a loner, yet he'd offered to assist me in breaking and entering. He'd questioned me about the murder, about how far the investigation had progressed, and was keeping a keen eye on my home and all of us. Why?

How long had he really been squatting on my land? Hmm. Had he truly believed the property was state-owned as a sanctuary? Not likely. Was he our intruder? No. What was his interest in Arty's house? Were he and Arty related? Possibly. Was something there that Andrew wanted? Maybe. And that line of thinking went on and on. Two pages later, I had exhausted Andrew's possibilities.

I moved on to the tall, thin, hooded intruder. He'd worn the hoodie before, leaving his features covered. Would I have recognized him if I'd seen him? I didn't know, but knew Rusty wasn't the intruder. Who was the intruder working with, if anyone other than the brute who tried to kill me and Bun? What did these people have against me? I didn't have a clue. Had he killed Arty? I thought so. Had he done it because he had to? Maybe. But what would make him have to kill someone, especially Arty? Had he searched for the key I found at the scene of Arty's death? Possibly. What had the document box held? That line of thought took hold and I hastily scribbled words. I reviewed what I'd scrawled and had difficulty reading my own handwriting.

Bun thumped his paw on the rug, his patience barely in check. Well, I had finished writing, hadn't I?

"Are you done yet? I can hardly wait to hear what you've written on that paper."

I set him on the chair next to mine and read all that I'd written. When I came to the end, Bun's ears drooped sideways, then bounced up straight again as though they had springs. Having never seen this reaction, I worried that he thought I might be on the wrong track altogether.

"I must say, Jules, that you have been very observant, that you've listened to what I've said, and made great mental note of it all. I couldn't have done better, if I had

written all this myself, if I could write, that is, but, I am only a rabbit, and that must be a consideration. One thing, though, you shouldn't take this to Carver. He'll say you're meddling, you'll get into trouble, he might even put you in jail, and then where will the other rabbits, and I, be?"

So very like Bun to turn things in his direction, I nearly laughed aloud. It wasn't easy to keep the laughter inside, but I managed a smile and thanked him for his input.

"You have such a knack for getting to the crux of a situation, Bun. I'm always impressed. As to where you and the other rabbits would be, um, let me think." I tapped my index finger against my lips, pretending to be thinking hard. "If I land in jail for interfering in an investigation, which is highly improbable, mind you, Jessica and the students will care for your and the other rabbits' needs."

I tossed the papers onto the table, picked my laptop off the corner desk in the living room, and made sensible notes out of my scribbled ones. If I were to talk to Carver about this, I'd need coherent and orderly notes. While I typed, Bun insisted I was making a great mistake by bringing such notes to Carver. Resolute in his belief these notes incriminated us as home invaders, he reminded me that such behavior was against the law. In answer to his griping, which might have been closer to a full-on rant, I said, "Don't nag, I know what I'm doing."

"There's no need to be rude, I'm not a nag. Someone must watch out for you, since you don't do it. Besides, if

you just let all those thoughts simmer for a day or so, you might come up with the solution to Arty's death. You'll even know who the intruder is and how this whole scenario fits together like pieces of a puzzle. Carver only complicates things and I've noticed he only has linear thinking. Typical, I guess, for a lawman. Not like us, Jules, we step outside ourselves and see the grand picture. Has Carver ever given you any concrete information? That would be a huge 'NO.'"

While Bun went on and on, he made sense. Still, in my determination to get Carver to share with me, it was clear the only way to do that was to put my information in front of him and see what happened from there. When Bun perked his ears in my direction, I knew he was about to start talking again. I pointed at his room in silence, wiggling my finger in that direction without giving him a verbal "go to your room" remark.

A disdainful sniff accompanied a dire warning of what to expect from Sheriff Carver. Rather than sunshine and roses, Bun muttered, I'd undoubtedly end up in a dreary jail cell because I couldn't mind my own business.

His attitude rankled, because he might be right. Stubborn to the core, I was certain I was doing right by Arty, and us, in taking what I knew to the lawman. The printer spit out three full sheets of notes that read better than an outline for a mystery novel. I'd managed to organize the information, and thought the sheriff would appreciate my efforts.

I folded the pages and tucked them inside a business-size envelope, and squirreled it away in my handbag along with Arty's handwritten note. I grabbed my spring jacket and went out the door just as Jess entered the kitchen.

"Going somewhere?"

"Just making a trip to see Carver. I shouldn't be gone very long. Bun's in his room, and everything should be fine in the barn. I guess the change of locks did the trick."

"Too bad we hadn't thought of it sooner. Anyway, I'll be here for the rest of the night. Don't feel rushed." Jess turned toward the living room and over her shoulder, she said, "Call if you need bail money."

"Very funny. I'll pick up something for supper." With a wave, I drove to the police station, with hope filling my heart that Jack and I could discuss what each of us knew and maybe bring the investigation to an end. I was fairly certain Arty's death and my intruder were connected.

CHAPTER NINETEEN

The desk sergeant took my name and rang Carver's office. It wasn't long before Jack ushered me into his office.

"This is a surprise. What can I do for you, Jules?"

"I thought we might talk about Arty's death and the investigation itself." I slid the envelope across his desk and watched as he withdrew the notes. Unfolding them, he gave me a cool stare and smoothed the folds from the paper before reading them. Within a few minutes, he tossed the papers onto the desk and teetered back and forth in his chair, an unhappy frown on his face.

"Do you have anything else to tell me?"

I shook my head.

Okay, so this wasn't going quite the way I wanted it to. Dang, I really hate it when Bun is right. There'd be no living with him if he found out I was on the hot seat.

"The only thing I did want to see, but didn't get the opportunity, was to check the contents of the

Bible at Arty's house. I had seen it on his dresser, but now it isn't there."

Heaving an enormous sigh, followed by a roll of his eyes, Carver asked, "And how would you know that?"

"We, uh, I, uh, peered through the windows of his house." It was weak, I know, but unwilling to admit I'd broken into the man's house, I had to say something.

"I see." He teetered back in the squeaky chair, his look disbelieving, and the shake of his head surely meant I was in for a lecture. "By 'we,' I take it you mean you and the rabbit?"

"Uh, yeah. It was just me and Bun."

"Did you see anything else in there that might have been helpful to *my* investigation?"

Hopeful that his sarcasm wouldn't lead to outright anger, I gave him Arty's notes.

He took them, then opened a desk drawer and handed the Bible to me. "This Bible?"

Nodding like a bobblehead doll, I stammered, "Y-yes, this is the one."

"Then why don't you have a look, and then we'll talk." He fingered the notes and gave them a quick look while I delved into the Bible. A family tree was listed on an inside page set out for just that. I scanned them once and then again, disappointed that none of the names were familiar to me. I ruffled the pages, knowing Carver had already done so and probably had his crime scene people check for prints. If he'd come up empty, then why wouldn't I?

"I have someone chasing down the names. You sure you don't recognize any of them?"

He took the Bible and slipped it into the drawer, then slammed the drawer closed. Oh, my.

"Didn't I warn you about interfering? Have you forgotten there's a killer on the loose, and that you could be a target? Look what's been happening at your farm."

"Sheriff Carver, I know you're upset, but I've been very careful. When I was at Arty's house this last time, a man was lurking around my car when I came back. I hid in the bushes and waited for him to leave. He was dressed in a hoodie jacket like the intruder at my farm was, has the same build, too. And, when he spoke on his cell phone, I recognized his voice as the same man."

The teetering of his chair stopped when Carver brought his full attention to the topic and slammed both palms of his hands on the desk. "Have you lost your mind, Juliette? What if he'd seen you, what then? Did you get a look at his face?"

I hadn't and said so.

Heaving himself out of his chair, Carver pointed at the door and yelled, "Stay out of police business, or I'll throw you in jail. Now, get out of my office."

I didn't waste any time making for the door. As I stepped over the threshold, I blurted, "Has there been any other news on Andrew Stone?"

His face red, his hand came up and Carver pointed. "No, just get out."

For fear of being locked up, I nearly ran from the station. Officers turned to watch when I rushed past. They had probably heard Carver bellow at me. My head down, I kept on moving.

Whose idea had this been, anyway? Oh yeah, that would be mine. Maybe I should listen to Bun's advice more often. He was rarely mistaken. The entire trip to see Jack had produced nothing. I'd gotten to peruse the Bible, if only for a moment or two, but it didn't matter, there wasn't anything of use in it that I could find. I leaned my forehead on the steering wheel and took a few deep, calming breaths.

Why hadn't I believed Bun when he insisted Carver wouldn't be all sunshine and roses? The rabbit had a bead on Carver, the way every animal could, by use of their senses. I'd have to own up, and it would be hard to admit he was correct, but then, he was, so why not let him bask in the knowledge? Bun never steered me wrong. I had to remember that.

Before I returned to the farm, I stopped at the market and bought rolls, a roasted chicken, and a bag of mixed salad greens for supper. Though I had no appetite, especially after escaping arrest, I was sure Jess would be hungry.

She and Bun greeted me at the door. Bun sensed my trip to Carver's office didn't go well, but he didn't carry on about it. He snugged up to my ankle and murmured he was glad I was home. Jess took the grocery bags and unloaded them. Meanwhile, I cuddled Bun.

"Shall we eat now? I set the table, thinking you'd be along any moment."

"Sure, has Bun eaten?" I set him aside and went into his room. Assured he had plenty of food and water, I went into the kitchen, washed my hands, and sat at the table.

"From the look on your face, I take it things with the sheriff didn't go as planned?"

"That's for sure. He ranted like a maniac over the fact that I had interfered in *his* investigation. Geesh, you'd think I committed an all-out crime. He wouldn't even discuss what he's found out."

Commiserating with me, Jess went into positive mode by pointing out that Sheriff Carver had his business to run and we had ours. She also mentioned the bookings for parties and spinning classes, and then exclaimed, "While you were out, you got a call from Mary Brickworth. Did you see her when she came to the open house? She was very excited over the rabbits, your educational programs, and is interested in setting something up at the library in conjunction with an author who's coming in to discuss her latest children's book that features a family of bunnies."

From under the table, I heard Bun moan. *"Good Lord, don't people know rabbits aren't people? These authors make them out to be something from Walt Disney."*

I asked Jess if Mary had mentioned anything else about the book.

"She has a copy, if you'd like to see it. I think it's great publicity for the library and the farm, not to mention the author. I don't think she's a local writer, though."

With all this positive talk, my appetite returned. We ate, talked, and ate some more, with Bun inserting his thoughts between our bites. For the most part, I ignored his comments, trying to keep the conversation light and focused on the rabbits.

We'd finished our meal when Jess asked, "Has Lizzy been around at all?"

"I haven't heard a word from her. Her boss might have her working on another super campaign."

She shrugged. "I wondered since the wool-spinning classes begin soon. She promised to handle that."

"I'll give her a call to remind her. I'm sure it's on her schedule, she's quite efficient. Have you set up an appointment to take your state license exam?"

"Not yet, but I'm going to have to do it soon. I can't afford to put it off."

"How many hours a day do you plan to be open? I know you mentioned appointments for afternoons mostly. Does that mean your off-site visits will take place in the morning?"

"That's what I hope for. With an afternoon schedule only, at least for now, I should be fine. There won't be any evening hours unless it's an emergency. Taking on too much, too soon can be a hazard, one that I'd like to avoid."

"You're right. When I started Fur Bridge Farm, it was crazy until I reached a point where I got the farm under control. I wouldn't recommend that to anyone. One step at a time is the best way to build your business, Jess. I'll help all I can, just as you've helped me. If I'm busy, feel free to ask the students to give you a hand. I don't mind at all."

Life at the farm ran smoothly and quietly for a few weeks. Getting into a pleasant routine was odd at first. So much had taken place, I was unsure whether this was the quiet before the storm. Jessica had passed her license exam and was now Dr. Jessica Plain.

A few parties were scheduled. I reached out to

Mary Brickworth about the author book signing and then paused before hanging up.

"Would you happen to know a puppeteer who could fill the gap left at birthday parties from Arty's death? I only ask because parents are clamoring for more than me and the rabbits to entertain their children."

"You know, a sweet woman comes here to entertain the kids when we have summer and other school vacation programs. Wait one minute, I'll get her phone number for you." The line went quiet and then Mary was back, rattling off the woman's name, address, and phone number.

"Mention that I gave you her information. Good luck, Juliette, I think you'll like Bailey."

"Thanks, Mary." I hung up, read the phone number, and called Bailey Kimball.

After I explained who I was and told Bailey of Mary's referral, the conversation went well. I couldn't gauge her age by the sound of her voice, but from the way she enthusiastically spoke of her puppeteering experience, I was sure we'd make a great team.

"Can we meet? I'd like to get to know you better and perhaps see your puppets."

"Good idea. I'm coming out your way tomorrow and can drop by, if that would be all right? Say around eleven in the morning? I have an engagement at the school later."

"I'll be here. This way you'll have a chance to see the rabbits, too. We'll also be able to tell how well our entertainment styles will work out. See you tomorrow, then."

I'd set the phone in its charger and started across

the room when it rang again. Bun, who had been silent up to now, hopped from his room.

"Geez, isn't anyone going to allow you time enough to feed me? I'm starving to death and fading fast."

I sighed at his dramatic tone and said I would be but a minute, but that he had already had a snack.

"Do you think you can hang on that long, Bun?" I chuckled, and answered the call.

One of the mothers I had booked a party with was on the line.

"Hi, it's Karen Sommers. I'm checking to see if you have had a chance to find someone to take Arty's place? Not that it's your responsibility, or anything, but I thought you might know of another entertainer who can accompany you, so you won't have to handle the children all alone, but will have a break."

"As a matter of fact, I've had a referral from Mary Brickworth and will meet the woman in the morning to iron things out."

Her squeal of excitement deafening, I held the phone away from my ear. When the noise ceased, I said I'd be in touch by the end of the following day.

"I'm so pleased. Can I tell the other parents about her?"

"After she and I have had a chance to meet, yes, but let's not be hasty in case she doesn't work out." Certain that I wasted my breath, I listened to her agree, knowing the phone calls would begin as soon as I hung up. Karen couldn't keep anything to herself, which might be just what I needed to learn more about Arty and his antics toward the end of his life. Karen and her husband, Dr. Sommers, hadn't attended the open house, which was a loss, because it could have saved a lot of snooping on my part.

Food filled Bun's dish and his water was replenished before I went to the barn to care for the rest of the rabbits. Halfway through the job, the school kids came in and took over the remainder for me.

The phone in Jessica's clinic was ringing when I opened the door. Jessica's face held a harried expression as she answered the call. Scribbling information on a notepad, she checked her schedule and made an appointment.

Not twenty minutes later, Jessica, Murphy, and his owner exited the examination room and Jess asked if I'd set a follow-up date for the dog. I nodded, took care of the appointment, and collected the fee. Jess invited another owner with a pet carrier into a different examination room. After Murphy was gone, I scooted into the empty patient room and gave it a quick clean. Each room was sanitized after each patient had been treated.

A short respite took place around three in the afternoon. Jess and I flopped into seats in the waiting area of her clinic and heaved a sigh when Molly Perkins stepped into the room.

"If you don't need me any longer, I'll be going. Ray already left, but I wasn't sure if you needed a hand, Jessica."

Her smile wide, Jess accepted Molly's offer and asked if she was able to work in the clinic at any other time during the week. I left them chatting and tended to my own business. A delivery truck pulled up to the barn doors. While the driver opened the truck's overhead door, I slid one of the barn doors open to receive the goods I'd ordered earlier in the week.

As a team, the driver and I unloaded bags of feed and bales of timothy hay. I took the bill of lading, signed off on it, and watched the driver depart. About to close the door, I saw Andrew Stone come up the driveway. He gave me a nod and turned in my direction.

"Got your feed delivery, I see. I'll give you a hand putting it away."

Before I could protest, Andrew had stacked a half dozen bags of rabbit pellets on the shelves where I stored them. I handled the timothy hay and we were finished before I knew it.

"Would you like a cup of coffee?"

He nodded and followed me into the house.

The pot set to perk, we sat at the kitchen table, across from each other. He wasn't one for small talk, but I had questions, and I didn't hesitate to ask them.

"Have you been keeping an eye on us?"

"I have. Nothing going on, though. I guess the lock changes did the trick."

"Seems that way, but that raises another question, doesn't it?"

With a keen stare, Andrew nodded. "Uh-huh."

"Just so we're thinking alike, what I'd like to know is, who gave the intruder the key or from whom did he steal it? Any ideas?"

"I'm certain none of your staff would willingly let anyone have their key, whether they knew them or not."

I poured mugs of coffee and set them on the

table. Andrew sipped his while Bun crossed the threshold of his room and entered the kitchen.

"What is he doing here?"

"Thanks for stopping by and giving me a hand with the supplies. Jessica's got her hands full with the clinic right now, so I can't count on her to come to my aid. The schoolkids are great, but they aren't always around, either."

"Least I can do." He slurped a mouthful of coffee and held the cup out for more.

Unusual for him to stay very long, I took advantage of the opportunity, just as he knew I would. I caught the quick gleam in his eyes before he peered down at Bun.

"This rabbit sure has the life. You take good care of these animals, you should be proud."

"I am. They get good care and are healthy because of it." Bun deposited his plump bum next to my ankles and sniffed. What his sniff was about was anyone's guess. I let it be.

"Getting back to the key situation. Who would steal a barn key and how would they do it? Very few of the kids had keys before and only Jess and I have them now. I can't figure it out."

"Have you considered who your employees have contact with? Take the high schoolers, for example." Andrew sat back, thought for a moment, and then said, "Has there ever been a kid from their school who caused trouble for either of them?"

"They've never mentioned it to me. They are great kids, popular, smart, both studied college-level classes, and graduated high school with honors. I've never heard a bad word about them. The same goes for Pete Lambert, my college student. Honors all the way, nice young man with a great future ahead of him. When it comes to my employees, I have lucked out. Never a spot of trouble, not ever, from any of them."

His smile stopped me talking. I clamped my mouth shut. "What's so funny?"

"You are. You were probably their best referral on their college applications, I'm sure." He chuckled, another unusual thing about him. The stars must have been in alignment or something of that sort for me to have had a lengthy and interesting conversation with this loner.

"You know, Jules, you do see the help through rose-colored glasses. I do think they are all super people, that you can always count on."

"Are you saying I don't see them clearly, or are you agreeing with me?"

"Agreeing, mostly. We've covered the students, so who does that leave?"

I opened my mouth as the phone rang. Raising a finger, I took the call.

CHAPTER TWENTY

"Hello?"

"Juliette, it's Lizzy. I'm returning your call."

"Where have you been? We've missed you."

"I know, life's been crazy these last few weeks. I haven't forgotten about the spinning classes, don't worry about that. How many students have signed up?"

"We have a few, and others are interested in doing so but have questions I can't answer. Could you come by later this evening to clear up a few questions?"

Silence hung in the air for a second or two before she said, "Uh, sure, about seven, or maybe tomorrow morning would be better? How about around ten or so, tomorrow morning?"

"In the morning, then. See you." I hung up and sat at the table.

"Something bothering you?"

The conversation with Andrew had gotten under my skin, aided by the one I'd just had with Lizzy.

Was I overreacting to something I had no clue about? Maybe.

"I'm not sure. The only two left are Lizzy and Jessica. I'm positive Jessica would never give her key to anyone, let alone allow what's been happening here at the barn to continue. She adores the rabbits."

Andrew pushed away from the table, stood, and zipped his jacket. "That would leave Lizzy. Thanks for the coffee."

"Thanks for your help."

He closed the door behind him without another word, sauntered across the field, and faded into the woods.

"He's an odd duck, a solitary figure, too. He sure has given us a lot to think about. Does he suspect our sweet Lizzy of being part of these terrible events that have taken place? Or is he casting doubt on her, so we won't consider him a suspect any longer?"

"I don't know, but he does make a good point. After all, what do we really know about Lizzy?"

"Fair enough, then. We know there's a connection between Arty and Andrew. We're both certain Andrew means us no harm, right?"

"I know I keep waffling back and forth about him, but deep down, I don't believe he's our intruder."

"Now that is clear between us, let's move on. Has Sheriff Carver mentioned if he's looked into Peter Lambert's background? I think he's the only person, other than Lizzy, who hasn't been investigated."

"I can't accept the idea of Peter being capable of these crimes against us, or of killing Arty, either. He's too shy, to begin with. A well-rounded person in my opinion." I hesitated and with a shake of my head, I said, "Not that my opinion is worth much these days."

"There's nothing wrong with your deductive reasoning. You willingly accept people for who they are, but you have a keen sense about them, too. Don't underestimate yourself."

Bun thumped his foot on the floor, a sign that he meant business. Endearing as he could be, I knew he wouldn't offer validation if he thought it wasn't merited. I scooped him off the floor, then walked through the corridor and into the barn as Jess closed and locked the door of the clinic.

"Done for the day?"

"With appointments, yes. I'm giving Molly a ride home before I pick up the medications I need for Mrs. Trumble's bulldog and run a few errands. Do you need anything? I can pick it up on my way back later."

"We're all set, thanks. Will you be back for dinner?"

"No, don't hold dinner for me. I'll grab something while I'm out."

She buttoned her jacket and waved as she went to her car. I gave a final wave before she drove away. Smiling, I contemplated the transitions ahead for Jessica, me, and both of our businesses. I wasn't sure I was ready for the differences these changes would make, but moving forward was the only acceptable direction for all of us.

Set for the night, the rabbits sprawled in their cages, while Bun hopped about double-checking all was well before he squatted next to me in the yarn shop. Bills for deliveries had been neatly stacked on the counter. I flipped through them, noting which ones required immediate payment and how long I had before the others would come due. Each delivery invoice had been meticulously signed by Lizzy.

I leaned my head against the back of the chair, let the warmth of the fireplace wash over me, and hoped that no one in my employ was part of the misery that had taken place these past few months. I couldn't possibly be so mistaken about the people who worked for me. I heaved a sigh, turned the heat down to low, and invited Bun back into the house.

"I think it's time for something to eat. What do you say?"

"You're right. Let's go." Bun set off toward the house. I chuckled over the way his tail puffed up and down as he bounced.

Bun's food ready for him, a few wisps of timothy hay accompanied the meal, and his water feeder was full, before I tended to my own meal. I could hear him crunch the pellets as I prepped a salad, added slivers of baked chicken, then salted and peppered it. I'd gathered the oil and vinegar cruets and took a seat at the table, facing the windows.

Darkness hadn't quite arrived, but was well on its way. I fussed with the salad dressings and had started to eat when I heard Bun say, *"We have company."*

Sheriff Carver's cruiser stopped next to my car. He got out and looked around before coming to the door. Curious over why he'd stop in since he lived east of the farm, I opened the door and waited as he entered.

"Evening, Jack."

He shrugged his jacket off, hung it on a peg near the door, and said, "Got any coffee, Jules?"

From the other room, I heard a series of warnings. *"Beware!"* was among them. Ignoring Bun's overreaction to Jack's visit, I poured coffee that had just finished brewing and handed him a steaming mug of it.

I took my seat and began picking at my salad again. The last time we had spoken, he'd been quite angry at my interference in his findings of Arty's death, his house, and possibly his son. I wouldn't start the conversation. This time around it was up to him.

Silence stretched, the thread of it tightening, but I held fast.

"I know I was outspoken and angry when we last met, Jules, but this silent treatment is downright rude."

"Really? You think I'm rude?" I dropped the fork onto the plate and nudged the dish away. "If I remember correctly, you kicked me out of the station, threatened me if I interfered one more time, and even yelled at me. Why would I be the one to start a conversation, Jack?"

He regarded the coffee in his cup, then slowly lifted his head to look at me. "I might have been out of line a bit, but I did warn you and as always you didn't pay attention to the warning in the least."

I pushed my chair back and folded my arms over

my chest. "If you've come to pick an argument, then get out of my house. But, if you have something you'd like to share with me, then just do it."

"That's telling him, Jules. Don't take any guff from him."

Taking the plate, I dumped the salad into the trash, gave Bun a look that conveyed more than words ever could, and went back to the table with the coffeepot and a warming pad to set it on.

Settled in my chair again, I fiddled with my napkin, waiting for Carver to get to the point of his visit.

"You can be quite stubborn. Are you aware of that?"

"You came to me, Jack, I didn't invite you over for a chat. What's on your mind?"

He withdrew a bunch of folded papers from his back pocket and smoothed them out on the table. I fought hard to refrain from snatching them up, and won the battle, but it was nearly my undoing.

I peered at them.

"I received confirmation that Andrew Stone is indeed a decorated hero, spent a few tours in the Middle East, came back with PTSD, was honorably discharged, and then suddenly dropped off the map. He was part of a Special Forces unit who took heavy fire with serious casualties to his unit at the end of his last tour."

"Okay, what does that mean to us?"

"Nothing, really. I just thought you should know in case there's an incident involving him."

"I see. Thanks for letting me know." My opinion of Andrew hadn't changed one iota.

"What else? There must be more to this visit than

Andrew. We had pretty well figured him out anyway."

He shrugged, drank the rest of his coffee, and got up to put his jacket on.

"I won't ask again, Jack."

He whirled back to me and crammed his hat on his head. "I guess I really got under your skin that last time we talked. I won't apologize again, Juliette, but my wife says I should be nicer to you."

I nearly laughed, but held it in at the last moment. Tipping my head to the side, I realized this was as close to a real apology as I was going to get.

"All right, sit down, and tell me what's going on. I have a right to know, this is my farm, my land, and Arty was my associate. It's all linked, we both know it, so let's put our heads together and figure this murder out and what it has to do with Fur Bridge Farm."

"That's just it, Jules, I can't come up with one single connection. It's frustrating as all get-out, too. Meredith says I'm driving her nuts with my cranky attitude, and that I should be ashamed of myself for losing my temper with you. Gave me a good tongue-lashing over that, I tell you. She was a good friend of your family's for years. Did you know that?"

I shook my head. "Mom never said much about that, other than she and Meredith had enjoyed organizing church events and such. How far back does her friendship go?"

"When she was young, she knew your grandparents. We attended your parents' wedding together, and your mother and Meredith became close. They had a great time at events, and socializing with the other women in their knitting groups and whatnot. Why do you ask?"

"Just wondering. I knew nothing much about that part of Mom's life, but then, I did go to a private academy rather than attend the local high school. I returned home after college, and then had my accident not too long after that. I guess I missed out on that part of my parents' lives."

He pulled a chair away from the table and sat down again. "Have you any other information that you'd care to give me about what you found at Arty's?" Carver raised a hand. "I promise not to get angry."

"There isn't much to tell. Just that the same guy who has broken into the barn and taunted us was at Arty's poking around the last time I was there." I got up, fished through my jacket pockets, and handed Carver the house key. "He didn't enter Arty's with a key, so if there was a break-in, that guy did it. I usually put the key back in its hiding place when I leave, but forgot this time."

His lips compressed, but Carver never uttered a negative word or admonished me for my own breaking and entering. Instead, he pocketed the key and asked if we were having any other problems.

"Nothing for weeks. Not since we changed the locks and kept the keys to ourselves. The kids work when we're here, and Jess and I alone have keys to get in."

He glanced around. "Where is Jessica?"

"Out and about. The clinic is open for business, so she has to do her vet errands in between all else."

"How are your other employees working out? Any problems?"

"None. The kids have worked their usual hours, Peter Lambert hasn't been around as much as he used to be, he's finished up his studies and has graduated college. Lizzy hasn't been around for a week or two, she's busy at her other job, I guess."

"What does she do there?"

"She's part of a marketing team. Smart girl, that one."

"Mm, well, I'd better be going. Meredith will be upset if I'm real late for supper. I'm glad we had this chat. Stay in touch, and if you hear anything, I will do the same. Keep this to yourself though, okay? I can't have anyone thinking we're working together to solve this murder and find the culprit who's tormented you, Jules." Carver bid me farewell and left.

"Wonder how badly he choked on that crow he's had to eat?"

I hadn't heard Bun come up behind me, but burst out laughing over his comment.

"You read my mind." I crouched next to him, fluffed his fur, then smoothed it again.

"It's still early let's put together an itinerary for Saturday's birthday party. Bailey Kimball is stopping by tomorrow, she's a puppeteer, to talk about entertaining at parties with us. I hope she's a good fit."

I hauled out the party book in which I kept pictures from past events and went through the pages one by one as Bun commented on the memories he had of each event. Close to the end of the book, I found a photograph of Arty with his back to my camera. He was speaking with another man, a lean, tall man in a hoodie. The side view of the man's face was visible, but not clear. Fuzzy, instead.

"Bun, look, I think that's the intruder."

Bun viewed the photo, backed away and then looked again. His ears turned downward. *"I can't see his face very well. Is the picture on your phone?"*

Scrambling to my feet, I reached into my handbag for the phone. It didn't take long to scroll through the photos and find the picture matching the one in the album. Plugging the phone into my laptop, I downloaded the snapshot and enlarged it as much as I could to sharpen the image. Still, the face was unclear. Whether it was from a cast shadow or the angle of the shot, I didn't know, but I couldn't get the picture any clearer.

Sitting cross-legged on the floor, I wondered if Carver's technicians were able to sharpen images. I planned to ask, and then loaded the photo onto a flash drive, which I stuffed into my handbag.

"Is that flash thingy for the sheriff?"

"His technical guy might be able to work more magic than I can. No harm in trying, right?"

"I guess, until he kicks you out of the police station again." Bun's whiskers jittered up and down.

I gave him a light nudge with my wrist. "Then he'd have to eat more crow, wouldn't he?"

CHAPTER TWENTY-ONE

Rabbits scampered to and fro in the huge play-pen. Jess and I cleaned cages, sanitized trays, and filled water dispensers and added fruit and veggies to feeders. We worked in harmony, completed the chores, and I swept the barn floor. With no early morning house calls scheduled, Jess prepared the clinic for her appointments.

"If you need a hand, I'll be out here, just give a yell."

She grinned, said she would, and left me with the rabbits.

Bun, in the pen with Walkabout Willy, remarked, *"Jules, this arrangement with Jessica is gonna be perfect."*

"I think so, too." I'd gathered the two rabbits, set Bun on the floor, and left Willy in his hutch when I heard a rap on the shop door. With a glance at the wall clock, I hung the broom on its hook and rushed to unlock the studio door to let Lizzy in, her arms loaded with bags.

"I hope I didn't interrupt you by arriving earlier than planned, Juliette. Maybe if I had a key, you wouldn't have had to stop what you were doing to let me in with all my bundles."

"Here, let me take some of those." I grabbed three of the bulkiest bags and set them on the countertop. "What's in them?" Like a kid in a candy store, I tipped the bag on end, waiting to see what came out. Two knit sweaters, one angora, and the other heavy wool, were a feast for the eyes. I squeezed them and listened to Lizzy giggle at my excitement.

"Wait until you see what the other bags hold." She repeated what I'd done and laughed aloud when I squealed with excitement over the contents. A thick white chenille knit blanket cozied up to a crocheted one of azure blue chenille. Two cable-knit lap blankets made of fisherman's wool sat amid the shawls. Lizzy's friends had been busy.

"Was this yarn from our supplies?"

Nodding her head, Lizzy laid her hand atop the blankets. "The women have been working like crazy to make enough samples to increase this end of your business. When classes begin, people from all over will want to learn how to make their own yarn to create items such as these."

"Is that why you haven't been around? You've been waiting until this merchandise was finished to bring it all at once?"

"I wanted it to be a surprise."

Her hesitation was so fleeting, I thought I had imagined it. "I don't know what to say, except, help me find a place to display all this. Do you have invoices for the work?"

As Lizzy rifled through her purse, I separated

the items and scanned the room for spots to display each piece.

Handing me the invoice, Lizzy explained who had done each item, saying they were listed separately, and noting a check for each individual person should be made. The total cost was more than I expected, but the work was superb, so I didn't complain.

"This should be enough for now, don't have any other garments or projects crafted until classes are underway, okay? The order for the spinning wheels should arrive this afternoon."

"Whatever you say, Juliette. I know this cost more than you'd anticipated spending, but you'll get more in return than you could possibly imagine. I promise."

A car parked next to Lizzy's. I opened the door to summon Bailey inside. She stood beside her car peering at each entry, seemingly confused about where to go.

I greeted her warmly, and instantly took a liking to her sweet face, brown hair streaked with shades of burnished copper, and the wholesomeness of her entire being. In worn blue jeans, a North Face jacket of cream and gray tweed, her scarf of mixed shades of blue, purple, and touches of pink set her complexion and blue eyes off to a T. Her reserved smile stiffened a tad as she glanced past me, but then returned to charming as she greeted me with a handshake.

"Juliette, I must stop in to see Jessica for a second before I leave. Gotta run, I'll call you later," Lizzy said, and stepped into the clinic and closed the door behind her.

We hadn't set the displays, or worked out answers potential spinning students had, and now Lizzy was gone. Annoyed at her sudden departure, I turned my attention to Bailey, who had also arrived earlier than expected. Must have been my day for early meetings. Hm.

After Bailey and I had introduced ourselves, we sat in chairs near the fireplace. Bun huddled on the hearth rug, intent on not missing a word.

"This is such a wonderful farm. I've been by on several occasions and was disappointed to have missed your open house. Mary Brickworth speaks very highly of you, Juliette."

"Jules, please."

"How long have you been doing rabbit events and education?"

We chatted on for a half hour until she asked if I would like to see her puppets. I slipped into my jacket, left Bun by the fire, and accompanied Bailey to her car. The hatchback opened with a click of her key fob. Funky and unusual puppets sat lined up on the rear seat as though taking a ride. I grinned when she said their names and knew she was going to be great entertainment for parties in the area. With a photo album of her past events, we went back inside, but not before I realized Lizzy had driven away, leaving the barn by way of the outer clinic door. My annoyance returned. What was her problem, anyway?

Bailey went through a few pages of the album, explaining her experience, who her audiences were, and how pleased she was to work with young and old people alike. I agreed, and mentioned the Easter egg hunt, and then Windermere's summer day camp, where elderly people visit a few days at a time each summer to enjoy the lake, the fresh air, and were fond of my rabbits.

Though Arty had never participated in the affair, since these elderly folks didn't care for mimes, I thought they might enjoy Bailey's puppets. It came as no surprise that she had done shows at the camp on days when I was absent.

"The elderly campers are characters in and of themselves, don't you think?" Bailey asked with a mischievous grin.

"That they are. I enjoy myself whenever I go there, and they adore the rabbits, too. Do you have time to see the rabbits, before you go?"

She glanced at the grandfather clock and nodded. "Sure, why not?"

On our tour, I explained where the rabbits came from, how they were cared for, and the way I educated those interested in becoming bunny parents.

"Is there a process you go through before a rabbit is adopted?"

"There is. The animal rescue team and I came up with a program that allows us to have thorough documentation on those who wish to adopt. Some of the rabbits were rescued from places they should never have lived in, and were abused, injured, or both. I don't tolerate that, and work hard to ensure their safety here and in a future home."

"I'm impressed. This place is so clean, and the rabbits respond to you when you stop and talk to them." Bailey poked a finger through a space in the wire and rubbed the nose of the rabbit. "I think I'll enjoy working with you, Jules."

We shook hands and agreed to meet at Karen Sommers's house on High Ridge Road on Saturday. I walked Bailey to the door and watched as she went toward her car.

"She left her book behind."

I grabbed the album and ran out the door, waving for her to wait. At the driver's side of her car, I held the book up and waited until her window slid down. "You forgot this, I didn't know if you needed it for your next appointment."

"Thanks, I would be lost without it. By the way, how well do you know Lizzy?"

"Not real well. She works here a few hours a week. She's done some great things for the business. Why?"

"I just wondered. I haven't seen her since, well, for a while now. See you on Saturday, bye."

The window closed. Bailey drove away before I could ask questions, of which there many, piled one on top of another. Why I'd become worried by Lizzy's behavior was anybody's guess, because I sure didn't know why.

Inside the studio, I applied what little talent I had for displaying the garments and finally, after hearing chuckling behind me, I stopped with a disgusted huff.

"Need a hand, do you?"

Her hand tucked into the pockets of her white coat, Jessica laughed aloud. "I thought Lizzy was coming to meet you today. She would have had these displays completed in no time flat."

"She came by. Didn't you see her?"

"No, I had appointments all morning."

"When Bailey Kimball arrived, Lizzy said she

wanted to check in with you and hurried off into the clinic. What the heck is going on with her?"

"Maybe she couldn't wait to speak with me in between patients."

"Hm, could be," I said with a shrug. "I think there's more to Lizzy than we know." I turned away to work on the display. Jessica gave me a hand until her next patient arrived. When she left, I struggled on my own until I was satisfied with the total look of it all. One blanket lay folded over a quilt rack, the other was suspended from one angled edge to another on a cord attached to the wall. I gave it a final viewing, threw my hands up in despair, and went into the house. Décor had never been my forte.

Lunch was on the table when Jessica walked in. Washing and drying her hands, she asked what I thought of Bailey.

"She's charming and funny. Her puppets are weird, they don't look like Punch and Judy puppets, but they're vibrant in colors that kids will love. I think she'll work out well. We'll meet at Karen Sommers's house on Saturday for her trial run puppet show. That reminds me, I have to call Karen after we finish lunch."

"Glad to hear she'll fit in. No one could mime like Arty, and a different venue is sure to be accepted by all. I'm certain Bailey will be a hit." Over lunch, we talked of her appointments before the conversation returned to the farm itself.

I retrieved the photo album from the living room chair and flipped it open to the page where Arty stood with the hooded man. Explaining my conclusion that this man was our intruder, I handed the book to Jess. She gave it a long, close look before giving it back.

"It isn't very clear, is it?"

"I'm going to ask Sheriff Carver to have his tech guy sharpen the image, if possible."

"Aren't you on Carver's naughty list?"

"Not really. He came by last night and we talked awhile. He seems as confounded by all this crap as we are. I think he's at his wit's end. If I come up with a smidgeon of info, he wants it. That's why I'll give him this picture."

"If nothing else, you have steady nerves, Jules." Jess offered bail money, should I overstep my bounds, yet again.

"This could be important. I don't know how, but surely Carver has dug into Arty's life deeper than I. This might be the one clue that will bring these mysteries to an end. I'm willing to try. I only hope he is."

"Remember, I have bail money," Jess said with a grin while I dialed Karen's phone number to give her the news about Bailey.

Saturday arrived, sunny and bright. A light breeze fluttered through the now fully budded tree branches. Many had sprouted leaves, and spring had arrived. We should all be thankful for the little things in life, right?

My chores complete, the rabbits and cages had been loaded into the van. Carry cages used for transport filled the better part of the vehicle. Regular cages, too cumbersome to take to events, were left in the barn. I folded the petting pen, secured the straps, and drove toward Karen's home.

Our arrival coincided with Bailey's. As we helped each other unload our vehicles, I could sense excitement in the air and heard children giggling. "Guess we're going to have a big turnout today."

Bailey laughed and said she hoped all would go well.

"It will, you'll see. If the kids are happy, the parents are, too."

Karen directed us to where she wanted us placed. I was on one side of the yard and Bailey was on the other, each with a clear view of what the other was doing. The rabbits happily chased one another, nosed their toys, and nibbled at hay while children stopped by to touch their fur and run a hand over their soft coats. Bun hopped to a spot close to my feet and asked, *"I'll keep my ears tuned for any talk of Arty, okay?"*

I knelt beside him, scratched his ears, and murmured it was a great idea. Karen came by to admire the beauty of the rabbits.

"They are darling, aren't they?"

"Yes, they are. Sociable, too. They like it when the children come over and pet them."

"The kids do love them. I'm so pleased to think Bailey will be able to step in since Arty can't be with us any longer. It would be so hard on you to handle a bunch of excited kids all day on your own. They are wearying after a while. Thank goodness the party will be shorter than usual. My older daughter has a dance recital that we are attending. Bailey is very sweet, isn't she?"

"She has a wonderful personality, I think her puppets will win the day."

The show had begun, the puppets were on the small stage with Bailey holding the rapt attention of the ten-year-old kids. I listened to her voice for each character and realized her act wasn't that far off from Punch and Judy, just more updated. Her puppets were also colorful enough to hold an audience's attention on their own.

The show over, the rabbits drew the kids in a swarm. I offered to let one or two kids at a time hold Jazz. She enjoyed contact, and I explained she needed gentle handling. Some kids asked questions while petting Jazz. I answered honestly, yet simply, to help them understand the ways of rabbits. I wasn't used to letting the kits be handled, but these creatures were docile, and all went well.

Karen herded the guests onto the patio for cake and ice cream, then said gifts would be opened afterward. I left Bun in the pen with the other rabbits while I joined Bailey, who stood on the fringe of the parents. Many regarded us with friendly smiles and greeted Bailey warmly when I introduced her.

The kids were noisy, their interest piqued when gifts were opened and shown to all at the table. I backed away from the hubbub, as did Bailey. We were walking toward the rabbit pen when I heard angry voices. One was feminine, the other was terse and masculine. We both stopped to listen.

I peered at the rabbit pen. Bun had risen on his hind legs, his head turned to the voices. The couple stood just beyond a lattice trellis, partially hidden from view.

"What's that about?" Bailey whispered.

"No clue. Maybe a marital spat."

Bun turned his head in my direction. *"I'll tell you about this on the way home. Stay where you are."*

I reached out and touched Bailey's arm. She gave a start and a wide-eyed look at me.

"Let's go over to your puppet stand. We should stay out of that." I dipped my head in the couple's direction.

With a nod, Bailey agreed. We packed up the stage and puppets, loaded them in her van, and then returned to the yard. No further angry words could be heard as we neared the rabbit pen.

"It's safe to come over. I can't wait to leave."

"The rabbits are so calm, and very soothing. I wish I had a place for one, but my landlady would have a cow if I brought one home."

"Feel free to come by and visit them anytime you'd like. We like company, don't we, Bun?"

He hopped around for a minute before stopping before me. I picked him up, put him in a small cage, and then did the same with the other rabbits. Leaving the van doors ajar, Bailey and I returned to the patio where Karen waited with checks for each of us. We marked our invoices paid before handing them to her.

She walked us off the deck, her arm tucked in my left elbow. "Thank you so much for entertaining the guests today." She looked at Bailey with a wide smile. "You can't do better than teaming up with Juliette, she's well known and well liked by the community. You two will be known far and wide if I have my way."

Her willingness to be so kind left us with smiles

on our faces as we parted ways. Bailey drove off. As always, I'd put Bun's cage on the passenger's seat. If I didn't, he'd get cranky and I wanted him to tell me what he had heard of the argument.

"Did you recognize the couple who were behind the trellis?"

"I never saw them before. The man was jealous over the attention paid to the woman by Dr. Sommers. There wasn't anything of interest to be gotten from that. A waste of time. I did hear another couple speaking earlier. They weren't real close to the pen, but you know how acute my hearing is, Jules. You might not have been able to discern what they said, but, of course I could."

Not wanting to ruin his self-adulation, I said, "You do have super deductive powers, Bun. No getting away from that."

"I know you appreciate my keen senses. That's why we're such a great investigative duo."

"I'm all ears, Bun. Tell me what you gleaned from the party."

"The man was watching you while you spoke with Karen. He told his wife it was because of you that Arty had been killed. We know that's not true, and I don't mean to hurt your feelings. His wife asked him how he knew that, and he said their neighbor had told him so. He said the neighbor knew you personally, and that he had proof you were to blame. Could the neighbor be Rusty?"

I shrugged. "I'll give Karen a call and ask her about the couple. You have to give me as much information about them as you remember, or Karen will get suspicious."

I turned into the drive of the farm while Bun

rambled on and on about clothing the couple wore, what they looked like, including their child. At the end, he mentioned the man had a moon-shaped scar on his chin.

"You're so smart, what would I do without you, Bun?"

"I'm exhausted from this busy day. The other rabbits are, too. They liked that you let the kids handle them. I know you don't usually like to do that."

Once in their own roomy cages, the rabbits chowed down on timothy hay and rabbit nibbles, and quenched their thirst before settling in for a nap. I'd finished packing away the pen when Jessica stepped into the barn from the yarn studio.

"How did it go?"

"We were a smash hit, especially Bailey."

"Great. I have news, too. Molly will work for us all summer until it's time for her to leave for college. Isn't that wonderful? I'll have to hire someone before she goes. She said she'd also work with you and the rabbits. You don't mind if she splits her time between both of us, do you?"

"Not at all. I had asked Molly if she wanted to take the summer off before leaving for college, but she had said she could use the extra money. If I need her to give me a hand, I'll ask. Your business is going to get busier, you just wait and see." Jessica was excited about the prospect of having Molly handle the office end of things. I was glad, but uncertain if I could deal with all the chores by myself. Maybe it was time for me to look for a helper who didn't have to bounce back and forth between Jessica and me.

"Now that you two have settled that, can I have something to eat? I think I'm fading fast."

"If you have time, come into the house, Bun has to be fed before he starves to death." I set off through the breezeway.

Jessica set the kettle to boil for tea while I poured food into Bun's feeder and added fresh water to his dispenser. When I was finished and joined Jess in the living room, I indulged in a cookie and a hot cup of Earl Grey.

"This tea hits the spot. All I've had today is water and a slice of birthday cake."

"I'll make a sandwich for you. It'll only take a minute."

I waved her offer away. "Don't bother. It's only another hour or so before we have supper."

Sipping her tea, Jess curled up in the chair. "What do you think will happen if Lizzy doesn't get her act together before the spinning classes begin?"

"I don't know, but I am worried about it. She seems to have taken an unexpected hiatus from her job here, and frankly, I'm not happy about her attitude. When Lizzy first started working with us, she was organized and willing to jump in where needed. Now, well, she seems to have lost interest. What do you think? You know her better than I do."

An odd look crossed her features. "Actually, I don't know her all that well. She's a friend of a friend, you know the sort of thing. Lizzy came recommended to me by way of a conversation we were having on a break from class at the college. It never dawned on me to ask for references. Sorry, Jules, I know I should have."

"Hey, I didn't ask for them, either. We might be blowing her actions out of proportion, instead of getting to the crux of why she's been behaving differently. I had hoped that she'd become part of our businesses and don't understand what's going on with her. Do you think she's got anything to do with our intruder and what's been happening?"

There, I'd put into words what I'd been trying to avoid saying.

Shock widened Jessica's eyes and her mouth formed an O as she hauled in a breath.

Flustered, she spilled tea down the front of her sweater, then dabbed the moisture with a napkin. "It never occurred to me. Oh, my goodness. I'm sorry, Jules, I can't believe she'd have anything to do with that."

"Just throwing my thoughts out there, to see what yours are. That's all."

"Let's invite her over for supper or lunch, maybe. If we have her in front of us, without interruptions, she might tell us what's going on. She could be going through a rough patch with a boyfriend, or her parents. You know, something like that."

"Sounds like a good idea. Why don't you call and invite her over for lunch when it's convenient for her? We'll see what response you get and take it from there."

"I will. What if she refuses?"

"We can't force her, Jess. All we can do is attempt to find out what's going on with her. Don't be nervous or she'll know we suspect that all isn't well with her, and she might not want to talk about what that problem is, anyway. Offer a simple invitation to lunch with us. No strings attached, okay?"

"All right."

"Stop wringing your hands. We'll all be fine with whatever happens."

CHAPTER TWENTY-TWO

It wasn't until two days later that Jessica and I had time to discuss the phone call she'd made to Lizzy. I'd been so busy with the rabbits and farm issues that I hadn't had a chance to ask. There'd been no sign of Andrew, and I awaited return calls from the sheriff and Karen Sommers.

Jessica's success with the invitation to lunch had been a struggle. Lizzy insisted she couldn't attend until the end of the week. I had hoped for a sooner, rather than later, opportunity to question her. I accepted what we could get in answer to the invite and thanked Jess for making the effort.

"I did my best. Lizzy's nervous as a cat about something. She wanted to know why we invited her to come by and asked if she was being fired. As if."

"I know, huh? She's worth every penny I pay her. The problem is, she's not doing the job I asked her to do. It has me worried."

"Me too." Jess returned to the clinic. I cleaned the kitchen before Bun insisted we get outside into the sunshine.

A break from routine gave us a chance to briefly leave the farm. My cell phone in my jacket pocket, Bun in his sling, I went toward the lake. The walk did me good, the sweet smell of spring refreshed my mind, and Bun never stopped talking for a minute. Blah, blah, blah. I had tuned him out until he poked his head out of the sling and craned his neck back to see me.

"Have you heard a word I've said? I know you're alive, because we're still moving, but you haven't uttered a sound."

"Sorry, Bun. I'm preoccupied with other issues."

"What issues could possibly be more important than what I have to say?"

"Yes, I know, you have been droning on about something. I can't fathom what it is, so start over, okay?"

"Huh, I don't think I will. You've ignored me all day."

"Don't be upset, I brought you out here with me, didn't I? That's far from ignoring you."

A sniff was his only response. It made no difference to him that I had brought him along. He was miffed over the fact that I hadn't hung on his every word. I reckoned there'd be no way to get around his attitude, so I fell silent and kept going.

Birds twittered and sang while they flitted from tree to tree. They'd finally come home after wintering down south. A movement at the far edge of the water caught my eye. Andrew reeled in a fish before he noticed us.

"Andrew is fishing over there," I murmured softly.

Bun poked his head from the confines of the sling and jittered his whiskers up and down a few times, then stiffened his ears.

"He hasn't been around the farm in a while. I thought he had moved on."

"Me too." I waved and headed in his direction.

His fish pouch held three good-sized fish. I peered at them and congratulated him on his skill.

"When you're hungry enough, you get good at catching your dinner."

"If you want to share, I'll cook these up for supper later. That is, if you want . . ." I trailed off, not knowing what else to add to my offer. Andrew was adept at making his own meals. He didn't need my help.

"That would be good of you, thanks. I do occasionally get sick of my own cooking."

I checked my watch, noted we'd been gone a good hour, and knew it was time to return home. "Come by around four o'clock, then?"

"Sure, the fish will be cleaned and ready. Thanks, Juliette."

If I wasn't mistaken, it seemed we'd come to be friends of a sort. I smiled, turned, and left with Bun, who objected to the idea of my inviting this man to our home for supper. We'd gone about fifty feet, when I whispered, "It isn't as if he hasn't eaten with us before. Get over it, will you?"

My cell phone jangled a merry tune until I pulled it from my pocket. Sheriff Carver was on the line.

"Been a while, Jules. What's going on?"

"Not much. I do have an interesting picture I just came across that I'd like to show you. Are you going to be at the station much longer?"

I heard a sigh.

"I'm at the farm, where are you?"

"On my way back from the lake. Stay put, I should be there shortly." Maybe within a half hour, but he could wait. I started to jog, quickened the pace, and went into a full run, clasping the sling to my chest so Bun wasn't bounced all over the place. I'd offended him enough for one day.

"Geesh, you're crushing me."

Lightening my grip, I ran until the farm came into view. Only then did I slow my pace to a walk.

Sheriff Carver leaned against his cruiser, basking in the sun. I raised my hand and pointed to the house. He got my drift, and walked on ahead of us, waiting on the porch by the front door.

"That was pretty fast. You must have run every step of the way. I expected to be here for an hour before you got back."

Breathing hard, I opened the front door, stepped into the kitchen, and answered the phone as it rang for the third time.

"Jules Bridge."

"Karen Sommers here, returning your call. How can I help you, Juliette?"

I gave her the rundown on the couple at her daughter's party, then asked if she remembered them. "The woman's husband seemed quite interested in scheduling an event for their own kids, but I didn't have the opportunity to get their name and address. Would you happen to have that on hand?"

"I know exactly who you're talking about. Wait one sec while I look them up in my address book."

Paper rustled, and Karen gave me the information. I thanked her and hung up.

Sheriff Carver leaned against the door, his hands in his pockets, waiting for me to explain. When I didn't, he asked, "That's how you get your information, huh? You're pretty good at finding out what you want to know. I've never seen you in action, Juliette. I bet you never spoke to that couple, did you? You overheard something that's been bugging you and you had to satisfy your curiosity?"

Leaving Bun out of my admission, I said, "Okay, I admit it. I heard them talking, but didn't have a chance to follow up with them. This was an easier way to do it. Have a seat, Jack, I'll get the photo for you."

I delved into my handbag for the flash drive I'd meant to drop off to him and then pulled the picture up on my cell phone. I showed it to him, explained what I'd come up with, and left him to figure out if his tech guy could work his magic.

Eventually, Carver handed the phone to me, slipped the flash drive into his pocket, and asked for a cup of coffee.

While it brewed, I asked if there were any new leads in his investigation.

"I'm afraid not. There is lots of conjecture, with no proof pointing to any one person. It's very frustrating. You'd think by now we'd have something to go on. What's with the name and address of this couple, then?"

"The husband made a remark concerning what his neighbor had said about me. His neighbor blames me for Arty's death and said he could prove it. I was worried this man might be Rusty, but the address Karen gave me is nowhere near Rusty's house. He hasn't relocated, has he?"

"Not to my knowledge." He dialed a number and ordered a patrolman to check on Rusty's address.

"We should know very shortly if he's still living in the same place."

"That was simple. I figured I'd have to see for myself, which isn't on my play list. I avoid the man if, and when, I can. He did his time in jail, I survived, and we've both moved on. I can't tell you how relieved I am about it."

"Have you been back to Arty's house?"

"Not since you threatened me. Besides, I searched every nook and cranny to find a scrap of evidence that might lead to his killer, and found nothing. How about you?"

With a shake of his head, Carver heaved a sigh. "What do you think that hooded man hoped to find?"

"I have no idea. Sorry."

"Stone been around at all?"

"Not lately, but I saw him down by the lake earlier. Seems in good spirits."

"Thought he might have moved on by now, wonder what he's waiting for."

"Jack, we both know he's connected to Arty somehow. I wouldn't be surprised if he was Arty's son. I found a scrap of paper at the house with Arty's handwriting on it, I showed it to you, remember?"

"The one about father and son?"

"That's the one. I think he meant Andrew, but I can't prove it and refuse to push Andrew to tell me."

"He wouldn't if he didn't want to. That man can keep his mouth shut and his thoughts to himself. I interviewed him all night when we arrested him for squatting, and he didn't budge an inch." Carver put his cup in the sink, then said he'd check on Andrew.

Without a word about Andrew providing dinner, I watched Jack walk through the field and disappear into the woodlands. Gone for some time, Jack returned, got into his car, and drove away without a look in the direction of my house. My curiosity ratcheted up a notch as I wondered if Andrew had even been at the campsite. How could I bring that into the conversation over dinner? I wondered.

At four o'clock, Andrew arrived with two fish in hand. I took them from him, added a spice and butter mix, rubbed it on both sides of each fish, and laid them in a pan to bake. The vegetables were ready to steam. Jessica had closed the clinic after her last appointment and set the table for three.

Curiously, Bun had remained quiet all afternoon. Probably sulking over his supposed unfair treatment. I checked his water supply, offered him a small thatch of timothy hay, and filled his food container.

"You've had an interesting day, Jules. I know I was rude earlier, and I apologize. Can we talk later?"

I smiled, ran my hand over his fur, and nodded, leaving him to enjoy his fare.

The three of us enjoyed the delicious fish dinner, and our conversation was smooth, rather than stilted, until Andrew put his fork on his plate and said, "Sheriff Carver stopped by my campsite this afternoon."

I hesitated but a fraction of a second. "He came by here first, wanted to know if I'd seen you and then said he wanted to check on you for himself. How did it go?"

"Not bad, really. He can be quite personable when he isn't trying to terrify someone into confessing to things he hasn't done."

"Like what, exactly?" Jess asked.

"Like when he arrested me for squatting and then tried to pin your intrusions on me."

"He did say you aren't easily intimidated," I said.

"I'm glad he realizes that. No harm done, we're on solid terms now."

"What are your future plans?" Jess asked before finishing her last bit of food.

"I'll be moving on in a week or two. I've only stayed to keep an eye on you and your barn. It's plain that the sheriff doesn't have enough manpower to leave an officer here all the time."

"That's nice of you. We haven't had any trouble since we changed the locks, though, so maybe our intruder has moved on to an easier target."

His blue-eyed piercing look stopped me short. "You and I know that isn't the case. This man has a reason for his actions and those haven't gone away, I'm certain of it. I think he's waiting for the right moment to return and begin again. The lock situation has only kept him at bay until he figures another way in without breaking windows or setting off an alarm if you have one."

Her expression filled with angst, Jessica asked, "You really believe that?"

His nod was his answer.

"We can handle what comes. Jessica and I aren't victims, nor are my rabbits. If this guy comes back, we'll be ready for him."

"If you say so. I'll do my best to remain vigilant." Andrew stacked the dishes, placed them on the counter by the sink, and retrieved his jacket from a peg near the door. "Dinner was tasty, thanks."

"Thanks for sharing your catch, and for watching out for us."

Jessica, standing by the door, opened it and wished him a good night. The minute he was out of sight, she rounded on me.

"I was no longer worried over this creep who's been breaking in, but now, well, that confidence just flew out the window."

Surprised, I asked, "You really thought we had seen the last of him?"

"Didn't you?"

"No, I have taken this break in his attempts to ruin me and my business as a temporary reprieve. Nothing more. The changes we've made have worked so far, but they won't work forever. If he has become desperate, then we'll likely have another visit."

The phone rang. Sheriff Carver assured me that Rusty was still at the same address. "I'll find out who this party guest's next-door neighbor is and take it from there. Have a nice evening."

While Jessica made a supply list for the clinic, I went into the barn to settle the bunnies for the night. Done with the chores, I turned back toward the breezeway to find Bun at my heels.

"Before we go into the house, Bun, I want to look over the supplies in the yarn shop."

He followed along behind me as I went into the huge room. The fireplace flickered, the flames turned to low, and I flipped on the light switch. The room brightened, colorful yarns caught my eye, bringing a smile to my lips. Yes, Lizzy had done a great job in bringing life into a sector of the business that had been lacking the vitality to encourage customers to spend their money. It would serve us all well to get to the bottom of Lizzy's problems.

"Lizzy is coming to lunch next week, right?"

"Supposedly. I hope she shows up."

"She will. I'm sure she's just got too much to deal with right now. She's smart, and a hard worker. You'll see. She was a bit scattered when she was here the other day. When Bailey arrived, and they saw each other, I could feel tension in the air. Lizzy couldn't get away fast enough. What do you make of that?"

"I thought I imagined it. You should have spoken up sooner."

"If you'd listened to what I was saying on our way to the lake today, we wouldn't be having this conversation now."

I halted mid-step, looked down at my furry mystery partner, and abruptly apologized. "I was trying to figure out who the party guest's neighbor might be. I should have listened, Bun. Sorry."

"The women know each other. They were surprised to see each other, too. Lizzy was shocked and fearful, then she was herself again and practically ran from this room."

"I caught the looks between them, but they recovered so fast, I figured my imagination was in overdrive. One thing that struck me as odd, though, was when I spoke with Bailey, she asked about Lizzy."

"Hm, curious. Might be worth looking into."

"That's what I thought."

We left the barn in good order, went through the breezeway, and found Jessica had gone upstairs. She'd scribbled a note saying she was having an early night. It was after nine o'clock when I finally sprawled across the sofa, covered with an afghan, and began to doze. I'm not sure how long it lasted before I was awakened by Bun.

In a frantic state he ran in circles, and hopped onto my body and off again to complete another round. All the while he repeated, *"Smoke and fire in the barn, smoke and fire in the barn. Get up, smoke and fire in the barn."*

I flung the afghan aside, rushed from the living room, and yelled up the stairs for Jessica to come quickly. I heard her door open as she yelled back, "I'm coming."

Grabbing my slip-on sneakers, I ran through the breezeway into the barn, stumbling as I ran while slipping the shoes onto my feet. Smoke billowed into the front of the barn as I came down the sloped breezeway. I flipped the switch for the air vent built into the roof to clear the air by drawing the smoke upward and out of the building. "Call nine-one-one, Jess. I'll roll the hutches close to the door in case the barn is on fire. I don't see any flames, but that doesn't mean they aren't there."

The sharp smell of vinegar permeated the air. Confused by the odor, I rushed toward the first cage, grabbed onto the stand, and wheeled it toward the double doors. Jessica followed suit as sirens screamed before falling silent.

Fists pounded on the doors as I pushed the fourth hutch forward. I opened the small door and allowed the fire and rescue team in followed by the police. I shut the door and continued to rescue the rabbits. Sheriff Carver followed me up the aisle, his questions terse, and my answers short.

"What happened?"

"I smelled smoke."

"Are there flames to go with this acrid smell?"

I stopped, and was about to answer him, when a firefighter stepped next to me. "The smell is from a smoke grenade. It has a vinegar odor that can be caustic. My men are pulling the rabbit hutches outside. You needn't worry about fire. Let's get moving, it can be harmful for the rabbits."

Everyone did their best to get the rabbits to safety. Jessica had her stethoscope out to listen to each rabbit's breathing. Firefighters and cops lined up, each holding a rabbit to make the job go faster. She listened, nodded, and moved on to the next rabbit. I was marching back and forth inside the barn, scrutinizing every inch of the space, when I stumbled upon the body of a man.

"Back here, somebody come back here. I found a body," I yelled.

Intent on getting the rabbits to safety once we knew the smoke was from a grenade and it wasn't a real fire, no one else had thought to search the rest of the barn except for me. EMTs rushed past, loaded with equipment, followed by two more guys rolling a gurney up the aisle.

Now that the barn was lit brilliantly, and the

smoke had been completely cleared, I attempted to get a look at the man lying crumpled on the floor.

"Is he dead?" the sheriff wanted to know.

"He's breathing, just unconscious." The lead EMT nodded to his men and said, "Let's load him up and get him to the ER."

Minutes later, the gurney, the man, and the crew were on their way out the door and then down the driveway in their rescue truck. The efficiency of these guys impressed me to no end.

A tap on my shoulder gave me a start.

"I have questions for you two." The sheriff dipped his head toward Jessica and then said, "After you get the rabbits organized, we'll talk. My officers can help bring the animals back in."

"Thanks, Jack." Directing the placement of cages, Jessica came up to me and reported the rabbits hadn't shown any signs of injury. She'd check them again in the morning.

"Did you get a look at the unconscious man?" Sheriff Carver interjected.

Jess shook her head while I mulled the question over. I had seen his face, albeit briefly. Although I was certain I hadn't seen him before, he somehow seemed familiar. It didn't make sense, but my gut said it was so. Seldom did I ever doubt my gut. It had proven helpful for years, just as Bun's superb senses did.

"Jules?"

I snapped back from my distracted thoughts and said, "I have no idea who he is. He seems familiar somehow, but I don't know any more than that. Sorry, Jack."

He asked a few more questions, for which we had no answers, and finally left, ordering all but one officer to get back to work. The last cop was assigned to stay for the night.

Once the sheriff drove away, I offered the man coffee and a snack. He grinned and said he'd take me up on the offer. In a flash, Jessica had put together a sandwich, some cookies, and the thermos I'd filled with coffee, and took it all out to the man. They spoke for a few minutes before she hurried back inside.

"It might be spring, but the nights are still chilly," she said with a shiver.

I picked up the phone and dialed the non-emergency number for the fire station. The team leader, Alphonse Bilodeau, wasn't available. I left him a message, asking for a return call. Determined to know who the stranger was, and what he was doing in my barn, I waited impatiently for Alphonse to call me back.

It took some time, but Alphonse called and apologized for the long wait. "I have no information to give you, Jules. The sheriff is adamant about that. I am sorry that I can't tell you anything."

"That's fine, I might have a word with Jack."

CHAPTER TWENTY-THREE

Dawn arrived, Jess went into the house for a cat-nap, and I took off into the woodlands for a chat with Andrew. I found him sitting on a tree stump, a fire in the firepit with steam emitting from the tin coffeepot's spout.

Expressionless, Andrew watched my approach, then lifted his cup and asked if I wanted some home-brewed coffee. Squatting next to him, my hands spread toward the heat from the fire, I nodded.

"Why didn't you come to the barn last night, or did you, and then leave?"

"You had enough help, mine wasn't needed." He handed me a sorry excuse for a mug, chipped, with a fine crack in the handle. I gladly accepted the coffee anyway. I sipped the strong, fragrant brew and let the caffeine work its way into my system. A long day stretched out ahead of me.

He tossed a dry stick of wood onto the flames. "Tell me what took place."

I gave him as much information as I could before I asked, "Were you in the barn at all?"

"Why do you ask?"

"We found an unconscious man."

"I saw a shadow moving about. Do you know who he is?"

I shook my head and handed him the mug for a refill. "Do you?"

"No."

"Did you stop him from setting fire to the barn?"

"I did."

"He might not have been planning to burn it down, but he set off a couple smoke grenades. I'm glad I had the roof vent installed. It sucks all the nasty smells out of the barn when I turn it on. That's what saved the rabbits. Thanks for protecting them and us."

He shrugged, handed me the filled mug, and said nothing.

"Are you Arty's son?"

He turned his head, gave me a long look, and admitted he was. "My mother left Arty when I was around four years old. She died of a heart attack not long after we moved away. I was put into care, a nightmare no matter how you look at it, while the authorities searched for relatives. When they couldn't find any, I was put up for adoption. I was lucky enough to have a nice couple take me in and raise me as their own."

"You were fortunate."

"I'm sure Arty was aware somebody wanted to ruin you and your farm. He wasn't functioning on all gears toward the end of his life, but if he'd been sensible enough and gone to the police with what he knew, I think Carver would have believed him."

"That's a possibility. I do wish he'd told me, though. All I ever got from Arty was ranting and raving, anger, and a bit of violence. Now that I know he had brain cancer in advanced stages, it all makes sense."

"I know this is only theory on my part, but your intruder might have thought he couldn't take any chances on Arty having a lucid period and took him out of the picture before he could report what he knew. I really think that was the case, Jules."

"I agree. Have you any ideas about the intruder? Where he might live, why he's doing this to me? Anything at all?"

"I don't know the man and never fully saw him until last night. Could he be connected to the farm in some obscure way?"

"Not that I know of. I didn't recognize him, but he was somehow familiar to me. Why is that, I wonder? Could he have been a friend to one of my employees?"

"It's worth considering. Tell Carver, I know he's anxious for a break in the case. He came by and yammered on about it yesterday. He's a good man, Jules, and has your best interests at heart. He'll investigate any and all information that comes his way."

We talked until the sun rose high.

"This guy may have used smoke grenades, but he also wanted to set fire to the farm. We scuffled a bit before he knocked himself out on pipe supporting a cage."

"I have no plans of telling the sheriff or anyone else what we've talked about today. I'll keep your presence at the barn to myself. The last thing you need is to be arrested, and the sheriff shouldn't be sidetracked from his investigation, either. I will say this, if any of this comes to light, and you're arrested, I will testify on your behalf. But . . ."

"I know, you want me to tell the sheriff that Arty is my father. I'll give it some thought."

I left him at the campsite knowing it wasn't likely that he'd confess to being Arty's son, or to anything else that had to do with my farm. I'd made a promise and wouldn't break it.

Arriving at the house, I found the farm swarming with people. Jessica and Molly were amidst a mad frenzy of shoppers interested in a fire sale. I stood on a bench in the back of the yarn studio and yelled for quiet.

"There was no fire, there is no fire sale. Our goods were not damaged in the least, nor were the rabbits. If you wish to make purchases, know this, nothing is on sale."

Half the crowd departed, their faces filled with disappointment. The other half bought merchandise and was excited to do so. Some had never been to the studio and registered for spinning classes. Happy to have the business, I smiled, took their class fees, rang up purchases while Molly bagged what they bought, and then realized Jessica had scooted into the clinic.

Shooing Molly off to help Jess, I handled the remaining shoppers and blew a sigh of relief when the last one left. Bun, who had squatted in a corner of the room, taking all the action in, came over to me and rubbed his ears against my ankle.

"You've been gone a long time. Are you all right?"

"I went to see Andrew at dawn. We had quite the conversation. He's Arty's son, just as we thought."

"We're brilliant, aren't we? I knew they were related." Bun attempted a backflip, but didn't quite make it.

"Did you hurt yourself?"

"I used to do backflips with no problem. I must be eating too much and getting fluffy like you. I think we need a diet, Jules."

I leaned in and whispered, "You wouldn't last a day."

"I know." His whiskers jittered and then he asked, *"Are you going to tell the sheriff about Andrew?"*

"I promised not to, but said he should admit the connection to Jack before it comes to light and causes problems."

"You smell like pickles. Have you showered lately?"

"Not today, but I will now. Glad you told me, I must have gotten used to the odor. I couldn't smell it on me at all." I scurried into the house, took the stairs two at a time, and scrubbed my skin with hot water and soap until I glowed bright pink. My hair clean, a quick blow-dry, I dressed in fresh jeans and a work shirt and went into the barn to see the rabbits.

A couple days later, Andrew showed up at the farm. Surprised to see him, I finished my chore and asked what he wanted.

"A ride to see Carver would be nice."

I washed my hands, changed from boots to sneakers, tossed the plastic apron into the trash, and grabbed my car keys on the way out the door. Leaving Bun behind, we drove into town and I parked in the rear lot of the police station.

"Would you like me to come in?"

"I know you can hardly keep your curiosity from taking over, so yeah, please do."

We sat side by side in front of Jack's desk. He surveyed us with a quizzical look, then asked, "What can I do for you today, either of you?"

"Jules gave me a ride into town, she doesn't have any business with you, I do. I am Arty's son, his only son."

Jack leaned back in his squeaky chair, rocked a bit, and said, "I thought that might be the case. Why tell me now instead of in the beginning?" He shuffled papers in order and set them aside. Then he handed a manila envelope to Andrew and said he should take a look at what the envelope held.

As he flipped from one page to the next, I caught bits and pieces of what the documents said. Andrew's mother had taken her maiden name back when she and Andrew left Arty. The sheriff had made the connection and let it slide due to not having enough time to question him in the past day or so.

"I should arrest you for the murder of your father."

I leaned forward. "He's not guilty and you know it."

"How do you know, Juliette?"

"My gut says so. Andrew's had more than

enough time to kill his father and destroy my business, but he hasn't done either."

"You still haven't answered the question," Carver murmured.

"I can't explain it, I just know he's innocent."

"You need to give me at least a kernel of something to go on, or I'll have to arrest this man."

The threat was empty, all three of us knew it. Carver was pushing me to remember a crumb of information, so he could dismiss us and continue his search for the real killer. I slumped back in my chair, propped my elbows on my knees, and cupped my face in my hands. Eyes closed, I mentally squeezed my brain for a nugget of truth to give the man.

I'd held my breath without realizing it. About to explode for lack of oxygen, I exhaled and sucked in air. I said, "The only clue I have is that one of my employees is connected to the intruder. He's also your killer, sheriff."

"Which employee would that be, Juliette?"

"I don't know, but you do, don't you? You've been sitting here working it all out these last couple of days."

"Don't get upset, it's more conjecture. Together we can discover the proof we need and bring these people to justice. I have officers checking your employees, their friends, families, and their backgrounds. Everything I can think of is being investigated. This has gone on too long, Jules, and the chief is on my back. Stone, you can leave, but stay in the area until this case is closed."

"Thanks, I will."

Before we walked out, I asked, "Who was the man in my barn? Have you identified him yet?"

"He's still unconscious. He took a serious hit when he landed against that post in your barn."

"If he regains consciousness, let me know."

"You got it."

We left the station and drove to Arty's place. The key had been put back in its place and I used it to open the door. I waited in the kitchen while Andrew walked around, giving the house a good look. When he returned to me, we left, locking the door and putting the key on the ledge.

"I don't think I'll live there. Instead, I'll sell the place and move on."

I didn't ask why, it was none of my concern. There could be bad memories that plagued him from his young childhood in that house. After all, if his mother left Arty, she must have had good reason.

We went our separate ways after our arrival at the farm. I entered the farmhouse while Andrew drifted off into the woods.

Over supper, Jessica and I discussed what had happened at the sheriff's office.

"You mean that Carver already knew Andrew was related to Arty and kept it to himself? What nerve. Now he's investigating everyone here at the farm and their families and friends, as well? Is there no privacy left in life?"

"Why are you so disconcerted about it? I think it'll clear everything up and put an end to all this nonsense."

"True, but I don't like it when they poke their noses where they don't belong."

"I understand, but it's important to solve this mystery."

"I guess, but what if the sheriff doesn't come up with the killer, then we'll never solve this case."

"Don't be silly, we're going to keep him on track, I can feel it in my bones."

CHAPTER TWENTY-FOUR

Expecting some normalcy to return, I was surprised to hear from Carver day after day, as if he thought I had a crystal ball that would help him solve his murder case. I began to grow annoyed. With no choice but to answer his calls, I was certain that if I didn't, he'd drive out to bug me in person. His boss pressuring him was the only reasonable explanation I had for his continuous interruptions.

"Have you spoken to the intruder, now that he's conscious? I called the hospital today and they said you'd been in to see him."

"I saw him briefly. That was my reason for calling, yet again, today. His name is Grady. Ben Grady."

The name of the man gave me pause. "He's my intruder? You have to question him, don't be nice, just beat the truth out of him if need be. I know he killed Arty. My farm, this Grady fellow, and Arty are all connected. Have you finished checking my employees yet?"

"I've gathered almost all the information I've asked for, why?"

"I need to know which employee he's associated with. It could be a matter of life and death, Jack. My life or death."

I hung up without waiting for him to speak. Good golly, couldn't he get a move on? I had to know in order to protect myself, Jessica, and the rabbits. My pacing got on Bun's nerves until he couldn't hold back any longer.

"You're a wreck. Let's go for a walk, it'll do you good to be out in the fresh air. Besides, if you aren't here, Carver can't annoy you, can he?"

The rabbit had a point. We went into the house, where I slipped the sling around my neck and strapped it across one shoulder. Once Bun scrambled inside, we went into the shop to let Lizzy, who had arrived out of the blue and worked for the day, and Jessica know we were taking a walk.

"Where are you going?" Lizzy asked.

"To the lake and back. It's a nice walk, and I could use the fresh air."

"Was that the sheriff on the phone earlier?"

"He's driving me nuts. But yes, it was him, that's part of the reason I should go walking."

Her chuckle light, she said, "Have fun."

I set off at a good pace, Bun kept up a constant stream of chatter over inconsequential topics. He was doing his best to help me relax, and I appreciated his efforts.

Our route the same, we traveled farther than usual. The sun, bright and warm, the breeze sweet with the fragrance of the forest just beyond the beach, I retraced our steps to return to the farm.

We'd come to the spot where I'd found Arty's body, when I noticed Lizzy sitting in her car in front of the chained fence. When I waved, she smiled and stepped from the driver's seat.

"The sheriff called and wants to see you right away. Jessica still has patients, so I offered to give you a ride. Molly is helping her until we get back. Hop in."

We climbed over the fence and got into the front passenger seat of her car.

"Did the sheriff say what's so important?"

Lizzy backed up and turned the car toward town. "There's been a break in the investigation and he wants your help."

My mind flew over the possibilities, one of which was if this was so important, why hadn't Carver called my cell phone? Bun popped his head out of the sling to watch Lizzy, his regard intent.

"I've always liked Lizzy, but I sense she's different somehow. Beware of her, Jules, she might be lying to you."

His astute senses never failed, and hadn't this time either. I didn't believe a word Lizzy said, and wondered what she was up to.

We struck up a conversation about the shop and sales. All the while, Bun issued warnings that something was amiss. Knowing he was right, I smoothed his ears and stroked the fur on his head, hoping to assure him.

At the intersection, the light turned green. Lizzy turned in the opposite direction, away from the police station.

"You missed the turn."

"I have to make a stop first, you don't mind, do you? It won't take a minute, I promise."

"Sure."

We passed the park where Bun and I had been assaulted. About to mention the incident to Lizzy, she glanced at me and said, "Isn't that where you two were set upon by a man who thought he killed you? You were lucky to have survived it."

Knowing neither Jess nor I had explained the episode, I merely said, "You've got that right."

Alarm bells weren't the only thing going off in my head. Bun was struggling to get free of the sling, while still warning of the danger we were in. I slipped the sling from around my neck, let the buckle slide down, and dropped the loose fabric into my lap.

"There now, be still, Bun."

Lizzy gawked as though I'd lost what marbles remained in my head. In my own mind, I knew we were in danger from this woman. Wanting to deny it, I couldn't.

Bun's paws and upper body protruded from the sling as he wiggled to make sure he could get away. Suddenly still, Bun said, *"I'm ready to make our escape when you are, Jules."*

"So, Lizzy, how do you know my intruder?"

Her laughter evil, Lizzy answered, "I thought you'd never work out my connection to Ben. We're siblings, of course."

"But . . ."

"I was married and then divorced, but use my married name. Ben and I are Gradys, does the name sound familiar to you?"

"Not really. I'll have to give it some thought. How do you know Bailey Kimball?"

"She had an affair with Ben. Thought she would

marry him, until I put a stop to it. She resents me for their breakup, but that's too bad. She would have gotten between me and my brother and what we are entitled to. Bailey is all about honesty and such. If she'd found out about Ben's activities at the farm, well, she'd have turned us in. No one is going to do that, not ever, not even you."

"Arty knew your brother was my intruder, didn't he? He was also aware you were behind what was happening at my farm."

"He was an interfering fool. Ben had to get rid of him before he became a liability. So, he did."

"Why me? Why my farm? I don't understand."

"We want the farm, of course. I knew you'd never sell, and that by ruining your business and burning the farm to the ground, you'd be dead. The land would then hit the real estate market, where it would sell for a mere pittance of its true worth."

"Why this particular farm?"

"Because, cuz, we're related to you."

"We are not, I'd know if that were so. You're lying." While I'd thrown out the accusation, I wasn't sure if I was right. Could she and Ben be related to me? How?

Her grin was as evil as her laughter. Lizzy withdrew folded papers from her pocket and flung them at me. The woman was unhinged. How had Bun and I not noticed something so evident?

"How could we know? She gave a stellar performance every time we saw her."

I straightened the papers and read them quickly while Bun insisted Lizzy's story had a ring of truth.

I'd reached the last page of the documents and saw my father's name, alongside that of a woman with the last name of Grady.

"My father and your mother are siblings?"

Memories flashed through my brain as I thought about my family. While I had been away at private school and then at college, I hadn't been able to get home as often as I'd wanted. Throughout my childhood, I hadn't been aware of strangers coming to our house. Only after we'd moved to the farm did I see a couple arrive in a car that had seen better days. Upstairs in my bedroom at the time, I watched from my window.

The driver, a man with a limp, was accompanied by a woman. They'd come to the door, but hadn't been allowed inside. I'd heard arguing, the front door slammed, and then they drove away. Having asked my father who these people were, he put me off by saying they were salespeople. My mother refused to discuss it when I approached the subject while we were shopping. Were they Lizzy's parents? Why had my father been so mean to them? What had caused the rift between him and his sister? I needed to know.

"My parents always dreamed of a life on the farm, especially my father. Dad was obsessed with it, but had always been refused by our grandparents, right up until the day he passed away. A few years later, our grandparents sold the farm to your parents. My brother and I approached your father with an offer for it. They flatly refused, saying that when you recovered from your accident, you would have the farm and they'd move to a warmer climate."

"My father never said a word about it. You should have come to me, talked it over, we could have come to some arrangement. I'm sure of it."

"Don't be stupid, Juliette. We didn't want an arrangement, we wanted what should rightfully be ours. What we were cheated out of all those years. While you grew up in a beautiful place, my brother and I were poor. We didn't go to a private school, nor were we put through college. I paid my own way, working two jobs while I did so. Have you ever lived like that, Juliette? I bet not." Lizzy's lip curled in a sneer.

"What was the problem between our grandparents and your parents?"

"My mother dated my father and became pregnant. Her parents were horrified and ashamed, which was normal back in those days, I guess. Mom wanted to get married, but she needed permission because she was underage. My father wasn't a minor, and your grandfather threatened to have him arrested. When Mom found out, she and Dad ran away. After I was born, they approached our grandparents and were tossed off the property for their effort to make peace."

"Why didn't you tell me all this?"

"Would it really have made a difference? Your father wouldn't even speak to my mother in all those wasted years. How ridiculous and small-minded is that? My father ranted and raved about it all, until he died from a heart attack. Mom passed on about a year later, never having been able to make her parents or her brother see reason. From that point forward, my brother and I hatched a plan to take our due from you." Her driving increasingly erratic, the car skidded on a sharp curve in the road and Lizzy hit the brakes.

I thought she was right about wasted years and righteous feelings. She and her brother had grown up in a sad and bitter household. Unfortunately for me, I might pay for their losses.

"How did Arty come into this?"

"Unwittingly, he overheard us discussing the plan. He tried to intervene on your behalf, to make us realize we were wrong. The poor sot, he couldn't get us to see things his way. Arty was very ill by then, and not making much sense at times. Often, he rambled on that your rabbits and all animals should be free. I think it was his way of trying to warn you, and everyone he spoke with, that something was afoot. He'd become mentally unstable by the time the frigid weather set in. In my opinion, Ben did him a favor by ending his misery."

Gripping the door handle, I shouted, "Watch out, you almost hit that post."

The car slowed, until it barely moved. Bun prepared to leap out, as did I. In one swift move, the door swung wide. Lizzy reached over, but only grasped an empty sling as Bun and I sought our freedom.

I rolled to the ground, got up, and started running. *Wait for me, Jules. I'm right behind you.*

I slowed a tad, reached down, felt fur touch my fingers, then closed them around Bun's heavy coat and swooped him into my arms. Scouring the sides of the road for a place to dash into the woods on even ground, I found we'd come to the exact spot where Rusty had left me for dead. Lizzy's car engine revved as she raced toward us. There was no choice but to jump over the guardrail and take our chances.

"Hang on, Bun."

We flew over the rail and skidded our way downhill, with me grasping at branches one-handedly. Catching my balance, I stood still for a second to get my bearings, until a shot rang out. Lizzy was a maniac, one with a gun.

We took off. At the sound of a second shot, we ran as fast as my feet would carry us in search of safety. Breathing hard, I crouched on my knees behind bushes. I pulled my cell phone from my jeans pocket. Luckily, I had service and dialed Carver's number. When he answered the call, I gave him what I thought our location was and urged him to hurry.

We kept moving as more shots echoed through the trees. Sooner or later Lizzy would run out of bullets, at least I prayed she would. She must have been a poor shot to not have struck us, but then, who knew what she was, other than nuts.

"Her desperation has made her crazier and crazier. Why didn't we notice? I should have known with my superpowers and all."

"Can we discuss your superpowers later?" I whispered, and peered past the new pile of brush where we'd taken refuge.

"She's coming, I think I can smell her. What if I draw her attention so you can attack her?"

Worried he might be shot, I said, "That doesn't sound too promising. What if she gets the best of me? Crazy people are strong, you know."

We squatted as close to the ground as I could get. We listened, Bun with his superior hearing and me with my human ears that were nowhere near as fine-tuned as his. The gunshots had ended, the silence nerve-wracking, so much so that I could feel sweat running down the sides of my face. Fear was trying to control me.

"Don't be afraid, if we're still, she won't know where we are."

"She will if we aren't quiet," I whispered.

He twisted his head around and peered at me while those long ears flopped forward. Bun had taken my words to heart. My legs cramped from crouching, I didn't dare move. I only knew that Lizzy had a gun, was off her rocker, and was hunting us.

"You know I'll find you, don't you, Juliette? I heard you talking to the rabbit. Stupid animal. I knew you two were going to make a run for it, I just didn't think you'd jump from the car. Maybe I'll shoot him first, so you will suffer more before I kill you. It's what you both deserve, you know."

Bun's ears perked up, his whiskers twitched so hard they almost spun. I touched the top of his head, loosening my grip to relax the muscles in my arms. It was a mistake, a big one. Bun leapt off into the brush, his feet so fast I couldn't have caught him if I'd tried. In an instant, I heard a scream and then a gunshot. Anger took hold. I rose from the brush and raced forward.

Not fifteen feet away, Lizzy lay on the ground, grasping her ankle with both hands while swearing to get Bun if it was the last thing she did. Nowhere to be seen, Bun had taken off to parts unknown, leaving me alone with this crackpot.

Lizzy hadn't seen me right away, and her gun

was closer to me than to her. I kicked it behind a rock and began to run. Now aware of my presence, Lizzy howled in pain as she attempted rise, all the while promising bad things would happen to me and Bun.

At least twenty yards away from her, I glanced over my shoulder. By the time I reached what I considered far enough away to be safe, I stepped into a muddy hole, twisted my ankle, and got up to keep going. Searing pain flew up my leg when I put my foot down. Lizzy and I were now on the same playing field. Limping forward, I took sanctuary behind a pine tree wide enough to hide two people.

In an instant, Bun was at my side and huddled against me. We sat there for some time, waiting, not hearing another threat from Lizzy. Had she found the gun? Was she sneaking up on us? Fearing the worst scenario, I focused on woodland sounds. I had wanted to have put serious distance between us, but I wasn't willing to take any chances by taking a peek to see where she was, or even moving on in this condition.

Shots rang out, I hugged Bun closer, closing my eyes, and praying we wouldn't be killed.

Moments later, I heard a mixture of voices and one that called my name. Sheriff Carver had arrived.

"It's Sheriff Carver. Come on, Jules, let's go," Bun said.

The voice grew closer as I hobbled toward his voice with Bun keeping watch for Lizzy.

"Juliette, come out, it's Sheriff Carver. We've been searching for you. You're safe now."

I peered through pine tree branches, clutched Bun to my chest, and answered Jack's call.

Shaking from our heads to our toes, the two of us made our way to Jack.

"Thank you for saving us. All of you," I said to the officers who had come for us. Nervous, I kept darting looks in all directions, waiting for Lizzy to show up. When she didn't, I accepted the officers help to reach the road where I saw a rescue parked several feet away. Thinking it was for us, I went toward it, but was stopped. The way forward had been blocked by a wall of policemen.

"What's going on?" I peeked through a small space between two men and saw a covered body being loaded into the rescue.

I stepped back, threw up on the side of the road, and then blew my nose when someone offered a hankie. I jammed the offensive cloth into my back pocket and apologized.

"Everything is okay, Juliette. It happens to the best of people who encounter these circumstances. Lizzy is dead, and her brother is our guest in cell number four at the police station. He's being charged with their crimes. It's all over, come on, let the EMTs take a look at you. Then I'll take you home." Carver put his hand on my shoulder and turned me in the direction of his car where a rescuer waited with an enormous medical kit.

Not completely comprehending what he'd said, I asked, "It's truly over? My rabbits and farm are safe? I don't have to worry about these two any longer?"

"No, you don't."

The EMT wrapped my foot and recommended I stay off it until I could get an X-ray.

I thanked him and scooted farther into the front seat of Jack's cruiser after the EMT was done with me.

Jack closed the door after Bun jumped into my lap. He got behind the driver's wheel and said, "Just relax. I'll take you to the emergency room. You're in shock over what's happened, and you're soaked from the rain. If you catch pneumonia I'll be in trouble with Meredith for allowing it to happen."

"I'm sure I didn't break anything, just take me home."

Jack opened his mouth to comment, but thought better of it and we started the ride home. It was a shorter trip than I remembered it being with Lizzy. Andrew and Jessica awaited us at the kitchen door, smiles of welcome and relief on their faces. Jessica hugged me tightly and drew me inside.

"Coffee's ready, anyone want a cup?" Jess asked as she brandished the pot.

I nodded, the sheriff took a seat at the table, Bun lolled across my lap, unwilling to leave me for a minute while we all settled in for coffee. As the story rolled out in detail, Carver said Lizzy had brandished a gun and was shot because of it.

My guess was that she had found the weapon I'd kicked behind a rock. Carver slurped the last mouthful of coffee in his cup and said he'd stop in tomorrow for a formal statement.

After he left, Jessica asked, "What happened? There are scratches on your face."

"Bun and I ran for our lives in the very same

spot Rusty left me to die. I bet Lizzy chose that location for a reason. I—"

Jess interrupted me. "Don't worry about it now. I knew something was wrong when Lizzy made a sudden excuse to leave before half the work in the shop was complete. Then the sheriff called looking for you. I grew worried and told him you'd gone to the lake. He said he'd find you there, it was imperative he speak to you."

"Lizzy showed up at the lake, said the sheriff needed me at the station, and offered us a ride. It wasn't long before I knew we were in trouble."

Jess jumped in when I took a swig of coffee.

"When Carver couldn't find you, he stopped by to ask if you'd returned. When I said you hadn't, he got worked up over your disappearance, and called out all the officers available to search for you. He left here in a hurry and we've been waiting ever since."

Filling gaps in the story, I said, "If anyone had ever told me Lizzy was unhinged, I would have thought they were wrong, until today, that is. I just don't know how they accessed the barn."

Her expression odd, Jessica fiddled with her coffee cup handle. "I hate to admit this, but I left my keys unattended on a couple of occasions. That could have been when Lizzy got hold of them. Her friend and I met for lunch once last fall. Lizzy stopped by our table and invited herself to join us. Of course, she was so charming, neither of us gave it a thought. The other occasions were when we worked in the yarn shop. I'd added my new key to the rest of the ones on my key chain and left the lot on the counter. She could have made an impression of it when I was out of the room. You know, both times Lizzy mentioned I should always be conscious of where I left my keys."

Silent during the discussion, Andrew said, "It's over now. Time to move on and create a happier atmosphere for yourselves and the rabbits. Isn't that right, Bun?" He looked at Bun, gave him a wink, and rose to leave.

I blinked when Bun said, *"You've got that right."* He leaned against my midriff and said, *"He heard me, I'm positive."*

I ruffled his fur, set him on the floor, and gave him a small tray of chopped fruit and veggies before he could whine about starvation.

We thanked Andrew and watched him stride into the darkness.

Jessica murmured, "He's a complicated man."

I wholeheartedly agreed.

The following day, Sheriff Carver came by to take our statements and told us Ben Grady would be tried and more than likely convicted of murder, assault on several counts, and a host of other charges. If found guilty, he faced thirty years to life in prison, without parole. Sheriff Carver said Ben lost control once he'd found his sister had died after being shot during their search for me. Ben's attorney might offer an insanity plea on his behalf, but Carver didn't think it would mean he'd get a lighter sentence.

On his way out the door, Carver said, "I guess a Realtor in town is going to buy Arty's house. Gordon Miller, the Realtor, operates one of those 'I

Buy Ugly Houses' kind of real estate companies. Andrew will be able to make a decent life for himself, and he deserves it."

"He sure does. Thanks for letting us know what's going on. I suppose I'll have to testify?" I asked.

"It's possible, so keep an opening on your calendar, Jules."

"Tell Meredith we'll be having a sale on yarn."

"Not gonna do it, Jules, I'm just not." Said with good humor, Carver marched out the door.

CHAPTER TWENTY-FIVE

A couple of days later, I spoke with my father. He had some explaining to do, and I refused to be put off this time around.

The phone rang three times before my call was answered. "The Bridge residence."

"Hey, Dad, how are you?"

"Great, your mother isn't here right now, do you want her to call you back?"

"I want to speak with you, not Mom. I've had quite a serious problem on my hands these past few months, you know."

"No, I didn't know. You should have mentioned it when you called. We're always willing to help you, Juliette. You know that, don't you?"

This was it, my one and only opportunity to learn the truth. I took a deep breath.

"Years ago, a man and woman came to the house. There was an argument and you slammed the door in their face. I now know—"

"You don't know anything."